PRAISE F
JOANNA CATHERINE SCOTT
AND
THE LUCKY GOURD SHOP

"Incisive. . . . Scott can really write—her sentences are lean and move with authority."

—The New York Times Book Review

"An excellent read."   *—Booklist*

"Arresting opening pages . . . wonderfully empathetic characterizations."

—Kirkus Reviews

"Scott's empathy for her vulnerable protagonist and her understanding of the cultural issues in Korean society make this an engrossing tale."

—Publishers Weekly

"Quickly shatters the reader's complacency. . . . A riveting, compelling, and disturbing novel. . . . Scott's descriptive talent is enormous."

—Library Journal

"The narrative voice of Joanna Catherine Scott and the intriguing structure of her novel combine in an irresistible concoction that crosses cultural and generational boundaries. Scott uses her acclaimed poet's eye to enhance the rich imagery of Korea as she deliberately draws the reader into her lilting narrative. . . . [A] fresh and compelling author."

—*BookPage*

"This gripping tale takes hold like a long forgotten, but often told, family fable. Anyone who has ever wondered about their ancestry, wanted names and stories to go with half-dreamed memories, will feel kindred to the characters in this story."

—*Foreword*

"There are really only two types of books suited to summertime. On the one hand, plot-driven novels—mysteries, say—that are fun, easy to read, and can be devoured in a day. On the other, however, are those rare . . . novels that offer a glimpse into a completely different world, without asking the reader to do anything but marvel—the simpler, and shorter, the better: Joanna Catherine Scott's *THE LUCKY GOURD SHOP* falls perfectly into the latter category."

—*The Christian Science Monitor*

Also by Joanna C. Scott

Charlie and the Children: A Novel of Vietnam

Indochina's Refugees:
Oral Histories from Laos,
Cambodia and Vietnam

Birth Mother: poetry of adoption

Coming Down from Bataan: Poetry of the Philippines

THE LUCKY GOURD SHOP

JOANNA CATHERINE SCOTT

WASHINGTON SQUARE PRESS
PUBLISHED BY POCKET BOOKS

New York   London   Toronto   Sydney   Singapore

This book is a work of fiction. Names, characters, places and incidents are products of the author's imagination or are used fictitiously. Any resemblance to actual events or locales or persons, living or dead, is entirely coincidental.

 A Washington Square Press Publication of
POCKET BOOKS, a division of Simon & Schuster, Inc.
1230 Avenue of the Americas, New York, NY 10020

Copyright © 2000 by Joanna C. Scott

Published by arrangement with MacAdam/Cage

Book epigraph is from the poem "Long From Now," published in *Modern Korean Literature: An Anthology,* compiled and edited by Peter H. Lee (University of Hawaii Press, 1990).

ISBN: 0-7434-3735-7

First Washington Square Press trade paperback printing November 2001

10 9 8 7 6 5 4 3 2 1

WASHINGTON SQUARE PRESS and colophon are registered trademarks of Simon & Schuster, Inc.

For information regarding special discounts for bulk purchases, please contact Simon & Schuster Special Sales at 1-800-456-6798 or business@simonandschuster.com

Cover design by Brigid Pearson
Cover illustration by Brian Bailey

Printed in the U.S.A.

for my children
and for their birth mother

Long from now, if you should seek me,
I would tell you I have forgotten.
If you should blame me in your heart,
I would say, "Missing you so, I have forgotten."

—*Kim Sowol*

FOR WEEKS WE HAVE WAITED FOR THIS LETTER from Korea. Now I sit at one end of the kitchen table with it open in my hand. My three adopted children watch me hopefully. The boy, Dae Young, is seventeen years old now and sits like an oriental patriarch at the table's other end. Li Na, sixteen, sits to my right, the youngest, Tae Hee, fourteen, to my left.

I clear my throat, "Dear Ma'am, It is pleasure of me to write a letter to you. I was very impressed for your husband to adopt our three Korean children, and grown up to be good men."

"Skip that bit," says Li Na. "What does he say about our mother?"

I clear my throat again. "I have made great and sincere effort to find the house in Inch'on where your children seemed to live. However, it is too long time of more than ten years now for me to find such a house. Inch'on used to be a small fishing port located approximately forty kilometers west from Seoul. Now it has been growing by itself as it is one of South Korea's foremost seaport. Your concerns are circumstances when your children were grown up in a small temporary house which would be described as follows: a room with kitchen and no toilet, nor bathroom, to be shared by all family members to be used as bedroom, living room, dining room. It was built with either wood or concrete covered with low quality wall paper. Asphalt papers or close to those were used as roof. Heating system is *ondol*, smoke and heat being channeled from the stove in kitchen through flues under the floor. Coal briquettes are used. Traditionally toilet were located outdoors and not considered part of house. Before flush toilets of Western style were introduced into Korea, there had been a strange-looking toilets for Western people at ground level and one were expected to squat over it. Your children might go to public bath twice a month or so. I want happiness will be with you and with your family all the time."

"That's all?" says Li Na.

"That's all, I'm afraid."

"That's nothing."

"No, not much."

I look at my children, at their smooth complexions, their tidy bridgeless noses, their exquisitely curving eyes, and I feel both relieved and sorry for them. From the first day we adopted them they pursued, almost obsessively, an American identity. When we met them at the orphanage, they stood before us in a row and bowed, but after they left their country they never bowed to anyone again. Within three months they sloughed off their native language like an outgrown skin.

Then they sloughed off the memories. They rejected their Korean names.

For a brief time, for parties and high occasions, the girls were willing to wear the brightly colored *hanbok* dresses of their culture, but soon they were embarrassed. They wanted denim, ugly little t-shirts, sneakers with soles as big as tractor tires. They cut off their lovely swinging hair. They played soccer. They chewed gum. Li Na, the older girl, insisted that her hair was brown, not black. At home she cried a lot, and flounced, and stormed off to her room. At school she moved inside a small protective group of pale-faced friends.

Her little sister, Tae Hee, looked despairingly at me and said, "The kids at school call me a Chink." She walked around the house with a finger underneath each eyebrow, a thumb below the lower lid, stretching her eyes to make them round.

The boy's head grew a baseball cap. They stood him in the outfield. He could move his legs so fast you could barely see them move. But he complained about them—they were too short. He drank chocolate milk six times a day and consumed entire cows, then lay down on the kitchen tiles—each one a foot—to see if he had grown. He didn't grow. He gave up milk and took to beating up on other children in the corridors of school. He never lost.

He was suspended, recruited to play noseguard for the local football team, and came home every weekend stomped and bruised and bursting with testosterone and rage. He fell in love with girls with yellow hair, pale skin, blue eyes.

But now we have moved house. The children's new school,

just north of Baltimore, is in an area where it seems that half the population looks like them. And now the process has reversed itself.

First, like an announcement of a new identity, their Korean names appeared on book bags. They huddled together on the floors of their rooms, heels tucked under in Korean style, and practiced the characters until they could write them as slickly as they wrote their American names. They addressed each other by them and insisted that we do the same. They joined the Asian Club, brought small parades of oriental faces home, stayed overnight with friends and came home smelling of garlic and hot peppers, speaking with an awed respect of grandmothers.

Then came Korean videos about wild Genghis Khan–style marauders, sitcoms with tears and lots of face-slapping, baby-faced Korean rock and pop stars twitching and moaning in the throes of broken-hearted love. They memorized the words, the meanings rising out of some subconscious well of memory, came home with language worksheets from their friends, huddled in their bedrooms over picture books with Korean words. Their language started to come back.

The boy announced he liked the way Korean girls' hair swung and shone, the way it was so black. The girls pinned posters to their walls of a rapper named Kang Ta.

And now, as adolescents will, they want to find an anchor in their ancestry.

I am sorry for this dead end we have come to, and yet I know that if they found their mother the chances of a happy ending would be slight.

Dae Young shifts in his chair and runs a hand across his close-shaved head. He is a taciturn young man, easily moved to anger, and has been difficult to raise. It took a long time to convince him that a woman was in charge, and even now he sometimes looks at me with an expression something like astonishment, as if to say, "How did it come to this?"

"We don't know anything we didn't know before," he says impatiently. "And anyway, we didn't cook on a coal stove. We had an electric burner, the sort that sits on the countertop and plugs into the wall."

"Just one burner?"

He thinks, and then he nods. "The *ondol* floor was raised. I remember there were three steps up to it. We left our slippers on the lower floor. It was cement and very cold. There was a metal flap in the side of the raised floor and you had to open it to shovel the coal in. I remember that it opened downwards and the handle rested on the floor."

"Was there no stove to cook on heated by the coal? No flues running from it underneath the floor?"

"No, none."

"No firebox even?"

"No. We just shoveled coal inside the flap onto the ground below the floor. When it was burned we shoveled the ashes out again. It was my job to clean the ashes out. I remember being very dirty from the coal." He holds his hands up like a just-scrubbed surgeon, turning his eyes down on them with fine disgust.

I am holding my breath now. This boy has spent almost

eleven years with me, and except for a brief rush after he broke the barrier of English, not a whisper of his past have I managed to winkle out of him. When I have tried to pry some information loose, his face has taken on that blank quality I have come to think of as "Dae Young's Korean face," and he has offered nothing.

"What else do you remember?"

"The toilet didn't work. There was a plastic trash can full of water with a scoop beside it."

"Go on," I say, too eagerly, and see that old familiar mask beginning to come down.

I prompt him—nothing to be lost. "Do you remember, when you first learned English, how you told me that the woman who came with your grandmother to put you in the orphanage was not your mother? How your mother worked in a coffee shop in Seoul? About the time she slashed your father's face? Do you remember telling me how you used to creep under the market stalls and steal food to take back to your sisters? And about the Christmas party the American soldiers hosted for the orphanage? How one of them gave you five hundred *won* and you thought it was a lucky coin?"

"I remember only one thing," Li Na interrupts, "how the big girls in the orphanage used to hit us on the head with sticks."

Tae Hee looks plaintive. "I don't remember anything."

Dae Young speaks again. Slowly, as if with an enormous effort, he begins to drag up twigs and sticks of memory and offer them to me. With a writer's instinct, I pull my notebook from the pocket of my jeans and click my automatic pencil.

South Korea,
a generation earlier . . .

SINCE MI SOOK LEARNED TO COUNT she had been found five times. Before that she did not know how many, two at least, but maybe more. Kun Soo was the sixth person to find her, also the first man. The others were all women, wives of owners of the Coffee Shop Utopia in Seoul.

The first time she was found she had been abandoned in the lane behind the shop. The owner's wife found her when she came to toss a paper bag of stale buns into one of the garbage cans that stood there in a row. There were eight back doors of shops along the lane and sixteen cans, all with their metal lids askew because the garbage men were rough with them. Whoever left Mi Sook could have chosen any one of these to leave her by, but for reasons no one knew or cared about, she was left on the ground between the first and second trash cans of the coffee shop, where she could not be seen unless one of them were moved.

She most likely would have died there if the owner's wife had not accidentally set the paper bag of buns down in a puddle of spilled coffee before she picked it up to bring outside.

This softened the bottom of the bag and it gave way, spilling stale buns onto the ground. One bounced off the skewed lid of the first can in the row and lodged in the space between it and the second. The owner's wife cursed, but only mildly because she was an easygoing woman. She picked up the buns that had fallen free and then moved the can aside to get the last so it would not attract more rats than already roamed the lane at night.

When she saw what she had found, she picked up the last bun and dropped it into the can with the others. She straightened the lid and pressed it down securely, leaning heavily on one side, then the other, to keep the battered edge from popping up again. While she did this she was looking at the baby by her foot. It lay perfectly still with its eyes open and she couldn't tell if it were dead or just looking at whatever it could see. Blood was on its head and its purple cord was trailing on the ground. She crouched down to look more closely, and yes, it was a baby, her eyes were not playing tricks on her, and yes, it was alive, and no, it could not have been there long because no rat had found it yet, and yes, the child was lucky even though abandoned because it was midsummer rather than midwinter, when it already would have frozen stiff out here and died. She picked it up and took it into the back room of the shop.

It never occurred to her to take it to the police or the hospital or to make any effort to find its mother. She simply wrapped it in a couple of green striped tea towels and a floral apron and set it on the floor of the back room. Then she went through to the coffee shop, where she mixed a little of the rice left over from her lunch with lukewarm water and, coming back, trickled it into the child's mouth with a plastic spoon. In an hour or so she did the same again, and then again. Later in the day she went down to the general store in the next street and bought a few supplies: a feeding bottle with a pair of rubber teats, some cotton diapers, a can of baby powder, an inexpensive quilt, a tiny dress—because the child was a girl—and when her husband came to the shop late in the evening she let him count the money and close up for the night while she put warm water in a bowl and washed the child, cut and bound the cord, and put on her new clothes. She fed her more rice water from the bottle, spread the quilt out on the floor, set the child on top, and brought it up around her in a kind of nest. Then she went home with her husband.

Things went on thus for several years. Every day the woman came to run the shop and care for the child and every night she fed her late in the evening, settled her down to sleep, and pulled the door closed behind her. It never occurred to her to take the child home, and the child, once she began to talk and could have asked to go, never thought to because she had always slept in the back room of the shop among the mops and brooms and boxes filled with coffee filters.

One day the shop changed hands and the child was found there by the wife of the new owner. She was sleeping on the floor wrapped up in her quilt and when the woman opened the door she woke and said, *"Ama?"* which means, "Mommy" and is what she used to call the woman who had left.

"Who are you?" the woman asked, and the child said, "I am the child," which was all the name she had. She was almost four years old.

This woman called her Mi Sook and bought her a small electric radiator and a blanket to go with her quilt because the floor was not *ondol*, a chest of drawers to keep her few clothes in, a toothbrush and a tube of toothpaste, a mirror to hang on the wall, a new brush for her hair, and a small round cardboard box of boiled fruit candies with pictures of the candies on the box and on the plastic lid. Then she put her to work doing odd jobs about the place.

This was the first time Mi Sook had been allowed to come out into the part of the shop where the customers sat, and she was charmed by them. She brought them coffee in thick white cups, carrying them one at a time on a little lacquered tray with her socked feet sliding cautiously across the floor, and in return they put little shiny round things in her hand or in the pocket of her tiny apron. These she took back to her room and stored in the candy box, which had been empty from the second day she had it.

At night, after the woman had put her to bed and gone off home, she would stand on her bedding and jump up and down, waving her arm in the air until she caught the string for the electric light. Then she would take out her little shiny round things and arrange them in patterns on the quilt and on the floor and when sleep overcame her she would put them all back, set the candy box on the chest of drawers, and jump and jump again.

One day that owner also left, another took her place, and Mi Sook was found again. And so it went. Each time the shop changed hands, Mi Sook changed hands too. She called each new woman *Ama* and never thought it strange, nor did it occur to her that she was lucky to have had a string of easygoing women who simply took her on as part of the coffee shop, like a display counter that has to be wiped from time to time or a floor that must be swept. They were kind enough to her and one or two were fond, but none loved her well enough to take her home.

One of these women gave Mi Sook an old television set and showed her how to turn it on and off, but she was frightened by the tiny people who lived inside this box and spoke to each other without making any sound. She examined it carefully all over to make sure there was no way they could get out in the night and do bad things to her while she was sleeping, and then she ignored it.

During this time she made friends with a dog who lived behind the slatted fence across the back lane. She would haul a trash can across the lane, climb up on its precarious lid to clutch the top of the fence, and raise herself onto tiptoe until she could see into the yard beyond. From here she would call to the dog, which came running to jump against the fence, barking and grinning up at her.

One day she discovered that one of the slats in the fence was loose and pulled it aside to let the dog into the lane. Every day for several months she did this, letting the dog out to play with her in the lane, then coaxing him back inside his yard and closing up the fence. He was a silly, loping, grinning thing, greyish white with black smudges on his rump and down one leg. Long stringy hair trailed in a fringe below his curving tail, which, when he saw Mi Sook's head appear above the fence, beat back and forth, the long fringe swinging underneath, his entire hind section caught up in the rhythm. When she released the slat, the dog would creep out on his belly with his back legs kicking out behind. Liberated, he would stick his haunches in the air, fringed tail swishing like a ribbon on a stick, and put his head down low, elbows on the ground, as though kowtowing. But his mouth would be grinning, his eyes rolling up at her. She would touch his head and he would propel himself against her, paws scrabbling at her chest, tongue slopping at her face. She would seize him by the paws and he would dance with her on his hind legs, lolling out his tongue, giving out little squeaks and groans of joy.

One night Mi Sook ate something bad and vomited all night and in the morning was not well enough to play. The dog, impatient, scratched against the slat until it moved aside, ran up and down the lane searching for his playmate, and was run over by a van making a delivery to the restaurant on the corner.

In the afternoon, when Mi Sook had recovered, she found him lying with his head squashed in. This distressed her greatly and she grieved for the dog. She fell to thinking about death and it occurred to her to see if the little people in the box were still alive. They were and she found that she was glad. She left the television set turned on to make sure they stayed that way and from then on they talked and ate and danced and fought and made up, all in silence, in the corner of her room. She never sat to watch them, just checked on them from time to time to make sure they were still all right.

Being near a university, the coffee shop had students as its primary customers. Groups of them gathered in particular coffee shops, where they would read the papers and discuss books and politics. Mi Sook's coffee shop, a favorite of the engineering students, was for the most part patronized by bright young men. From the first time she appeared out in the front part of the shop she had become a favorite with them and it was from them she learned, piecemeal and in an elementary way, to read and write. She also learned an oddly assorted collection of facts and opinions about what went on in the world outside the coffee shop. One student taught her the names of the three Korean dynasties, making her repeat after him, "Silla, Koryo, Yi," in a kind of chant, the sound of which so delighted her that she went about the place singing it under her breath like a favorite nursery rhyme. Another told her about Confucius and Buddha and Jesus Christ but she got the stories mixed together in her head. This same student gave her a statue of the Buddha with his arms flung up and a big smile on his face. Mi Sook liked him because he was happy but she did not like the way he carried his belly in front of him like a huge ripe melon or the way his breasts and earlobes hung down low, and when this same student appeared one day with a tiny crucifix for her she liked that better because the man's ribs stuck out in the same way hers did when she raised her arms before the mirror on her wall and sucked her breath in hard.

The next student to undertake her education had a different interest. He taught her to count. When she had mastered the numbers up to ten she started a new game at night when the *Ama* had gone home. She began to count her shiny things, which she now knew were coins called *won*. She also knew that the small pieces of colored paper the students gave her for their coffee were called *won* as well. These she was not allowed to keep. All the paper *won* must go to the *Ama*.

As the faces of the women Mi Sook called *Ama* changed, so did the faces of the students who patronized the coffee shop. Each year some vanished and each year new ones came, but no matter who came or went there was always a core of them Mi Sook knew well. By the time one group left the ones who had been new the year before were steady customers.

One day Mi Sook went with her current *Ama* to the general store in the next street and watched her trade coins and paper money for cigarettes, a tube of lipstick, and a little book with lines across its pages but no writing. Later that week, when she had done her morning tasks, she took her box of money and slipped out of the coffee shop. She had never been out on the street alone before but because no one had ever been unkind to her, she was not afraid. She trotted down the sidewalk, crossed the road inside a crowd of legs, went along the sidewalk of an intersecting road, crossed another road with another crowd of legs, and at last made her way to the general store. Here she traded some of her money for a *juju* bar and walked back to the coffee shop sucking at it.

As she grew bolder, she wandered further on the streets and one day found herself before a very modern store, its shining windows filled with all kinds of merchandise. What fascinated Mi Sook, though, was a display of candy because the round boxes were the same as the candy box she used to store her money. The name on them was *Lotte*, she recognized the characters.

The next day she came back with her box, and pushing through the big plate-glass door, walked up and down the aisles until she found a display of these candy boxes on a counter that stood higher than her head. A shopgirl leaned across the counter, looking down at her. She was very pretty, with curled hair and bright red lips. "Hello," she said. "Where is your *Ama?*"

"Hello," said Mi Sook, ignoring the part about the *Ama*. She pulled the top off her box of money, and reaching as high as she could, set it on the counter. "I want another one like that."

The shopgirl smiled and put her finger down into the box, stirring at the money. "It is not enough. You must have more."

"What number?" Mi Sook asked, and when the girl said the number, she memorized it so she could ask the students to teach her how to count that high.

Over time, Mi Sook made friends with the shopkeepers up and down the lane. The dressmaker next door became a special friend. She had a box with the same little people that were in Mi Sook's box but hers spoke aloud. This fascinated Mi Sook and she came often to listen to what they had to say to each other.

One day the dressmaker, whose name was *Madame*, said, "Do you have no television of your own, child?" and Mi Sook said, "Oh yes, but my people don't make any noise."

Madame laughed and showed her the volume control knob and told her how a television worked and after that Mi Sook sat in the evenings when the *Ama* had gone home and listened to her people talk. She learned many things this way and always turned the set off before she went to sleep.

Sometimes when her tasks were done, she would go next door and *Madame* would pay her a few coins for helping to clean the upstairs workroom where the clothes were made. She enjoyed this work because there were no cups and saucers to wash up, no tables slopped with coffee to wipe down, and also because after the sewing girls had gone home there were only *Madame* and *Madame*'s sister in the shop. *Madame* talked to her as though she were a grown-up person, and although her sister was a little birdlike thing who never spoke to anyone, she always smiled and welcomed her.

To clean up, she hauled the empty fabric bolts down from the upstairs cutting room and stood them in one of *Madame*'s garbage cans out in the lane. She gathered the leftovers of unbleached paper from which patterns had been cut and tossed them in the other can. The scraps of fabric littering the floor she sorted into two piles, one to keep and one to throw away. The pile to throw away was made of tiny scraps that were no use for anything. The prettiest of these she kept for herself and soon had a coffee carton full of multicolored scraps: pieces of crepe and satin, brocade, sheer embroidered nylon, bits of ribbon and lace. These she would spread out at night, fingering the textures and making them into patterns on the floor. *Madame* gave her a needle and a spool of thread and soon she learned to stick the needle in and out, attaching this piece of fabric to that, pulling this one into gathers, folding this one over on itself. She had no doll but if she had she might have made it clothes. Instead, she made herself strange ornaments and tacked them on her wall with straight pins she had picked up off *Madame's* floor.

Madame's shop was called Madame's Bridal Fashion Elegance, which was why she was called *Madame*. She told Mi Sook it was French and when Mi Sook asked did she have a Korean name, she said, "A French name is all I need for *haute couture*," which Mi Sook knew had something to do with dresses because *Madame* said it often when women brought their daughters to look for designs to copy out of *Vogue* or one of the other foreign fashion magazines she kept on a small round table in the window of her shop.

Sometimes *Madame* made traditional *hanbok* wedding dresses, the sleeves of their short jackets striped in yellow and bright blue, their long skirts like pink bells billowing, but she specialized in Western style. Her brides were decked in lace and flounces and gleaming white satin, with pert little veils and fingertip veils and veils that seemed to trail forever on behind. She stood them on a little platform in her shop before a three-way mirror, and with a tape measure draped around her neck and around her wrist a bracelet made of red felt into which were stuck straight pins, she studied them, walking this way and that, draping samples of fabric from their shoulders to see how their skin responded to the different textures.

Sometimes she would say, "White, yes, definitely white," and sometimes, "Ivory, this bride is ivory," and if the bride's mother offered an opinion she would draw her eyebrows tight together and sweep back and forth with one hand at her chin, looking at her over stout, black-rimmed half glasses until the woman learned to have no opinion of her own but to trust *Madame* entirely. She had many happy customers. They sent her photographs and she hung them on her walls.

Madame was not beautiful, being short and squat, with legs that bowed out like the two sides of a barrel and a square face from which her wide flat nostrils stared like a second pair of eyes. She had no daughter and no husband either.

"Bah," she said when Mi Sook asked her why. "I have no time for men. What good are they to me? When I was younger and my business growing, the matchmakers would come to me with photographs, but always I said to myself, here I am with two strong arms, a strong back, I can sew, I can make myself a business, I can please myself. Why should I give up all my profits to a man? Why should I wake each morning to make his coffee, to cook for him, to clean his house, to listen every day to his mother telling me how to do this and that, to lie on the floor screaming and bursting out in blood to give him sons? Three cousins I have, all married, and what do they do all day but worry about what their husbands have to say? And always they must be asking his permission before they can do some tiny thing. And when they have done this tiny thing they must run home quick to cook his food, to wash his clothes, to bow low to his mother, to break their backs carrying his children up and down the road. And then they come to me. 'Ileh, why are you not married?' they say. 'All day you sit in your store making wedding gowns for others and you yourself have never had one on your back.' But I say to them, 'Let others have the wedding gowns. I will wear dresses in bright colors, I will buy myself silk and copy the designs from *Vogue*, from anywhere. My belly will never stick out like a sack of rice, I will never wear a black eye or carry bruises on my cheeks, and I will go anywhere I want, answering to no man. One day, perhaps, I will even go to America. I will see Niagara Falls.'"

Mi Sook listened to all this with big eyes and said, "I will be like you. I will have a business too and never answer to a man."

But then *Madame's* voice would grow soft. "Ah, child," she would say, "you are too pretty not to marry. Many men will come for you and one day I will make a gown for you. It will be a gift. See, here is lovely fabric. It is cotton voile. See the little holes made into daisies? Here, stand up before the mirror. Look at that. Is that not so becoming on you? And see how this tulle is pretty round your face? No, child, you are not like me. One day you will have a veil and blush like all the rest."

Then Mi Sook would go away confused because the only men she knew were the students, who were always kind to her, and it seemed not so bad a thing to have a husband, but on the other hand she admired *Madame* for her independent ways and the beauty of the clothes she made, and especially for the way women came to her store and put money in her hand, and she wanted to be like her.

As a child, Mi Sook was a pretty little thing but as she grew prettiness gave way to something more substantial. She was not a beauty in the classic way, her face being too mobile, her mouth a little large, but something seemed to glow inside her that made men turn and look when she walked by them in the street. The students, however, who had always regarded her as a sort of little sister, did not treat her with familiarity when she became desirable but continued to show a brotherly courtesy. From time to time some stranger who had come with his friends to drink coffee would speak coarsely and pull at her, treating her the way he might treat a coffee shop girl in a provincial town. At these times the students watched carefully and if things went too far they all stood up together and approached the table where the stranger sat. In this way they protected her and she was grateful to them. Along with the current owner, they were the closest thing she had to family. However, because to her the concept of family was a shifting one, she grew up a kind of oddity, not a misfit but that rare creature in her society, one who did not draw her sense of self from fixed relationships with others. Yet she was not at all un-happy.

Eventually, one of Mi Sook's *Amas* asked if she would like to be the manager of the coffee shop and she agreed, so a girl was hired to be her helper and Mi Sook was given a wage for the first time in her life, not much, but she was proud to tell it to *Madame*. Each night when the last student had gone home, she would lock the front and back doors of the shop and unlock the till. Emptying out one curved metal pocket at a time, she would count the takings for the day, stacking the piles of notes and coins along the counter. She never wrote down numbers as she went but kept them in her head, labori-ously recording the final total on a small gray pad. That done, she scooped the coins off the counter into one of two worn leather drawstring purses kept only for this purpose, bound each pile of notes in a rubber band, and, setting them on the coins, tore the total off the pad and set it on the notes. Then she pulled the drawstring tight and hid the purse inside a box of coffee filters in the back room, where it would be safe until the *Ama* came by next day to collect it for the bank and return the other drawstring purse. Occasionally the *Ama* came by for other necessary things, but less and less as Mi Sook assumed more responsibility. Soon Mi Sook stopped calling her *Ama* and ran the shop all by herself. It was the only job she ever had, the back room her only home, and she was happy because it did not occur to her that things might have been otherwise.

Not, that is, until Kun Soo came along.

When Kun Soo first set eyes on Mi Sook, it had never, in all the time he had been married, occurred to him to take a mistress.

In those days he was miserable. His wife had given only daughters, five of them: an oldest, a set of twins, and then three more, the last born dead. The next year she bore again and when Kun Soo saw it was a son, also born dead, he went out and squatted on the narrow front veranda of the house with his back against the wall. He lit a cigarette, and filling up his lungs with rancid smoke, put his head down on his knees and moaned.

But then his mother was beside him with a smiling face and the old midwife behind her, also with a smiling face, and when he went inside, there was his wife with another, living, baby in her arms and her face turned up for his approval. "It was twins again," she said. "I have given you a son at last."

He was happy when that son was born. He called him Joo Yup and shouted out his wife's new name, Joo Yup's Mother, laughing aloud for joy. He quickly caught himself and frowned, but the damage had been done. The demons heard him laugh. They waited three days and then they came by night from underneath the eaves and sucked out the boy's breath. In the morning he was blue and there was no life left in him.

When Kun Soo's wife saw this, she burst out wailing, tearing at her hair and beating her head against the floor. His mother, though, snatched up the child and shook him upside down, slapping her hand against his back and rocking him violently. His breath came back, but not all of it. The demons had swallowed some and it was gone. From then on it was clear the boy would be a simpleton.

Kun Soo was ashamed. He knew it had been his own fault for showing his happiness before the demons, but a man cannot lose face before his friends. And so he blamed his wife and drank and cursed her bitterly for giving him this son with a lumpish head and a body squat and fleshy like a toad.

When one hundred days had passed, his wife came to him with her eyes turned down, suggesting that he hold the customary celebration. That day he beat her. He never had before.

Eight years earlier, he had been hauling bricks on a construction project near the Inch'on harbor when he was approached by a matchmaker with an offer of a wife who brought with her a house. True, it was one room only and half built and, true, the wife that came with it was almost ten years his senior, but the matchmaker had been persuasive. "Just the thing for you," she said, smiling her negotiator's smile. "You are young and strong. You know the building trade. You can lay your hand on many odds and ends of wood and stone from your construction sites. You can make a fine thing of this house." When Kun Soo pulled his face down at the photograph she showed of his prospective wife, the matchmaker stood up from the stack of lumber where they sat and looked down at him with condescension. "So," she said, "she is a little old, a little plain, but how else is a man who is nothing but a builder's laborer to own a house? It is a step up in the world for you. Look at you. You are a man with nothing but a pair of hands. Now you will have a house, a wife, a flock of sons, a mother—yes?—she will be proud."

When she put it that way Kun Soo saw that maybe she was right, but still he hesitated. A house was well enough, but he would still be nothing but a builder's laborer. How would he feed this wife, this flock of sons? He sent the matchmaker away and worried over it. He thought about his mother in their village in the countryside, about how she had labored in the fields to feed and care for him as he grew up, becoming stooped and old before her time. He remembered his frustration with the lack of any way to make a decent living, of how frustration reached explosion point and he burst out of there to join the movement of workers to the cities, trying first this work, then that, until he found he had become a builder's laborer. It was a humble job providing humble income, but the entire country was rebuilding and he was rarely out of work for long. Each day he rose before the dawn and each night came back to his lodgings aching in the marrow of his bones, dreaming of the day he would bring his mother to the city, where she would never have to work again. More than anything he wanted to be a good son to his mother.

So how to solve the problem of the wife and house? He worried on it for a week. The matchmaker came back. "You must decide," she said. "I have another offer." She gave him one more day. He went down to the wine shop after work and happened to fall in with Mr. Shin, who ran a fish warehouse. They drank together all that night, Kun Soo outlining loudly, then more loudly, the predicament in which he found himself. Mr. Shin was sympathetic, ordering more wine and belching in his face. When dawn crept in the sky he rose, smacked Kun Soo on the shoulder, and offered him a part-time job as driver of a fish truck. It would be a change from hauling bricks, he said, and he would get to travel all around the country.

That day Kun Soo took a bus home to his mother's village in the countryside and set the proposition out in front of her. What did she think? She thought it good. She also thought that she was lonely in this village since her husband's parents had died. The farm was too much work. She missed her son. Of course, he said, a man must have a mother in his house. And so he took the house and took the wife and the three of them set up together, the two women working at the market stall, Kun Soo going job to job, hauling bricks in wooden wheelbarrows, running up bamboo scaffolding, pouring cement, balancing on roofs, and when his shift was done, hurrying away to drive a truck for Mr. Shin, finishing the house whenever he found time.

At first he had been happy with his life, imagining that all this work, like a building rising on a firm foundation, would bring him something he could look at with his chest puffed out and proud. As each child came along, he swallowed his dismay, not just because it was a daughter but at the way the money he brought in seemed more and more sucked from his hand. And yet, each time his wife began to vomit in the morning and her belly started to grow large, his step would lighten and he would throw himself into his work, coming home each evening to talk and talk about the son that he would have.

These days, though, since Joo Yup had been born, a demon seemed to live inside him. Sometimes it slept. Sometimes it woke and raged and he could not control it and hammered at his wife. A flock of sons, where was his flock of sons? His wife had given nothing but daughters and a toad.

The first two years of his life Joo Yup lay on his back, attempting nothing. In his third year he learned to understand words a little and tried to speak, but all that came out were grunts and strange garbled noises like an animal. When he was four, his back was strong enough to hold him sitting up. He made no attempt to learn to walk or even crawl, just sat like a lump wherever he was put and every night peed without waking. Because of this, he could not be put to sleep with his sisters and the rest of his family but was wrapped at night in his own quilt and set to sleep on the cement close up against the warm side of the *ondol* floor. That way he was kept warm in the winter but could not soil the bedding of the other members of the family.

The smell of him could not be kept away, though, and no punishment or any sort of training helped. Once such a child would have been sent out to neighbors to beg salt to shame him but with Joo Yup it would have been a waste of time. Even if all the neighbors had beaten him at once it would not have taught him to control his water in the night. Even in the day he gave no warning that he needed to be taken to the outhouse in the yard. He simply peed or soiled himself and sat in it.

Because his sisters feared him and his mother went to work each day down at the market stall, it became his grandmother's duty to see that he was taken to the outhouse regularly, but no matter how many times she took him or how she watched his face for signs of urgency she couldn't catch him every time. She used old rags and pieces of cloth for diapers and fashioned for him a pair of waterproof overpants from a yellow plastic bag. Every morning after she had cleaned him from his night's soil and before she began her other tasks, she washed his rags, scraping them first over the outhouse toilet, screwing up her face against the biting smell. Each day he grew bigger and heavier for her to carry, and still he did not walk.

During this time Joo Yup's mother cried a lot, sometimes even bursting into tears while she was working at the market stall, and Kun Soo went often to the wine shop, where he drank all night, cursing back along the alleyways at dawn to plant a new bruise on her face.

· · ·

Joo Yup never learned to walk as other children did. One day when he was five years old, he just stood up and ran away. His grandmother had been sitting on the floor, pressing a pattern into the outer skin of an ornamental gourd, when she caught a movement in the open doorway from the corner of her eye. She glanced up but the door was empty. With sudden knowledge she looked behind and Joo Yup wasn't there. Quickly she set down the gourd and ran to look out the door. No one there again, but Joo Yup's yellow plastic bag of rags squatted like a shed cocoon beside the gate.

For some reason now the old woman felt urgency slip out of her. Slowly she stepped into her rubber shoes and slowly stepped off the veranda, slowly went out to the gate. And there was Joo Yup running on his tiptoes down the alleyway in the strange staggering way he would always run, elbows tucked against his sides with forearms raised so that his two hands flapped at shoulder height like a pair of useless wings. His naked buttocks twitched back and forth, the round pale flesh trembling underneath his shirt. When the old woman saw this a great weariness overtook her and she could barely drag her limbs along the alleyway to bring him back.

From that day on Joo Yup became like a heavy stone she had to carry on her back. Not only did she have to care for him in all the ways she had before, but now she had to keep him caged either in the house or in the yard. For his part, he had no desire on earth except to run. It was as though he realized that he had lost five years and wanted to catch up the time. Every day became a contest with his grandmother. If he woke before her, he slipped out of his stinking wad of rags and ran out of the house. If she woke first, he would bide his time until he saw some moment of opportunity. His grandmother became more and more exhausted from waking early and from watching him all day.

One day she brought home a rope and, winding it securely round his waist, tied him like a dog in the backyard, and all that day he howled and rushed violently to the end of it, only to be brought up with a jerk. The next day he did the same and the next also, but then he seemed to learn and on the fourth day he sat quietly, looking around the yard and mumbling to himself.

For a while this solved her problem and she would sometimes lie down in the afternoon and sleep. Or if she could not sleep she would smoke and think about her life, comparing this part of it with that, trying to persuade herself that after all, things now were not so bad. At least she did not have to labor every day the way she had when Kun Soo was a child, struggling beside her husband's parents to drag a rice crop from the rocky soil and mountainous terrain, bending all day in the chafing wind to plant the rice and in the searing sun to tend it and pull it from the mud when it was ripe. And no hope of marrying again. Who would have married her? The war with the North had taken all the men. Their village had become one of grandfathers and children, and women who carried all the labor on their backs. No, she would not like to go back to those days.

She thought wistfully about the time after Kun Soo's first

daughter, Eun Hye, had been born. He had made himself content with that. "Eh," he told his wife, "do not concern yourself. One daughter, it is nothing. Soon you will have a flock of sons." That was when the old woman had quit the market stall and become the grandmother. It had been a pleasant time. She had tended to the child and cooked and cleaned the house, growing decorative gourds against the garden wall in her spare time. And Kun Soo had done well enough. When construction work could not be had, he could always drive a truck for Mr. Shin. It was lucky work for him. Although the money he brought home was low, he often filled her cooking pot with unsold fish no more than three days old. She was proud of her hardworking son.

But then there was another daughter, and another. If only Kun Soo had been satisfied with them. They were healthy girls, although not beautiful. But no, he had to chew his heart out for a son. So came more girls, more mouths to feed. And now he had his son, an animal tied in the yard.

Not tied for long. Joo Yup chewed through the rope and ran away again. His grandmother went after him but instead of catching up to him and bringing him back home she watched to see what he would do. All day she watched while he did nothing but wander in the streets, eventually coming home of his own accord.

That was the day she gave up trying to keep him caged, and from that day on Joo Yup became a wanderer in the town. He looked so strange, slobbering on his chin and making his loud wordless noises, that the other children thought he was a goblin. When they saw him coming they ran away or sidled past with their backs against the fence. Sometimes he followed, coming up behind some child to catch him unawares and wrap his arms around his body, refusing to let go. He was very strong, but he did no one any harm and as long as he could wander in the town he was content. Eventually he even learned to control his water and his bowels by day, going behind a tree or in the lane behind a store, no worse than a dog.

He was doglike, too, in his affection, pawing at people or creeping up to set his head down on their knees where he would rock back and forth, moaning and drooling on their clothes. His sisters watched him warily, avoiding him inside the house by staying on the *ondol* floor, where he was not allowed. Outside, they ran away from him, sometimes poking him with sticks to stop him following.

With the storekeepers, though, he became a sort of good-luck charm. They would sometimes give him an apple or a peach or a piece of sticky candy. One day he discovered his mother working at the market stall and after that he often came to squat beside her with his hands resting on the ground on each side of his knees, waiting patiently to follow her back home.

As Joo Yup grew older, his behavior toward his sisters changed. He watched them in a new way that was at the same time less and more affectionate. When they bathed themselves out in the yard he came creeping to crouch on his heels and stare and at last they kept him at bay by appointing two to guard the others while they bathed. These two would stand one at each back corner of the house and poke him with a stick when he came staggering to see.

Soon he began to bother them at night. One or another would wake to find his heavy body pressed against her, the odor of his peed-on clothes sharp in her nose. Then his father would rise in anger and drag him back down to his place on the cement, but he would come again. Night after night it went on until at last he was set to sleep locked in the storage shed out in the yard, where he would howl and wail for hours until he fell asleep.

From this time on the girls talked incessantly among themselves about how one day they would have houses of their own.

When Eun Hye, the eldest, was seven years she had gone to help her mother on the market stall and her sisters followed one by one. When Eun Hye was fourteen, a woman came by the market looking for young girls to be housemaids for wealthy families who lived in the foothills around Seoul and also in other cities. A small group gathered and Eun Hye, curious, pushed through to the front, where she stood with her face turned up and listened carefully.

Those lucky ones who chose to come with her, the woman said, would be paid on alternate weeks and have their food and clothes for free, a day off once a month, a room to share with only one or two other girls who would soon become their friends. Those who worked hard would be treated well.

Some of the girls asked questions, worrying about this and that, and the woman answered everything easily, making it all sound like a grand adventure. When everything had been asked and said, she looked down into Eun Hye's upturned face and made a question out of hers. Eun Hye turned, went back to her mother, and held her arms tight around her neck. Her grandmother, who had come down to the stall that day with a basket of her decorative gourds, watched this with a heavy heart because she understood what would happen next. She whispered anxiously to her daughter-in-law, who made a shushing sound, brushing her objections to one side. Eun Hye turned to her grandmother, hugged her also round the neck, and went off with the woman.

One year later she came back to Inch'on when her father was not home. She bowed to her mother and to her grandmother and spoke softly to her twin sisters, who were next to her in age. Then she helped them pack their belongings into two small bundles and, bowing her good-byes, led them off along the alleyway. One year after that she came for her next sister, and then the youngest. She never came back home again.

Nor did her sisters. But from time to time when Kun Soo was at work, a small parcel of money appeared beside the door with their mother's name written on it in an unfamiliar hand. Neither of the women mentioned these gifts to Kun Soo, although sometimes he would look about him with suspicious eyes when something new appeared—a bowl or basket for his wife, maybe a little pot of glittering lacquer for his mother's ornamental gourds.

The girls' mother wept each time a daughter left and then she dried her eyes and went back to working at the market stall. She never mentioned these departures to her husband and Kun Soo said nothing either.

In those days Kun Soo often saw Joo Yup when he was going to a building site or driving a fish truck through the streets and he was ashamed because this strange lumpish thing was his. He never stopped to pick him up or lead him home but turned his head away. Many nights he spent down at the wine shop, and many early mornings were welcomed by his voice out in the alleyway, singing loudly and shouting accusations at the dogs along the way. They threw their throats up to the sky and Kun Soo trailed their agitated barking home like a triumphal cloak. There he would leap onto his wife and when she complained that he was hurting her he made it worse.

The day he first saw Mi Sook, Kun Soo had made a delivery of fish to the back door of a restaurant in Seoul. It was a fine day and warm, so he left his truck parked in the lane and strolled out to the street, rolling his shoulders in the sun and looking at the people walking back and forth in business suits and brightly colored dresses.

He passed the front door of the restaurant, paused to gaze at a display of handsome rattan furniture in the window of the shop next door, peered in at the window of the beauty shop, at the women lined in rows with curlers sprouting from their heads, admired the swift efficient manner of the clerk sorting piles of crumpled shirts and dresses in the window counter of the dry-cleaning shop. He stepped more quickly past the coffee shop, looking slit-eyed and suspicious at the students talking earnestly behind its plate-glass window, then slowed again, nodding in a friendly fashion at two headless women decked in bridal finery in the window of the wedding shop. At the souvenir shop window he stopped to click his tongue above the price tags on the eelskin wallets, then stood transfixed before the diagram of acupuncture points in the window of the shop next door.

That was the last shop in the block and now he waited at the traffic light to cross the road. But before it could turn green, the thought of his delivery schedule turned him round and he went strolling back the same way he had come—past the acupuncturist, the souvenir shop, the wedding shop.

She was standing in the doorway of the Coffee Shop Utopia, beneath its bright green swinging sign. She had a yellow flowered apron tied around her waist and seemed to be neither coming nor going but just standing in the warmth, looking up and down the street with no particular purpose, relaxing in the new spring day. From this he understood that she worked in the shop. As he passed, he felt her look at him and a strange vibration seized his body the like of which he had never felt before. He forgot his truck and wandered in the street outside the coffee shop for more than an hour so that he had to drive like a madman to catch up with his schedule. As he went, he examined his face in the rearview mirror of the truck and saw that it was handsome still, the teeth whole in his head, a few gray hairs along the sides but otherwise a face that still could pass as young.

He stopped drinking entirely. Instead, he paced out in the yard at night or walked about the streets clenching and unclenching his fists, not making plans of any sort but dreaming in a wild, incoherent way. One time, late at night, he heard a noise, and turning, found a goblin lurching behind him, its eyes glinting with the moon. Kun Soo's breath all rushed up into his chest and he ran with his feet making a loud echo in the silent street. Then he stopped, cursed beneath his breath, and going back, led his imbecile son home. It was the only time he did.

His desire for this unknown young girl became like an inflammation of the brain. Inside his head it itched. He saw the world through a half-transparent image of her face. She went before him driving down the road and when he balanced on a beam at a construction site she floated in the air in front of him. When he lay down beside his wife it seemed to him that she had been transformed into this girl and he seized her in a way he never had before, but when it was done and she lay flaccid and exhausted at his side he became angry with himself because he had seized the wrong woman by mistake. The rest of his night would be sleepless and he would rise in the morning heavy with a feeling that might have been called emptiness, or sorrow, or it might have been some sort of blind resentment. But then, when he went outside and looked up at the sky, it seemed to him higher than before, and clearer.

He began to notice things: the tiny splayed feet of a sparrow fluffing out its feathers on a stone wall in the alleyway, the flower pattern of his breath against the morning air, the touch of cotton on his arms and back like a young girl's caress, the song of spinning rubber on the road.

He smiled at people unexpectedly and felt a warmth like wine inside his stomach when they gave him back his smile. Walking on the road, he felt as though his feet were made of rubber and sometimes he seemed to walk behind himself, watching the way his back moved and his arms and legs swung easily. He never ached from labor anymore and he became kinder to his wife. One day he brought her a gift, the head of a sunflower, fat and ripe with seeds. He had watched it for some time, its head stuck up above a fence, nodding to him like a friendly face each time he passed, and one day when it was ripe and heavy, almost at the point when it would turn its head down, spilling its seeds like tears onto the ground, he looked left and right, then reached across the fence and broke it off. He had never stolen from another's yard before but the flower had been like a young girl trying to seduce him, waiting for him there all summer long behind the fence, smiling and nodding when he passed, begging him to take her home with him. And so at last he took her. What can a man say against the invitation of a lovely girl?

When his mother saw this sunflower, she looked at Kun Soo with a question in her eyes. As though to stop her asking it, he brought home next day a handsome brand-new kimchi pot and gave it to her as a gift. She had four already, but one had cracked the year before even though he had buried it well for her and the winter was no worse than usual. When spring came and the ground thawed, the kimchi juice leaked out and soaked away.

She was pleased with this new pot because it was bigger than the others. It stood higher than her knee, of rich red-brown earthenware. Kun Soo told her that she should do as all the neighbors did and keep her pots above the ground, offering to build her a special stand. But no, old country habits clung to her and she insisted that this pot be buried also. All one afternoon it took to dig the old pot out and get the new one buried to her satisfaction. When it was done she could not stay inside the house but kept going out into the yard to walk behind it and in front of it, crouching to pull off the lid and set it back again, smiling and sucking at her cigarette and blowing smoke about. Then her old friend, Jung Hee's mother, came to visit, and the two old women went jostling outside like children on a feast day and crouched and smoked together, nodding to each other, laughing and pulling off the lid to peer inside. A fine pot it was.

After she got that pot, Kun Soo's mother went every day to market, buying carefully. He could not give her enough money to buy all the vegetables she needed to fill her pots in one great welter of November kimchi making as women with wealthy sons and husbands and many pots could do, but she was well known at the market and one vendor or another would think of this old woman in her long white threadbare skirt and her jacket whose seams had rotted out and been resewn so many times it was growing tight beneath the arms, and he would set aside a wilted cabbage head or a turnip with the rotten part still small enough to slice away, some limp spring onions, or a giant radish slowly turning black. These he would offer to her at a reduced price and when she was done arguing and spitting sideways in disgust at the advantage taken of a poor old woman, the price would drop lower. Then she would shrug and turn her back and walk away, muttering angrily beneath her breath, and the stallholder, knowing that these half-rotten vegetables would not last another day, would call out after her, "Grannie! Grannie!"

Coming back with a great show of reluctance, she would pick up the items one by one, curling her lip until the stall-holder became angry and began to jerk his hands or, if it were a woman, to plead for some consideration of her children, hungry and in need of winter coats. Then the old woman would know that the price was down as far as it would go and she would count it out, hesitating over each note and coin as though hoping the stallholder would change his mind. At last the outstretched fist would close on the little pile and the stall-holder, smiling now, would bow to her receding back, happy to have gained a little money for spoiled goods.

Kun Soo's mother would come home then and the chopping would begin, and the mixing with garlic and hot peppers and a little ginger root and, if she were fortunate, a few handfuls of tiny salted shrimp. After that would come the careful storing in the pots, the rising smell of fermentation in the yard.

One day, sitting with his back against a half-built wall to eat his lunch, Kun Soo noticed that the ball of sticky rice his workmate unwound from a piece of cloth was nothing but a poor man's lunch. He examined this man and saw that he was a coarse fellow, with rough hands and foul-smelling breath. He thought about this for several days and the next time he was paid he went into the general store and bought a cake of scented soap, a toothbrush, a small tube of toothpaste, a hand mirror, a comb, and a bottle of black hair dye. These he carried into the storage shed in the backyard, where he propped the mirror on a crossbeam of the wall and peered at his reflection.

He was not growing old, he told himself. It was just the heavy labor of his life that had made his hair turn gray, not much, just here and here a little on the sides, and a little here in front. But see how much better it looked now. And he carefully screwed the lid back on the bottle of hair dye, hiding it behind a piece of wood.

With his mouth tingling from unaccustomed toothpaste, he examined his four t-shirts hanging by their corners on the clothesline in the yard and went inside to argue with his wife that they were not clean enough, what use was a wife to him if she could not get his t-shirts white as they were meant to be?

She whined at him, "All day you crawl around in the dirt on some construction site and after that you set boxes of stinking fishes on your head and the blood and grease run down. How am I to get your t-shirts white without a little bleach?"

So Kun Soo gave her money for some bleach and she took his four shirts off the line and the other one he owned out of the chest of drawers and washed them carefully. Next day she washed them all again, and the next day too, holding them up to him each evening to inspect.

"Look now, are they not white and beautifully washed?" she said, and each evening Kun Soo said, "Do it one more time."

This went on for a week, during which time Kun Soo rose very early, and without asking either of the women for help, set water to heat in the largest cooking pan. While it heated he went out to the storage shed, hauled out the metal basin used for bathing, and filled it with water from the hose his mother kept for watering her gourd plants. He went back for the heated water, and pouring that in also, stripped off his clothes and sat down in the basin with the cake of scented soap and a rag and washed himself all over thoroughly. Each night he did the same except the two nights he drove the fish truck out of town. On those two nights he paid a little money for the public baths.

While Kun Soo was away at work, his mother poured some of the bleach into his bathing water and soaked Joo Yup's rags to get rid of their bad smell. At noon she wrung them out and hung them on the line, carefully rinsing out the basin. She also funneled some of the bleach into a small bottle, setting it aside to wipe her ornamental gourds, by this means producing a lovely smooth pale surface.

At the end of the week Kun Soo's wife asked him for more money for bleach and because he was pleased with her for making such an effort with his shirts, he made no complaint.

When he was satisfied with the whiteness of his shirts he went back to the coffee shop where Mi Sook worked and drank a cup of thick dark coffee, watching her and looking around the shop. Noting that not just coffee but also buns and cakes were sold here, he came up with an idea and the next day came back with a sample of Mr. Shin's new line of pressed fish cakes, drawing Mi Sook's attention to their pretty beveled edges and the swirl of pink at each one's heart, trying to secure an agreement with her to carry them in the shop.

"Very good to eat with coffee," he said, but Mi Sook laughed, refusing them. "What place have fish cakes in a coffee shop?"

So Kun Soo went away, taking the fish cakes with him. But he had made her laugh and when he came again to sit with coffee in his hand, she came smiling up to him. "You would like fish cakes with your coffee, yes?" and they laughed together at her joke.

That winter Kun Soo began to drive the fish truck out of town a great deal more than usual. His trips became longer and more complicated and he had to stay away overnight more, but when he did come home he was happy and kind to his wife. He even brought her another gift, this time a stiff bamboo fan, lacquered shiny black and decorated with a flying heron. She began to sing about the house, never once complained about his absences, and never thought to wonder why, if he had so much work, he had less money than he had had before.

His mother, though, having seen such things before, understood what Kun Soo's new behavior meant. She was sorry for her daughter-in-law because of it but glad that Kun Soo was being kind to her these days, not coming up the alley drunk and singing in the miserable gray dawn to bruise her face or black her eye again. When her daughter-in-law came to her smiling and said, "At last my husband has forgiven me for the son I gave to him," the old woman smiled and pressed her arm. "Yes," she said, "he is being kind to you again." But secretly she pitied the poor woman for her innocence, putting away the thought of what might happen if Kun Soo's mistress had a son.

When Mi Sook became pregnant and gave birth to a son, Kun Soo was careful. He hung hot peppers across her door in the back room of the coffee shop and also across the front door to the street and the back door into the lane. He turned his mouth down at this son, saying bad things about him in a loud voice. He was too small, too ugly, he had a flat head at the back, he had a stupid look. He glowered at the boy and shouted at Mi Sook for giving him a weakling son, but secretly he watched the child and was proud.

After three days the demons had not come. After seven days the boy still breathed. Two weeks, two months. When a hundred days had passed he allowed Mi Sook to invite her friend *Madame*, who had helped with the birth, and they made a small celebration, setting out steamed rice cakes at the four corners of the shop for the customers to eat with their coffee. *Madame* worried that the cakes were not enough. "Do you not want long life for this son of yours?" she asked Kun Soo. "Do you not want good health? You must buy one hundred cakes."

Kun Soo felt anger climbing on his neck. How could he

afford so many cakes? He began to make excuses but Mi Sook seized a knife and cut the cakes up into tiny pieces, pressing them on every customer who came in through the door until she was satisfied that one hundred people had shared the celebration.

Now Kun Soo knew that the boy was safe. He smiled at him and was proud, calling him Dae Young. He was a fine son.

Mi Sook had been dismayed to find herself pregnant but when it was a boy she was happy enough. Kun Soo was pleased with her and said that he would marry her soon, as soon as his savings were sufficient. He began to call her *Yubo*, which means "wife," and although Mi Sook resented this for reasons she could not explain, she said nothing. Kun Soo had told her he was a building contractor, and although he did not lie to her exactly, led her to believe he owned the building company, or at least a part of it. When she said, "Why do you drive the fish truck?" he said, "Building does not take every minute of my time. A man must work at anything he can to get ahead." And so she thought that driving the fish truck was simply his way of making extra money between working on contracts for houses and apartment buildings and high-rise offices. He smelled of fish from time to time but she respected him for his hardworking ways.

Because he spoke of saving, she thought he must have an account with a credit union and was setting aside money each time he was paid to build a nice house for his new wife and son, so she tried not to worry too much over the extra expenses that the child brought her, although she was a little dismayed that she had to use the money in her candy box to buy him clothes. She thought of how she used to walk about the town in her time off, carefully buying this or that she had saved her money for, exploring stores and buildings she had never seen, enjoying the admiring looks of strangers. Sometimes a man would speak to her or brush against her in the street and this produced in her a feeling of excitement. Always, though, she gave back only a slight turn of the head, a demure look, a curving smile.

Sometimes, in the tourist areas or near the U.S. military base, a foreigner or an American soldier would approach her boldly. She had watched the girls walking in these areas and discovered that many took money to go with these men, especially at night, and it would have been easy enough for her to do the same, but these enormous men alarmed her. She saw the clothes the girls wore who went with them, the makeup too, and sometimes she would see one sitting in an elegant black car, or getting in or out, going on the arm of someone with decorations on his uniform into a hotel with doormen and red carpet from the curb up to the door. But because her strange upbringing had made her cling to solitude, and because she had discussed the dangers of this way of making money with *Madame*, she never went with anyone, satisfying herself with wandering the edges, watching the other girls and enjoying the approaches of the men while holding herself aloof.

Now, when she sometimes ventured on these night excursions with the child slung on her back, no one approached her anymore and she watched the other girls with a curious wistfulness. But, she told herself, soon she would be a married woman with a handsome, hardworking husband. It was not so bad for her. And anyway, this was not such a good time to be roaming through the streets. The students seemed more angry than they ever had before. All day long and late into the night they rioted, surging up and down and shouting, throwing stones and bricks and homemade fire bombs at police and soldiers who threw tear gas back at them and tried to break their heads with truncheons, dragging them off through their own blood to wagons taking them to jail.

By the time the riots had calmed down again that year, Mi Sook was pregnant for the second time. *Madame* pulled down her face and disapproved. "For two children you need a husband," she said.

"Soon Kun Soo will marry me."

"And when is soon? This week? Next week? Next year?"

"As soon as his savings are big enough."

Madame snorted.

When Mi Sook's second child was born, *Madame* came again to help, this time bringing her sister and her sister's friend, who chattered all the time as though to fill the void of *Madame's* sister's silence. While the commotion of the birth went on in the back room, Kun Soo hung more peppers on the doors and stood guard at each one in turn with his arms folded and his face drawn into a heavy scowl to keep the demons off.

But then it was a girl and he was disappointed. Mi Sook took the name of an actress she had seen on television and called the baby Li Na. In her heart she felt a welcome for the little girl that she had not felt for the son, but Kun Soo stayed away for several weeks. He came back, though, because after all Mi Sook had given him one son and so he knew that she could give him others. One daughter, not so bad. This woman had sons inside her.

Mi Sook became frightened and angry when he stayed away but when he came back she forgave him. She wanted to ask him for a little money for extra food because what she made in wage was not enough, and she did ask him one time.

He flared his eyes at her. "How can you expect me to put together my nest egg if I have to pass all the money I earn out of my hand?"

After that she didn't ask again but sometimes took a rice cake or a sticky bun from the display counter to keep her strength up for feeding the boy, who was now past two and very hungry, and also the baby girl. Sometimes she let the boy eat food left over on the students' plates. More and more often she thought of what *Madame* had said about needing a husband.

She had always been a favorite with the students but now they became extra kind. As well as leaving coins for her on the table or slipping them into the pocket of her apron, they sometimes brought gifts of cookies or candy, occasionally a piece of fruit. "For the boy," they would say, or, "Here, little sister, this is for your strength."

The third time Kun Soo made her pregnant she was frightened that it would be another girl and Kun Soo would refuse to marry her, so she went next door to the wedding shop, where she consulted with *Madame,* and then confronted him. "Consider your children," she said. "How can you let them grow up like this without a proper father? Your son will be ashamed when he is grown. He will not respect you as he should. Is that what you want? You must marry me as you have promised."

Kun Soo did not turn away so she went on boldly. "This new child is another son, I know it. We must give a name to him."

Kun Soo's eyes flickered. "How do you know it is a son?"

"It feels the same inside me as the first. Two sons to be ashamed of you. Is that what you want?"

He turned away. "I will consult a fortune-teller."

The next day he did not come to the shop and by evening Mi Sook began to give up hope because she had lied to him, telling him that the child inside her felt like the first, the boy, when in fact it felt like the second, the girl.

That night she did not sleep at all. When the boy and the baby girl had gone to sleep she went out into the town, walking up and down the streets in great distress because by now the fortune-teller had surely told Kun Soo how she had tried to trick him into marrying her. She would never see him again but would be left here with yet another child and not even enough wage to feed the two she had. She struck her hand against her head and moaned, staring into the dark as though she might see there the way her life would go now. She had wanted to be like *Madame* with a business of her own, but with three children how could this be done?

She thought of how *Madame* had flung her hands up, saying, "Men? I do not need them. All they bring is trouble," and when Mi Sook said, "But do you not want children?" she said, "Better go childless than to starve." Now Mi Sook feared that she would starve from all these children Kun Soo had put in her. She wished she had never let him tease her with his foolish fish cakes, or let him come into the back room of the shop, or lie down on her bedding on the floor. She wished she had not had any of his children.

She envied *Madame* in her bridal shop sketching wedding dresses on her pad, cutting out fine fabric with her sharp scissors, going about the city seeking out the best buttons and pieces of lace and buying foreign bridal magazines. Each morning she came to her shop and each evening went home and lay down to rest herself on satin bedding—Mi Sook knew it was satin because *Madame* had told her so—and never did she have to wash the soiled bottom of a child or listen to it crying in the night or have to give her breast to it when she was tired from working. She remembered how she used to close the coffee shop at night and go into her back room and count the money in her candy box or watch her people on the television, and she wished it was like that again.

Now delivery trucks began to rattle in the alleyways and

she realized she was very tired. She sat down for a moment on a step, but the moment grew into another and another. She woke with a jolt, shivering, and made to rise, but her belly felt too heavy to carry all the way back home and she sat there blinking at the morning mist. Then she thought of her two children, who might have awakened and be calling out for her and crying in the dark, so she heaved herself up and went back to the coffee shop.

The children were still sound asleep, curled up together in a ball, so she lay down on the bedding next to them and had barely fallen into sleep when a man making an early-morning delivery thumped on the back door and woke her up again.

Later in the day, while she was wiping down a table in the shop, Kun Soo came in from the lane. She heard Dae Young call out to him and then they came in together and stood behind the counter looking at her. All her worries from the night before fell out of her head because Kun Soo was smiling. When she came behind the counter he drew her into the back room and put his face against her hair. "We will call the child Sun Dool," he said, "because he will be a second son."

"The fortune-teller has told you this?"

"And the shaman. The shaman also said that I should marry you."

Although Kun Soo had been intoxicated by Mi Sook, intoxicated also at the thought of all the healthy sons she might produce for him, he had up till now thought of marrying her only in an imaginary way, never having applied his mind to the logistics of such an undertaking, namely, having to divorce his current wife. He did not hate this wife. In fact, he would have been perfectly content with her if she had given him even one good son. He would not have asked for more. To have five daughters is not so bad if a man has one good son. She was an obedient wife too, never making trouble for him. He got angry with her sometimes, even beat her, but if he spoke honestly with himself, she was a good enough wife, better than some. Besides, divorcing a wife of many years was not something to be taken lightly and he did not want to fall foul of the angry spirits of her ancestors.

The promises of marriage he had made to Mi Sook he did not consider lies and in a sense they were not. He did not say to her, "marriage," intending nothing, but on the other hand he had no intention. His were the promises a man makes to a woman he would like to have but cannot and yet does not want to lose, setting up by them a sort of imaginary world. But now he had been pressed to make a choice.

First he had consulted with a fortune-teller near his house in Inch'on, a shrewd old man approaching his one hundredth birthday who wore the traditional white baggy pants and shirt and slippers turned up at the toes. He had a hair almost a meter long growing from his chin and Kun Soo had been to him before, getting good enough advice.

The fortune-teller came to meet him at the door of his small shop, shuffling one step at a time behind his knobby cane. He bowed and greeted Kun Soo, and drawing him inside, slowly folded his creaking knees and hips until he was kneeling on the floor with his charts of astrology spread in front of him. These he turned and folded, unfolded and turned again, peering and muttering, asking a question now of Kun Soo, now of himself, now of some star or planet, punctuating all this with a flow of information and advice.

Kun Soo listened to all he had to say, waiting for each new thing with a sense of expectation, as though the thing he would say next would be the key, as though it would take from him the burden of having to come back to Mi Sook with a decision. He did not expect to hear him say, "You must marry Mi Sook," or, "You must divorce your wife." His thinking was not yet this clear on the decision to be made. He simply listened blindly, hopefully, and finally with disappointment because everything the fortune-teller had to say was ordinary.

When it was all said and the fortune-teller had folded up his charts and coughed politely with his hand held out, Kun Soo paid him because he must be paid, thanked him because he must be thanked, and bowed before he left because it was the civil thing to do. But he was restless and dissatisfied and that night clung to his wife in a way he never had before, not like a husband but more as a child would cling to its mother, and she opened her arms to him and let him lie inside their warmth.

In the morning he went off to work, walking briskly in the chilly dawn with no intention but to drive a load of fish to Kwangju. However, as he passed the vendors setting up their market stalls, his eye fell on a woman selling chickens. They

were all white and she had tied them by their feet to a metal
rack of the sort that clothes are hung on in a store. They hung
together in a row with their wings flopping, red combs hanging straight down off their heads, red wattles puffing down
across their throats like tiny cushions bent on suffocation. The
row of black beaks pointed at the ground, the row of sharp
eyes winked as though astonished at this new view of the
world.

As he passed these chickens it occurred to Kun Soo that in
a village in the countryside near Kwangju, not so very far from
where he must make his delivery that day, there lived a shaman
known in the area as the White Shaman, and that she had a
solid reputation. It might be prudent to take a chicken to her
and ask for some advice.

By this time he was past the market stalls and almost to the
warehouse, so he turned, and making his way back, argued
with the chicken vendor until he got one at a price he could
afford. Taking it by the feet, he carried it along the road, and
the chicken, having flapped its wings a time or two and made a
few complaining clucking sounds, pecked once at his knee,
and then the inner membrane of its eye came up and it relaxed
into its fate.

Kun Soo was frightened when he first saw the White Shaman.
She was like a ghost, or one of his bleached t-shirts. She wore
a long white gown like a monk's robe and every part of her
that he could see was white—long hair falling out from under-

neath the hood, bird's face half hidden by its folds, tiny hands and narrow forearms, tiny naked feet. Her eyes, though, were a strange pink color, like the inside of a mouth, and she was blind.

A young girl of about fourteen years, ragged and very thin, led her by the hand to meet him at the gate and left the two of them to talk about their business while she seized a stick and chased away the half-dozen or so children who had run beside his truck as he drove slowly up the rutted lane to where the thatched roof of the shaman's house could be seen above the village rice fields.

She had not been hard to find. The White Shaman was famous in these parts, not just for her skills but also for her unearthly looks. Her voice also was unearthly, like an indrawn sigh, and she seemed neither young nor old. Her skin was smooth like a young girl's, yet she had no teeth and the way she moved was like a woman who has lived through many years.

She listened to Kun Soo's request with her head on one side, asking a soft question now and then, and while he made his answer, examining his face and neck and hands and every part of him with her pale pink unseeing eyes until he felt that she could see clear to his soul and knew he could not lie to her. When an arrangement had been made, she called the girl to take the chicken by the legs, and setting one hand on her shoulder, followed her back to the house.

Kun Soo was pleased. The White Shaman had been kind and yet the questions she had asked had been perceptive. He wrestled with the truck to turn it in the narrow lane and jolted back along the ruts with the village children once more running at his side and told himself that tomorrow he would have the answer to his problem.

Next day he came back. Everything was ready. The chicken, with its head cut off, hung from one of the wooden crosspieces supporting a trellis above the little courtyard by the door. Gourd vines much like the ones his mother grew climbed across the trellis, making a dim arbor underneath. A patterned rattan mat was set on the ground below the chicken, and on the mat a large white porcelain bowl into which the chicken's red blood slowly dripped, making a spattered pattern up its sides.

The bowl was now half full. Arranged around it were various objects—a bunch of herbs, a knife, a feather, a small bundle of string, some smooth black stones, a scoop made from a gourd—and behind it knelt the White Shaman, wearing the chicken's head like a tiny crown. The girl knelt on her heels off to one side.

The White Shaman did not use astrological charts as the fortune-teller had. Instead she performed rites with the bowl of blood and the objects set around it. Mumbling to herself, she took the bunch of herbs in her left hand, and holding it above the bowl, tore it into pieces with her right, letting the herbs fall down into the bowl, where they floated on the surface of the blood. Then she dipped the feather in the blood, pressing it down below the herbs, and passed it in a complicated shape through the air above the bowl. She took up the knife, dipping it likewise, and made a single cutting motion in the same place in the air. The stones she dropped one by one into the blood, then with the scoop withdrew them and set them in a ring around the bowl. The string she cut with the bloody knife into three lengths, knotted each one on itself, dipped them one by one into the blood, and set them at equally spaced intervals around the stones.

Watching this, Kun Soo expected to see heavy magic and so was disappointed when at first the interview went quietly, the White Shaman telling him essentially the same things as the fortune-teller. There was hardly any difference at all. Both swore the child would be a boy. Both warned him to name the child at once, by this means securing his spirit to his body. If he did not do this there was danger of a female spirit nudging him aside. Both said not to wait until the birth to hang red peppers at the door but to do so at once and to be sure that they stayed clean. If dust should settle on them, making their colors dim, they should be washed, and if they faded or grew brittle, they should be replaced. Both said he must be careful not to praise Mi Sook or to boast to anyone that he was going to have a son.

Kun Soo listened with a doubtful face. "All this I did for my mistress's last child and still it was only a girl."

On this point the fortune-teller and the White Shaman agreed in their advice. "This mistress is not like your wife," the White Shaman told him. "Your wife was made susceptible to girls because she had a girl first. That girl attracted the spirits of other girls. This mistress, on the other hand, is prone to boys. You know that because it was a boy she had first. I will give you a recipe that you must have her drink each day, also a list of magic charms. With these together you are guaranteed a son."

"But what if this new son should be an idiot like the other one?"

"There is no fear of that."

"How do you know?"

It was at this point that a difference between the fortune-teller and the White Shaman began to be apparent. The fortune-teller had reassured him, saying, "There is no danger of that because it was through your wife's line that the bad blood came. It did not come from you." To this Kun Soo had said, "How do you know this thing? Five daughters I have had from her and not one of them an idiot. They have all gone off, abandoning their father in his difficulties, but not one of them is an idiot." The fortune-teller had had no satisfactory answer for him on this point.

The White Shaman, though, scoffed at what the fortune-teller had said. "Bad blood did not come through your wife's line, or through your line either. Any fool can tell you that. You have told me yourself that it was demons who came in the night to suck the child's spirit up into their nostrils. This is why his brain is not right. It is for lack of a complete spirit. And you have also told me that you laughed and boasted when this child was born. So his misfortune is because of you."

Kun Soo flung out his hand but as though she had felt his movement the shaman raised her own hand in a reprimanding gesture, turning her pale eyes toward him. "Did you come for my advice or did you come to argue?"

Kun Soo began to speak but then he looked down at his hand stuck out in front of him and set it on his knee. "I have come for your advice."

"Well then, if your first son's misfortune was because of you, it is clear that the outcome for this latest son is also up to you. If you follow my instructions carefully he will be safe. Oh, and one more thing. To be completely secure, you must divorce your wife and marry your mistress without delay."

"But this is the main problem I came to you to solve. If I divorce my wife, will not her ancestors be angry? What if they should seek revenge on this new son? I am fearful that no matter what I do they will be too powerful for me." Kun Soo's voice took on a tremor of self-pity. "I do not want another idiot."

There was silence. The White Shaman seemed to be listening to something inside her head.

"What is it?" Kun Soo said.

"Wait," said the White Shaman in an agitated voice, "someone is coming."

Kun Soo looked around. "I see no one."

She did not reply. Her head rolled back and her eyes turned up in her head. The girl sprang to support her from behind. The White Shaman's throat worked and writhed and Kun Soo saw a shape move up it as though something were struggling to come out. And now a presence seemed to stand in the air above the bowl of blood, in the same place she had painted with the bloody feather and sliced through with the bloody knife. Kun Soo looked fearfully at it and it seemed to him that the air there was not quite as transparent as the surrounding air.

A small child's voice spoke out of it. "Greetings, my father."

Kun Soo jerked his eyes to the White Shaman's mouth but although it hung open she was gasping in a way that seemed to indicate that the voice had not come out of her.

"Who is it speaks to me?"

Now the White Shaman seemed to take a fit. She fell back into the girl's arms with her back stiff and her arms and legs beating at the ground and her eyes completely turned up in her head so that the pink was gone and they were white like all the rest of her. She gasped and sobbed and then her tongue fell out and she began to drool. The spasm stopped and she rose up in a crouch, then stood, the small of her back curved in so that her bottom stuck out in a neat round ball, elbows tucked against her sides, forearms raised so that her two hands flapped at shoulder height like chicken's wings below the chicken's head attached to hers. She staggered on her tiptoes around the bowl of blood with her head swinging side to side as though searching for someone, whimpering and talking to herself in an incoherent language Kun Soo recognized.

He leaped up, backing violently away. "Joo Yup," he cried in a terrible voice. "What can this mean?"

The White Shaman seemed neither to see nor hear him. She went on past, out of the shaded arbor to the open yard, where she stumbled up and down, searching and weeping aloud now, the tears falling down her face and dripping off her lolling tongue. Her nose ran loose clear mucus and she let it run, not so much as wiping the back of her hand across her face. And all the time she repeated and repeated in a mournful voice like a dirge what Kun Soo realized was not some string of incoherencies but the words, "*Ama, Ama, Ama.*"

"What can this mean?" Kun Soo cried again, and as the White Shaman swung toward his voice, he cried, "Joo Yup, do not harm me. Pity me, my son," and flinging his arms around his head as though to protect himself, he turned to run.

But suddenly the White Shaman was herself again. She called sharply to him, "Do not run away. The chicken you have brought me has good blood. I have seen your dead son."

"I have seen only Joo Yup, the imbecile, and he is not dead," said Kun Soo, standing ready to back off again.

"Come, come, sit down again with me. I have seen your other son."

Kun Soo looked at her. "Dae Young? The son of my mistress?"

"No, it was your dead son I saw."

"I have no dead son."

"Did you not hear him speak to you?"

"That first voice? I did not know it. That one was a stranger."

"Not a stranger. It was Joo Yup's twin brother, the stillborn son."

"Joo Yup's twin brother, do you say? But that child never breathed."

"No matter. He will now be an advantage to you."

"An advantage? How so an advantage?"

"You must make a special offering and pray. Your son has recognized his father and will help you."

"How will he help?"

"He will restrain the demon spirits. He has this power because he never lived inside a body and so is like a monk who has never had a woman."

"But what about my idiot son?" Kun Soo said impatiently. "What about Joo Yup? I saw him here today."

The White Shaman looked puzzled. "No, no. There was one spirit only."

"But I saw him. I saw him in your body. He was searching and crying loudly, *'Ama, Ama, Ama.'* What does this mean?"

But the White Shaman professed to have no memory of it. She insisted that there had been one spirit only, the spirit of Joo Yup's twin. The more he pressed her on the matter the more adamant she became.

"Come," he said at last, "tell me truthfully the meaning of this thing or else I will not pay your fee."

The White Shaman rocked back on her heels. "It was nothing," she said in a wheedling voice. "You had a vision, that is all."

"What does it mean?"

"Eh! Do not think of it at all. It cannot be explained to someone who is not familiar with the spirit world."

Kun Soo looked hard at her with a frightened, dissatisfied face. "I think it was an omen. I think I have done myself great harm by coming here today."

The White Shaman said nothing, just fell to mumbling to

herself, but the girl, who all this time had said not a word, crept behind her and whispered in her ear, occasionally looking up at Kun Soo as she spoke.

The White Shaman held her head in a listening position, pursing up her mouth. "Of course," she said. "Of course."

"What now?" said Kun Soo.

"My girl here is a very clever girl. One day she will also be a shaman. She has told me that what you say is true, that Joo Yup's spirit did seem to be inside me. But it was not the spirit of the Joo Yup who lives with you, it was not your idiot son. It was the part of him the demons stole, a part that has become fused with his dead brother's spirit. For a time they separated but now they are together again. It is not a matter for concern."

"So what was the meaning of it?"

"Meaning? It was a kindness. He wanted to show you that what I told you was true, that he is now a very powerful spirit and will help you. So do not be afraid. I have done nothing that will bring harm to you." She smiled, showing her white gums. "If I should hurt you, how would I be paid?"

Kun Soo let himself be persuaded by this line of reasoning and after he had consulted with the White Shaman concerning the exact nature of the offering he should make to Joo Yup's twin, he paid her fee.

As he was turning to leave, he said, "It is a hard thing to ask a wife of many years for a divorce."

The White Shaman lifted her shoulders and rolled her head from side to side. "It is up to you."

MI SOOK WAS SO RELIEVED Kun Soo had agreed to marry her that she put off worrying about how he might react when the child was born a girl. By then she would be in a secure position with him, and anyway she might be mistaken about it. Had not both the fortune-teller and the White Shaman said the child would be a boy? Had they not already named him Sun Dool, which means "benevolent second son"? Surely it would be a boy.

When the helper came, Mi Sook left the shop to her and went next door to tell *Madame* the good news. "Finally he has agreed to marry me, *Madame*. Are you not pleased for me? I will no longer have to live crowded with my children in the back room of that coffee shop. I will be a married woman and perhaps not have to work at all."

Madame looked up from the piece of fine silk onto which she was sewing beads. "Why would you not want to work? Is it not from work that you gain money? Will you spend your life begging from a husband?"

"Well then, I will have a business of my own."

"What sort of business will this be?"

"I do not know." She turned away, looking out the window of *Madame*'s shop between two headless brides in satin finery.

"Then you must apply your mind to it, child. Setting up a business is no easy thing. You must have a line of goods, and a shop, and a little capital to start. Perhaps this new husband of yours will give you capital. It is not the usual thing, but perhaps if he is as successful as you say, he will see the wisdom of it. Then you can pay rent in advance and buy your stock. You must think about it, child. It is a good life, running a shop. See how I have my clients coming to me with their purses open and their daughters at their heels? Already I own this shop myself, and also the souvenir store next door, and next to that the acupuncturist, so these two must pay me rent, and one day I will say, 'This whole block belongs to me.' Yes, I have made a good life for myself and for my sister. I recommend it to you."

Mi Sook stood staring at the window. The evening was falling down outside and she could see herself reflected between the headless brides. She imagined that she was the owner of the shop and it was a good feeling to her, but then she thought about how she could not sew the clothes, so she tried to imagine something else standing in the window instead of brides. She saw a grand display of something gleaming but could not determine what it was. She wanted to be in charge of selling something beautiful, something that women would come and open up their purses for as they did with

Madame. Yes, she would like a shop. She peered at the gleaming display of merchandise to see what it might be but it was only the headless brides again.

She swung away. "But, *Madame*, I will have my children to care for, and my husband also. Obviously he loves me because he has agreed to marry me. Come, *Madame*, I want you to be happy for me."

"Then I am happy for you, child. Come here and look at these new beads I have found. Are they not delightful?"

Madame was disappointed in Mi Sook's wedding. "All this time I had planned to make you such a bride," she said, "but now you have only the smallest ceremony with no gown or veil."

Mi Sook laughed at her. "Better to be married with the smallest ceremony than not to be married at all. And anyway," she said, setting her hand against her swollen belly, "a big ceremony would not be appropriate."

"But gifts would be appropriate. Where is the messenger coming from your fiancé with the box tied to his back?"

"I am just a poor girl in a coffee shop, *Madame*."

"But you say this husband is successful. Why does he not send the customary box of gifts?"

"I do not know, *Madame*."

"I think I do not trust this man."

"But *Madame*, he has agreed to marry me."

"Still child, I tell you honestly, there is something in all this I do not trust. I think you do not know this man."

"I will know him soon enough. Tomorrow I will be his wife."

"Ah, child, from his wife a man hides many things, but many more are hidden from the wife who first was mistress."

Kun Soo took her home to Inch'on in the fish truck and as they went she imagined herself living in a nice house with two stories, *ondol* on every floor, a four-ring gas stove, and a gleaming white refrigerator. She would also have an electric washer and a private yard so that her clothes and underwear would not be pinned out dancing on a rope for all to see.

She imagined how the laborers would come each morning and squat out by the gate, waiting for her husband to finish his breakfast soup and dumplings and fine black coffee and come to give them their instructions for the day, how at night he would come home and talk to her about his business, asking her advice.

During the day she would care for her children and go shopping at the market, where she would be respected because her husband was rising in the town and one day would become wealthy—maybe he would even become the mayor, or at least the deputy mayor. She would come home and cook him rice and fish and *bulgoki* and many side dishes, maybe fifteen for one meal, flavoring it all with garlic and spices and hot pepper paste.

Sometimes her husband would bring home a toy for his children or a gift for her, maybe a necklace or a pair of embroidered slippers. She would bear him many sons and he would love her and soon they would move to an even bigger house. It would be on the side of a hill and would have court-yards filled with cedar trees and gingko trees and pines, and purple lilac and azaleas, and every sort of summer flower. Its tiled roof would be jade green and curve elegantly up at every corner. The room behind the coffee shop seemed small and shabby to her now.

But then Kun Soo pulled up and stopped in a street no wider than the lane behind the coffee shop. Mi Sook looked across at him, expecting him to start the truck again and continue on, but no, he took the key out of the ignition, opened his door, lifted out his little son, and carried him across in front of the truck, calling out to someone behind the stone fence to Mi Sook's right. Above it she could see a small house of the old type, made of stone and the roof of asphalt tiles splotched here and there with growths of roof fungus. The top part of a narrow veranda could be seen running across the front of the house. A vine grew on the fence, dangling its arms across the top.

Now Kun Soo came out of the gate, beckoning to her with his hand turned down, and with a heavy heart she opened the truck door and slung the baby on her hip.

The house had a tiny narrow strip of yard in front and on the veranda stood a small stooped woman, very old and wrinkled. She wore the traditional long white skirt and blouse with ribbons holding it across the breast, both made of the cheapest cotton. On her feet were white rubber slippers with turned-up toes and her gray hair was pulled back in a bun. She smiled, stepping down off the veranda.

"Welcome, Daughter."

Mi Sook was overcome with confusion. She bowed abruptly and the baby, frightened by the sudden movement, gave out a dismal wail. She felt strange, as though she were dreaming and would soon wake. But the old woman was not paying her attention. She was reaching for the boy, her old face cracked open in a smile. "Ah," she said, and, "Oh, so beautiful," and while Kun Soo talked and talked, telling the child's name and making boasts about his strength and intelligence, and the old woman rocked him in her arms and smiled and smiled, listening to Kun Soo brag, Mi Sook, like a sleepwalker, went past them with the baby on her hip, up to the veranda, where she slipped off her shoes and went into the house.

She looked around. Where she stood the floor was of cement. To her left, beside the door, was a row of metal hooks with coats and jackets hung on them, and below, a row of shoes and sneakers, a pair of padded boots. Beside them, in the corner, a low square serving table leaned against the wall behind a wide flat-bottomed basket full of ornamental gourds. From the corner, running along the wall, was a kitchen area—a sink with single faucet, a high bench with a portable electric hotplate set on it, stacked pots and bowls, a fat glass jar out of which stuck wooden chopsticks and long-handled metal spoons.

Above the sink was fixed a row of cheap wooden shelves. They went all the way up to the ceiling and along them sat dozens of ornamental gourds with round fat bellies and long tubular bellies and necks of every shape and size, some elegant as swan necks, others twisted, knotted. They were green and brown and yellow, red and orange, and in every shade, some dark, some pale, some almost white, and some were smooth, some mottled, and some flaking. Some had patterns scratched into them. Others had been stained or carved, or painted with characters that said *Long Life* or *Fortune*. Beyond them, in the other corner, a large wooden box stood with the handle of a shovel sticking out of it. Nothing else was on the left side of the room.

Mi Sook turned to examine the right side of the room, which was completely made up of a raised *ondol* floor with an oiled paper surface and three shallow steps for climbing up. In its side was a hinged metal hatch with a handle. She stared at this and then went across, and reaching down, took the metal handle in her hand. It was warm and she lifted it upwards to release it from the two supports that held it in place, then lowered it and peered inside. A few ashes stirred and fluttered where a fire had been. She peered lower, looking for the pipes for funneling hot air below the floor, but there was nothing, just the space below the floor and this metal hatch for shoveling coal inside.

She closed it, her mouth set in a line, and looked around her at the walls. At this end of the room they were covered with a bamboo-patterned wallpaper, which now was brown but might once have been green. The edges of the strips were peeled away as far up as a child could reach and hung like little flags around the room. On the front wall was a window with a shabby yellow curtain on each side, and against the back wall a small red chest of drawers and a yellow plastic wardrobe with a zipper down the front. A roll of bedding lay against the far end wall.

There was no more to the house, just these two sections of one room, the whole thing no more than twenty feet long and fourteen wide, barely twice as big as the room Mi Sook had lived in all her life, and with five people and soon another child to share it.

She turned her back on it and went outside, where the old woman was still making much of her grandson, Kun Soo still bragging as though he would never stop. Mi Sook slipped her shoes back on, walked the length of the veranda to the left side of the house, and stepped down, making her way along a narrow walkway no wider than the length of her arm.

Behind the house was a tiny yard with a row of buried kimchi pots and a single strung-wire clothesline with three white t-shirts pinned to it. A small shed was to the right with wires strung up it to support more vines, which clambered up onto its roof with their load of ornamental gourds.

Two doors were in the shed. Mi Sook pushed the right one and it opened to a storage room. Inside were shovels, a wooden ladder, some pieces of wood, other odds and ends of construction material, and a large metal bowl with handles, rusty in a circle where the bottom joined the sides. Beside it stood a plastic soap dish with a cake of soap and above it on a hook a small white towel.

The left-hand door opened to a toilet, set low against the

floor. Beside it stood a yellow plastic trash can full of water with a bobbing orange scoop. A faucet on a drunken pipe stuck out from the wall, dripping down into the trash can with a sharp metallic *plink*.

Mi Sook turned and looked at the back wall of the house: rough stone with not even a small window. She counted the kimchi pots: four and one broken in the corner of the yard. She looked at the three threadbare t-shirts hanging on the line. She stepped out to the middle of the yard and looked up at the gourds on the roof. They looked back down at her like squatting frogs.

So, she told herself, I have been tricked. My husband is nothing but a poor man after all, a builder's laborer who drives a fish truck on the side. He has no four-ring burner, no refrigerator, no electric washer, no bath or shower, just a metal basin to be filled with water, and only half an *ondol* floor with not even any cooking stove attached, and on top of that an old woman, a mother-in-law, to share it with. In all this time it had never occurred to her that she might have a mother-in-law.

Mi Sook hated Inch'on. She missed the coffee shop and her back room, the bustle of activity, the back-and-forth of jokes and conversation with the students. She remembered how they used to call her little sister and protect her, slipping coins into her apron. At the coffee shop she had had a room all for herself and an inside toilet. Also she had had a shower, just a nozzle sticking from the wall and a drain in the center of the floor, but still a shower. Best of all, at the coffee shop she had been in charge. She told the helper what to do, and when her work was done she pleased herself. Here she must please everyone else: her husband, her husband's mother, her demanding children.

Every day she was angry and upset and refused to tell Kun Soo why. His mother helped her get a job working on a market stall and she worked there until the baby's birth, but she was dissatisfied with it. She did not want to wind a towel around her head and work down at a market stall with foolish women who did nothing in their lives but bow their heads. She scorned Kun Soo's mother for the way she crouched down on the floor, scratching patterns onto gourds, staining them with shoe polish, spending all her time arranging them on shelves, turning them this way and that to dry evenly. And what did she get for selling them? A pittance.

Sometimes she regretted ever having children, but then her little son would come striding through the yard on his short legs and her heart would swell up in her chest, or her little girl would cry for ribbons in her hair and she would sit down on the floor with her and lose herself in scraps of red and pink and green, the soft smell of the child's skin. At night she would lie with her hand on her belly, feeling her third child kick and squirm, and when she fell asleep she would dream she was holding it, a perfect little girl. After that dream, she would wake happy, but then she would see how Kun Soo did all the things the White Shaman and the fortune-teller had advised to make sure this next child would be another son—setting out charms, every morning having her drink a draft made from the juice of kimchi mixed with ginseng tea, going every day to the temple to pray and make an offering— and thoughts of an abortion came inside her head. But she had no money of her own and no one to help her. She longed to see *Madame* and began to dread this birth because she was sure now it would be a girl.

So it turned out to be. Kun Soo went back to the fortune-teller, who was sitting on a low stool outside his shop. When he heard Kun Soo's complaint, he pulled the long hair of his chin, rocked onto the back legs of his stool, and came back down onto the front ones with a thump. Then he took a stick and drew some lines and circles on the ground. It was Mi Sook's fault, he said. Had she taken the draft each day? Yes, she had taken the draft. Kun Soo had watched her drink it every morning with his own two eyes. The fortune-teller rocked again and thumped again, spat in the dust. The girl must have had another lover. The child had not been fathered by Kun Soo.

This so enraged Kun Soo that he did not waste time traveling to consult again with the White Shaman. It was the first time he beat his second wife. He had not beaten her before because she was young and very beautiful, and because she pleased him. But now she was just a wife. And she had been with another man. He beat her well for that.

In all Mi Sook's life no one had raised a hand to her or

even been unkind, and she resented this man beating her. She lay down on the bedding and refused to feed the baby, and for three days and nights it screamed and screamed until Kun Soo's mother took it up and went with it to a friend whose daughter had a new child, asking her to feed it until her daughter-in-law got her wits together.

During this time, the old women who were Kun Soo's mother's friends took the baby and examined it. They looked into its eyes and down its throat. They examined the shape of its ears and ran their fingers down its spine to feel the shape of its bones. They touched it all over gently, singing to it to keep it calm. They did this every day for five days and at the end of this time Kun Soo's mother brought it home. "It is your own child," she told Kun Soo. "You are the true father. That old fortune-teller is a fool."

Now a man may beat his wife, but he must respect his mother, so Kun Soo took the baby as his own even though it was nothing but a girl, and Mi Sook got up off the bedding and fed it, and the little girl became her favorite. She named her Tae Hee and treasured her above both her other children, taking her everywhere.

Seeing this, Kun Soo thought she was afraid that he would kill the child if she did not keep it near her and this made his anger rise. To make things worse, there were strikes and union trouble in the building business at that time. Down at the construction site he and the other laborers squatted in the dust and smoked, watching the foreman go back and forth in argument with the man sent from the company who had con-

tracted for the building. At the end of that week, all the laborers got up and went in search of other work. Kun Soo went
with them but work was hard to find. Every morning he had to
stand in line before the dawn, his belly clamoring with hunger,
and beg for every day of work he got.

He asked Mr. Shin, the fish warehouse manager, for extra
work, but it seemed that every man in Inch'on who could
drive was asking too and Mr. Shin used this as a means of
keeping down the pay. "Eh," he said the one time Kun Soo
mentioned his low pay, "there are others. Every day they come
to me and ask for less."

After that Kun Soo kept his mouth shut and was sure to
arrive on time and stay on schedule and never deliver a short
order or leave the truck door standing open in the street for
passersby to help themselves. Consequently complaints were
few on the routes he drove but when they came, however
minor they might be—a mistake in billing, some undersized
crabs slipped in at the bottom of a box, some tuna fish a little
ripe—he bowed and bowed, apologizing and apologizing, and
at night waking with a shout from dreams of losing this job
also.

He began to drink again, a little here, a little there, just
enough to get him through this hard time. But by the time all
the arguments between the foreman and the contractor had
been resolved and he went back to work at the construction
site, it was too late—he had become the man he had been
before he met Mi Sook. With a little money in his hand again,
he stayed late at the wine shop every night and every morning

came home raging and accusing her with spittle flying from his mouth.

Beating Mi Sook, though, did not become a habit with him as it had been with his first wife because the White Shaman had been right about one thing: Mi Sook was not like his first wife. She screamed back at him, and hit him, and accused him too. He had lied to her, she said. He had tricked her. He was nothing but a common man, a builder's laborer who drove a truck and stank of fish. And so, although Kun Soo might get up a fine resolution to beat this second wife of his, he did not often do it. Instead he shouted louder than before.

The children cried loudly while this went on, adding to the commotion. The boy developed a kind of flinching quality, the little girl stopped running to her father, and the baby screamed if anyone but Mi Sook picked her up.

Kun Soo's mother, who had been kind to Mi Sook, became distressed. One night Mi Sook was sitting at the warm end of the room feeding the baby. She heard someone crying softly, and thinking it was one of the other children, looked down at them. But no, they were both sound asleep on the quilt beside her with their arms flung out. Then she realized the sound was coming from behind her. Turning, she saw that the old woman was crying and talking softly to herself as she stood over the electric hotplate stirring the soup with one long cooking chopstick.

Mi Sook pitied her because Kun Soo's mother had been kind to her and now her son's house was full of trouble. She set the baby down and went to stand beside her.

"I am sorry to have brought you trouble, Mother."

The old woman was busy talking to herself and did not hear. "He should be grateful that the one son she has given him is not an imbecile," she said.

"What is this you say about an imbecile?"

The old woman looked up with a start. "It is nothing, Daughter, nothing."

"But what is this you say about an imbecile?"

The old woman said nothing, just stirred at the soup.

"What is there, Mother, that you do not tell me?"

The old woman still did not speak but Mi Sook pressed and pressed her until at last she gave a sigh and said, "Well then, better perhaps that I should be the one to tell you because eventually you will hear it from others. They will tell you garbled versions and you will never know the truth. Better, I suppose, that you hear the truth from me. You must swear, though, never to tell my son that I have told you."

Mi Sook was frightened because the old woman's face was very serious, and she swore never to tell Kun Soo one word.

The old woman twisted her hand in the cord of the electric hotplate and jerked the plug out of the wall. "Come and sit with me and I will tell you, then."

"Ah," the old woman said, "he did not do it kindly. He had been away all night, taking a load of fish to Kwangju. Early in the morning, he came into the house, where his wife was chopping royal fern and boiling rice to make a special breakfast for his return. 'Wife,' he said, 'this son you have given me is an imbecile and worthless. You must give me a divorce.'

"As soon as the poor woman heard that she dropped the knife and burst out crying. 'But I thought you had forgiven me.'

"'You must understand,' Kun Soo said to her. 'My mother had three sons and two of them were killed during the war. I am all she has left and you have given me no son to carry on my father's line. But my mistress in Seoul has given me a healthy son and now she is pregnant with another. I have been to the fortune-teller and also I have taken a chicken to a shaman and both have assured me that the child will be another healthy boy. So you must understand my predicament. If I do not marry this woman, my old mother will die without the comfort of her grandsons in her house. How can I do that to her?'

"I was angry with him then—for using me as his appeal. I had always liked that wife and now she would think I had conspired against her. So I said to her, 'No, no, this has nothing to do with me, I know nothing of it.' 'You know nothing of it?' she said, and I swore to her, 'Nothing.'

"My son's first wife was a very humble woman who always kept her head turned down before her husband, but now she stood up straight and looked him in the eye. 'How old is this healthy son you say you have had with this girl?' she said. And Kun Soo said, 'Almost four years old.' She said nothing for a long time while Kun Soo looked to this side and that, making coughing noises in his throat, and then she said, 'For almost four years now I have been thinking that you have forgiven me for Joo Yup because you have been kinder to me and have brought me gifts, but now I see the truth.'"

The old woman drew her hand across her eyes. "I felt very sorry for her because I loved her, and I felt angry with my son because he used me as an excuse to ask for a divorce, but what could I do? I just stood there helplessly while the rice boiled over and went hissing down onto the hotplate so that afterwards I had to soak it in water because the rice had burned onto it and blackened."

Mi Sook was so angry at hearing all this that she could hardly keep herself from jumping up and running back to Seoul with all her children. But she knew that she was trapped. It had not been possible to feed even two children on her wage and now there was a third.

"Where is this first wife now?" she asked.

And now it was even worse. Kun Soo had made his demand early in the morning when the gourd flowers on the fence were closing their white faces. Then he went away, and while the old woman watched, his wife turned without a word and took the roll of bedding from where she had just set it up against the wall and rolled it out again and then lay down and seemed to go at once to sleep.

The old woman pitied her and left her there to sleep.

She slept all day.

Late in the afternoon the old woman thought of Joo Yup. By now he would be squatting by the market stall, waiting for his mother. Once before when she had been taken ill and come early home from work, Joo Yup had waited all night by the stall, forgotten. The old woman went to find him but he wasn't there so she inquired among the stallholders and learned that he had come there at his customary time and waited in his customary way, squatting quietly with his hands beside him on the ground.

After some time he grew restless and began to talk to himself and jerk his head around inquiringly, and after a while longer he got up, and with his tongue lolling from his head and his hands flapping at his shoulders, ran up and down on tiptoe in front of the stalls, crying and calling quite clearly in an agitated voice, *"Ama, Ama, Ama."*

When the old woman heard this story she questioned it because Joo Yup had never in all his life said *"Ama"* clearly, or any other word. He talked constantly, but only in the language he had dreamed up for himself, which no one but his mother understood.

Now, though, all the stallholders swore to it. Yes, they told her, they all heard him say it.

And so what happened then?

And then he ran away.

Where did he go?

But no one knew, only that Joo Yup had gone off into the town distraught.

Mi Sook shivered. "He did not come home?"

"He did not come. I have thought about this often since and it seems to me that by some instinct Joo Yup knew what had happened to his mother that day."

"Happened? What?"

"I came back home. My daughter-in-law was sleeping still and I went across to wake her, but looking down, I saw her two eyes staring up. Her mouth had fallen open and her cheeks had fallen in. Already her head looked like a skull. I ran to the house of Mrs. Park, our neighbor over there who has the telephone, but there was no use in it. When the health officer came from the clinic, there was nothing for him to do but write the death certificate. When Kun Soo came home late that night, drunk again and with a swaggering walk, he found his house full of mourners, his wife already washed and bound up in her shroud."

Mi Sook felt horror take her by the throat. "It was the same day he came to me and said that he would marry me, I know it."

Kun Soo's mother rolled her eyes and turned her hands palms up. "Of this I knew nothing. I had suspected my son might have a mistress—it is the way of men and none of my concern—but I knew nothing then of any talk of marriage to her, or of another son." And the old woman put her hands before her face and wept bitterly.

Mi Sook refused to let her weep. She took her by the shoulders. "Where is this first son now?" she demanded, because she was afraid that he would come creeping through the door and she would have to be the mother of an imbecile. "Tell me, Grannie, what has happened to the son?"

The old woman became very quiet, sitting with her eyes turned down.

"Tell me, Mother."

"Who knows? He vanished. Simply vanished. No one thought to mourn for him."

"You think, then, that he is dead?"

"All the women at the market stall say so."

"But you, what do you think?"

The old woman looked at her. "I think that he is dead."

For a while after this, Mi Sook became afraid to go outside at night because she would imagine the mad drooling figure of Kun Soo's first son creeping out at her from every shadow, but then she learned to live with the knowledge of him and could go out again.

The first wife, though, she still feared and could not sleep at night on the bedding where she had died. She grew gaunt and thin and tired and even more discontented than she had been before. Her milk dried up and she had to wean the baby. She took to pacing in the night, her feet slap-slapping up and down the narrow front veranda of the house. Because of her promise to her mother-in-law, and because she now feared and despised her husband, Mi Sook said nothing to him.

Madame, though, she missed with an increasing urgency, the way she would stand squarely in the doorway of her shop, greeting the passersby with stolid cheeriness. Man or woman, she didn't care, she greeted everyone, spitting on the ground behind the churlish or those who thought themselves above her. She had been a squatter in a shantytown beside the highway in the dreadful years after the war when no one had a home above their heads. Seoul had been laid flat by the army sweeping from the north and most of its inhabitants had run off toward the south in terror for their lives. *Madame*'s family had fled with them but on the way they were taken by surprise, her father clubbed to death with rifle butts, her mother flung onto her back across a rock and raped repeatedly, she and her little sister raped beside her on the ground. When it was all done and the soldiers had gone off into the night, hitching up their pants and calling to each other, she had bunched the cloth of her skirt between her legs and rubbed and rubbed until the blood and slime and mud were all rubbed off and she was sore. She called softly to her mother and her little sister, who was only five years old, but neither answered. Her mother was dead, back broken, her skirt wrenched up across her head. Her little sister was still alive, although she never spoke again.

That was the story *Madame* had told to Mi Sook when she was old enough to ask. Before that she had simply taken for granted the tiny birdlike woman who sat day after day at the big black sewing machine in the upstairs room of the bridal shop, squinting at the passage of the needle through the fabric, guiding it with expert hands while her foot went up and down, playing the machine as delicately as a pianist toes the pedal. She had no name of her own but was called *Madame*'s sister, and she supervised the sewing of a changing group of half-a-dozen girls, using her fine expressive hands to give instructions. As though in deference to *Madame*'s sister, these girls did not chatter as they worked. The construction of

Madame's creations went on in silence save for the rattle of machines, the clack of scissors, hiss and snap of thread.

At the time *Madame* told her this story, Mi Sook did not understand what it meant to be raped, but now that she had to sleep night after night with a man she no longer cared for, she imagined what it must be like and thought of *Madame's* sister with pity and a sort of awed respect. She wanted to go down the lane behind the coffee shop and, patting the door first with her hand, push it open, calling to *Madame*. She wanted to hear her loud confident voice and watch her eyes squint thoughtfully while she turned a young girl by the shoulders, making a picture in her head of how she would look in this style or that, assessing her mother's pocket by her rings and the quality of her clothes. Mi Sook wanted to talk to her, she wanted to complain, to tell her everything—about her husband's poor house, his job, his poverty, the way he went at night and drank and then came home and jumped on her, breathing stinking fumes into her face. Especially she wanted to tell her about his dead first wife and how she could not sleep for fear of her.

Early one morning, when she had paced most of the night, churning and churning her frustration in her head, she told herself that there was nothing left for her to do but kill herself. She crept into the house and brought back out the old woman's sharp knife that she used for slicing vegetables and paced some more, holding the point against her heart with tears running down her face. She came to the end of the veranda and stopped there, staring off into the dimness with both hands wrapped around the handle of the knife.

But then she heard Kun Soo come singing down the alleyway. Dogs barked behind the fences, one taking up after another like a triumphal announcement. She turned and saw him silhouetted in the gate against the harsh light flung down by the bare globe of the street lamp. She saw him swagger through the gate and come toward the house. He did not see her but swung his legs onto the veranda, kicked off his shoes, and pushing through the door, called out, "Wife! Wife!" in that voice he used when he wanted to lie down with her.

Mi Sook stepped toward the door, the blade of the knife turning itself away from her to point toward Kun Soo. When she came into the house he was bending over with his legs apart, pulling at the shadowed blankets. He swung around. "Ah, there you are!" And reached for her.

She swung out with the knife.

She had not meant to do it and she was afraid that she had killed him. She sat staring into the window of the bus at her own reflection but seeing Kun Soo's left cheek open eye to jaw. She had moved too fast to see the blood. In the microsecond of his shocked flesh she jerked away and ran. Now she imagined the well of blood and the wail of the police car coming after her, but nothing came, and she was almost back to Seoul before she realized she did not have the baby in her arms. She jumped up in a panic, but the bus was on the bridge across the river and would not stop again until it reached the other side.

She stood beside the door, clinging to the pole and peering out into the half light through the window at the front, as if by willing she could make the bus reach the next stop more quickly. When it did, she leaped down and ran across the road to the stop for buses going back the other way. Not until one hove into view did it occur to her that if Kun Soo was dead the house would be full of policemen, and if he was not dead, they might be waiting for her anyway. Either way, she could not go back inside the house.

The bus clanked open its door in front of her. The driver looked at her. She didn't move. He reached to close the door. "No, wait." She clambered up, digging in the pocket of her jeans. But she was out of money and the driver twisted in his seat and stuck his foot out to prevent her going down into the bus.

She climbed back down and stood irresolute. To walk all the way to Inch'on would exhaust her and even if she succeeded in stealing the baby away, how could she carry her all the long way back to Seoul? It would be foolish to attempt it.

She turned and headed through the silent streets toward the coffee shop.

When Mi Sook appeared in the front window of the shop, rapping on the pane, the owner's wife, who had been mopping the floor behind the counter, looked up with a disgruntled face. When she saw who it was a big laugh burst out of her. She leaned the mop against the wall and came running to unlock the door. Seizing Mi Sook by the wrist, she pulled her inside and flung her arms about her, laughing into her neck. The new girl who had replaced Mi Sook as manager looked up sourly and clashed a pot into the coffee machine. The owner's wife rolled up her eyes and jerked her head and Mi Sook followed her into the back room of the shop.

The new girl was no good at all, the owner's wife told Mi Sook with a hiss. She had let the place become filthy and brought soldiers into the back room at night, giving the coffee shop a nasty reputation. And she could not be left alone for one whole day. Money disappeared, food went bad, the coffee was too weak, too strong, the students all complained. Within minutes Mi Sook had her old job back. She even had a small raise in pay.

By now the coffee shop had opened and the early rush of students was already there when Mi Sook came out front. They turned their heads and looked at her, then, as if acting from a single impulse, they all stood up and cheered. They had not liked the girl who had taken over from Mi Sook and had been discussing other coffee shops where they might go instead. This was a delicate business as the Coffee Shop Utopia had been the gathering place for engineering students for some years now and groups of other students had long since laid claim to all the suitable places close around the university.

Now they forgot about their plans to find another coffee shop and fell back to arguing with each other over politics the way they always had. When Mi Sook set a cup of coffee or a bun down on a table, they looked up at her and smiled and gave her extra tips. Mi Sook became flushed and vigorous, bustling back and forth with trays. She beamed on the students, humoring them and lingering a little when this one or that put a hand on her arm or on her hip. The helper, who was the same one she had had before, hugged her and clung against her, smiling and smiling as though her face would split in half.

That day was a great triumph for her. When it was done and all the students had gone home, she cleaned the coffee pots, scoured the machines, replaced filters, ground beans ready for the morning, washed down the counters, even washed the walls and windows. And all the time a loud triumphant voice was singing in her head.

That night she dreamed about her baby, Tae Hee, and from then on, each time she was paid, she set the extra amount that was her raise into her candy box and hid it underneath the counter in the shop in case Kun Soo came and found it. She had heard that he was still alive and knew that sooner or later he would come.

The first time he came he was angry with her. He had bound his head up tightly in a rag and the seepage from his wound had patterned it in shades of brown and red and sickly clear. He pushed it at her through the door, making accusations, demanding to know what good a wife was to him if she was not in his bed when he came home at night. She closed the door on him.

The next time he came the rag was gone but the two sides of his wound had not healed together evenly and his face seemed not to fit him anymore. A purple ragged ridge angled eye to jaw, and Mi Sook could see it throbbing as though it had a heartbeat of its own. He pleaded with her to come home, saying he forgave her everything, calling up the names of her children, tormenting her. Now she saw a way to get her baby back, and she lay down with him. In the morning he was calm and treated her once more like a lover.

On her next day off she took the bus to Inch'on, bracing herself for argument. But it was easy. Kun Soo was not home and his mother passed Tae Hee to her without a word.

Back at the coffee shop, the students laughed and flirted with the child, passing her from hand to hand to be tickled and examined and praised for her good looks—just like her mother—and for her intelligent forehead—just like her mother too. Even though she still had Kun Soo like a shadow at her back, Mi Sook thought she had never been so happy.

Before long things were much as they had been before Kun Soo married her. She lived in the back room of the shop and worked there, and he came in the fish truck to visit her sometimes at night. On her days off, two or sometimes three each month, she went home to see her other children and in between the old woman cared for them. Thus everything settled down into a routine and each time she was paid, Mi Sook set aside a few *won* in the candy box.

This situation was not completely satisfactory to Kun Soo but in some ways he found it a relief. Not only did he not have to provide for Mi Sook and her baby but she brought home a little extra money when she came. She was not in his bed each night to warm his back, but she was not there in the morning either, to scream at him or slash him with a knife. Also, while he could not lie with her so frequently, he liked that he could lie with her in privacy. He feared her a little now and never hit her at the coffee shop. Even when she came home with her head swollen up from listening to the talk of students, and their opinions on her tongue, he held his hand because he knew that it would do no good.

But Mi Sook mocked him in her heart. Because she did not love him any longer, her desire began to swing like the needle on a compass. Eventually it settled on a student named Hyun Joon, who had taken a particular fancy to the baby Tae Hee. When he came to the coffee shop he would demand to see her and then he would sit in the window, drinking his coffee and arguing, with the little girl sleeping in the crook of his arm or slung across his shoulder. When she woke he would play with her, passing her reluctantly to Mi Sook to be fed, demanding her back when the feeding was done, sometimes even asking for the bottle and feeding her himself.

These attentions to her baby girl charmed Mi Sook. She watched Hyun Joon surreptitiously, comparing him to Kun Soo, who paid no attention to the child at all. She found herself noticing the days he didn't come or when he came later than usual.

And then one day he brought the picture book, a gift for Tae Hee.

"What is this?" said Mi Sook. "The child is far too young to read. She is not even old enough to hold a book."

"But she will grow. And you have the other little girl, the little boy also. You must teach them all to read."

Mi Sook turned the pages of the book. "But I do not read so well myself," she confessed, and then, on an impulse, "I would need someone to teach me first." She held her breath and kept her eyes turned down because she had seen an image of Hyun Joon and herself sitting together with the book open between them and their heads together while he said patiently, "Repeat. Repeat."

Hyun Joon only laughed. "You must practice, little sister. This is an easy book to read. You will have no trouble if you take the time."

Even though he laughed, it was not unkind, and Mi Sook

told herself that Hyun Joon had really wanted to give a gift to her but because she was a married woman he gave it to her child instead. She told herself he fancied her and she began to make up fantasies about him in her head, even imagining sometimes that Kun Soo's accusation had been right and he was not Tae Hee's father after all. She wanted the father to be Hyun Joon—look how he doted on his baby daughter. And so she favored him, bringing him the best cakes and the freshest buns, making sure his coffee cup was always hot and full.

The other students noticed this and sometimes they teased Hyun Joon, saying, "Here is your little sister come to fill your cup again," and they would tilt their heads and laugh. But because it was done in good humor Mi Sook was not embarrassed. She did not even blush, just flounced her hips a little when she turned and was a little cheeky to them. Hyun Joon ignored them and little by little Mi Sook came to feel that there really was an unspoken bond between them.

Soon she was so anxious to see Hyun Joon every moment that she could no longer bear to be away from the coffee shop, even for one day. Each time she went to Inch'on she went more reluctantly. Her children became of secondary importance. Her breasts swelled up and ached. The space between her hips became electric and all her skin more sensitive. She laughed and cried more easily and was constantly aware of how her body moved. Hyun Joon was all she thought about.

When he did not appear as usual at the coffee shop, she watched anxiously for him and when he came it was as though the sun came in the door. While he was there she walked with a light step and was full of energy. She laughed a lot and felt witty and intelligent. When he was gone she wrapped herself in fantasy, imagining that he walked beside her when she wandered in the night, that he lay beside her on the bedding on her floor. She even once imagined that he was standing in the door and, putting her arms around the wooden jamb, she kissed him tenderly.

Other times, she imagined ways for Kun Soo to die. All were very tragic, mostly violent, and none of them her fault at all. She imagined how Hyun Joon would console the weeping widow, how he would touch her sympathetically, on the hand at first, but as her sobs increased he would put his arms around her, kissing her on the neck and cheek while she kept her head demurely turned aside. He would pursue her then, his passion fully up, but she would turn away and mourn. After the mourning period had passed she would take off her white clothes and once more put on pretty things and Hyun Joon would fall down and beg for her to marry him. Still she would hold back, prettily devoted to her children, and Hyun Joon, a modern man, would spread his arms and take them all against his heart. Then she would agree to marry him.

Every day Mi Sook waited for Hyun Joon to linger after the other students had gone home but he did no such thing, just went on spoiling the baby and smiling at her, calling her little sister, slipping coins into her apron pocket. On one hand she was puzzled by this behavior, but on the other she thought that perhaps it was a good sign. It showed that Hyun Joon was an honorable man who did not want simply to take advantage of a pretty girl with no money. He must be from a wealthy family because he went to university and slipped her coins as though his pockets overflowed, and so he would be successful in his life. Perhaps he would work for a big company, Hyundai or Dae Woo maybe, or he would have an engineering business of his own. His wife would . . .

But here she caught herself. Even though he might fancy her for her pretty face, a man like Hyun Joon would never become serious about a poor girl living in the back room of a coffee shop, and with three children too. At most he would ask to lie down with her for a while, maybe stay a whole night from time to time.

She began to wait for this, planning in her head what she would do when at last he came to ask, dreaming up ways she might trap him because, she reasoned to herself, if she could just be lucky and make his longing for her high enough, perhaps she could run away with him. She would divorce Kun Soo and marry Hyun Joon after all.

All this she thought in one side of her head. In the other she knew very well that it was impossible. If she ran off with anyone at all, Hyun Joon or some other, Kun Soo would not let her see her children left behind in Inch'on. He would be so angry that perhaps he would even steal Tae Hee from her. She would lose all her children.

When she had thought about that for a while she became concerned about a different thing. If she ran away, perhaps Kun Soo would not come after her at all. He did not care about his baby daughter Tae Hee, but he did not care about his other daughter Li Na either. Perhaps he would abandon her, keeping just the boy.

This thought occurred to her when she was carrying some trash into the lane. The pile tilted and a paper sack of damp coffee grounds fell onto the ground. She dumped the rest into an open can, and mumbling underneath her breath because the garbage men had buckled the lid again, bent to retrieve the fallen sack. It had split a little on one side and coffee grounds were oozing out, so, mindful of rats, she swept at them with the fingers of one hand. As she did so, the story of how she had been found seemed to come alive. Her first *Ama* had told it to her when she was a tiny child and Mi Sook had repeated it to each *Ama* who followed so that as the years went by it seemed as though she herself had found the naked baby in the lane who had grown into Mi Sook. Now she saw it happen once again.

It had been another hard gray dawn, with heavy clouds across the sky. The air hung dank and hot and breathless, full of fumes and dust, the stale smell of urine mixing with the smell of cooking oil and garlic. No curl of breeze, no glint of blue above. The city thundered as it always did, with cars and trucks and the hard rattle of pneumatic drills, the creak of cranes, the roar of bulldozers. Construction workers called their sharp commands, a policeman's whistle shrilled, and the steady hum of many voices overlaid the steady drum of feet.

Now, around the corner of the lane, a figure hurried with a bundle in its arms, crouching low as though afraid of being seen. It came toward her and she saw that the bundle was a baby, small and skinny, with a bloody head and dangling cord.

The figure stopped behind the coffee shop, and turning its head this way and that, nudged aside a trash can with one knee and set the baby on the ground, then nudged the can back into place, and rose, and hurried off.

Mi Sook looked down at herself, pale and bloodied as her own babies had been at birth. She lay quite still, as though dead, and she could see the tiny purple heart beating in her chest. Tears knocked at her eyes and she turned abruptly, seized the buckled trash can lid, and began to beat it into shape against the wall. Three ringing whacks and she stopped, drawing her breath in sharply, because it had just dawned on her that this figure she had watched had been a man.

She had always imagined that it was her mother who had left her in the lane, some young girl who had been afraid or some married woman who had given birth to her lover's child. But perhaps it had not been her mother after all. Perhaps it had been her father. Perhaps he had been a man like Kun Soo, interested only in sons, and when his wife had given him a daughter he had taken it and thrown it out like trash.

This made Mi Sook even more angry toward Kun Soo, blaming him as much as if he really had left his little daughter in a lane. Before she had despised him for his poverty and his bad temper. Now she began to hate him. When he came knocking on the door at night she sometimes let him knock.

At first Kun Soo suspected Mi Sook of no more than a little innocent flirtation with the students, nothing serious. What really exercised him was his suspicion that she was holding back a portion of her wage from him, more even than what she wasted on a new blouse here, a tube of lipstick there. From time to time he searched her room behind the coffee shop but so far had discovered nothing.

Then one day, the second of her two days off for the month, Mi Sook brought home the book with colored pictures. She came in the evening with all her lovely swinging hair cut short and done up into curls, a gleaming silver clasp shaped like a bow holding them in place. The acrid smell of permanent solution clung to the air about her head.

When they first were married, Kun Soo had been more tolerant of such frivolities. Mi Sook was, after all, little more than a child. He chided her from time to time about the waste but secretly he liked to see her all dressed up and pretty. He was proud that he had been able to secure for himself a young wife with a beautiful round face and a body slim and graceful as a dragonfly. He liked to be the envy of his friends. But now, with the children always growing out of shoes and coats and hungry all the time, it worried him that she did not seem to understand the difference the little bit of money that she earned could make. And yet the hairstyle and new silver clasp were not what caused the very bad part of the trouble. That part was caused by the book.

He did not even notice it that evening. In the morning, though, when he came in from the yard before he went to work, he saw Mi Sook with her back toward him, sitting on her heels at the warm end of the house, her new curls springing out around her head, the baby settled on the floor beside her. As he was setting his shoes against the wall he called across his shoulder, "What, do you plan to sit all day in your fancy hair letting my mother carry all the work on her old back?"

Mi Sook made no answer so he came to stand in front of her, and that was when he saw the book. He set his feet apart and his fists in bunches on his waist. "What does a girl who can barely take an order on a pad want with a book?"

She did not look up, just went on reading with her lips moving and her finger edging character to laborious character.

"Where did you get that book?"

She stopped her finger on the page and looked up at him with blank, unseeing eyes. "From a student in the coffee shop." She turned her head back down and her lips and finger moved again.

"So now these students give you gifts? And what do you give in return?"

She hesitated. "It was not a gift. I paid for it."

"You gave *money* for this book?"

"It was cheap." She closed it with a smack, holding it with both arms across her chest. "It is an old Korean story. He said I would enjoy it." She flinched away from him, her voice rising with his rising hand. "He said when I have practiced it I can read it to Dae Young. He said I could teach him how to read."

"He said that, did he, this student? And who is he to tell my wife what she should do with my son? What else does he suggest that you might do?"

"He says Dae Young is old enough to go to school. He says if he goes to school and studies he can get a good job with a high wage when he is grown. He also says that the girls should go when they are old enough. He says there are many women at the university, and it is true. I see them in the streets and sometimes they come into the coffee shop. They have books and talk about them with each other. The men listen to their words and do not mock at them."

Kun Soo flung out his hand. "Give me that book."

She clung hard to it but he bent her fingers back. "It is I, the father of this boy, who will decide if he will learn to read. I will be the one, not some student who has hot eyes for my wife." And he flung the book against the wall.

Mi Sook jumped up from the floor, screaming and beating at him with her fists. Behind him he heard his mother gather up the two older children and go scolding through the door, and the red blood flared inside his head. But Mi Sook dodged under his arm, and, snatching up the baby with its shawl, she ran off into the street with her white-socked feet slapping on the ground.

Kun Soo ran after her but he lost some seconds stepping into his sneakers. As he darted out the door, a truck came down the alleyway, and when he swung out of the gate it was between him and Mi Sook, filling the space from the stone fence on one side to the edge of the storm drain on the other, its left wheels barely an inch from the sharp drop.

By the time it reached the corner, Mi Sook was flying for the bus, the baby bouncing and screaming in her arms and the shawl jumping along the sidewalk behind her. Past the general store she ran, with Kun Soo, clumsy in his unlaced sneakers, close behind, past the window filled with socks in bundles, rolls of elastic, toothpaste stacked against a giant set of smiling teeth, lined pads of grayish paper in a pile, pots of brightly colored pencils, past the Heavenly Estate Agent, the Dragon Photo Studio, the Best Food Supermarket, the Inch'on-dong Odeon where movie stars ten times as big as life stared down at them with lust or hate or searing rage.

The street where they ran jostled with people going to and fro, tumbling out of buses, scrambling onto them, people shouting and waving at taxis, sidewalk traders shouting and waving at everyone, people with packs and parcels on their heads, their backs, held in their arms, a man with a club foot swinging over wooden crutches, women holding parasols, men sitting in chairs outside a noodle shop, laborers going up and down in heavy shoes, swaying in the backs of open trucks like clumps of weeds blown back and forth before the wind. As

Mi Sook rushed toward them, the people flowed aside, and as she passed, they closed behind her. Then, as Kun Soo came, they flowed aside again, and back again, paying no more attention to these two runners than water flowing around stones.

And yet, although the crowd of people gave him room to run, it seemed to Kun Soo that the shops themselves prevented him. The smell of meat flew out to stop him from the butcher's shop, the whirr of dryers from the Lovely Lady Hair Salon attacked his ears like bees, the dressmaker's flapped yellow wooden shutters in his face, the laundry reached out steamy arms, the paper shop stuck out its feet of bundled newspapers to trip him up.

And so Mi Sook made it to the bus ahead of him, slapping up the high step in her soiled socks, the baby's shawl trailing on the step behind. Kun Soo saw her speak agitatedly to the driver, saw the driver look at him, sweep out his arm. As he reached the door it smacked shut in his face with the tail of the baby's shawl trapped tight. He seized the shawl, pulling and jerking at it in a frenzy. Mi Sook dropped the other end and vanished with the baby down into the bus. And now the driver was shouting at him with a big mouth and words he could not hear, waving both hands at him as though he would sweep him away like dirt. Then he set his left hand on the steering wheel, and smacking the gear lever with the flat palm of his right, he propelled Kun Soo, still holding tightly to the shawl, into a crazy run beside the bus.

Fortunately for Kun Soo, the bus had to stop almost at once to keep from running down a man whose bicycle was piled so high with baskets that it was taller than his head. He pedaled slowly and deliberately across the road with his back held straight and his knees turned out to balance his precarious load. The driver honked at him but he kept his eyes fixed on a point in front and did not change his pace.

While this went on, Kun Soo resumed his tug-of-war with the shawl but when he felt the bus jerk into gear again he gave it up and contented himself with standing in the street, shaking his fist and flinging threats and spittle up into the air, describing loudly to the blank receding window of the bus the nature of the beating he would give his wife next time she came home from the coffee shop. But in his heart he knew that no matter how he blacked her eyes or bruised her face, he would never have her underneath his hand.

Mi Sook sat jerking on the bus. It had been a mistake to take the picture book Hyun Joon had given her back to Inch'on. She had known that when she picked it up to go. A mistake also to appear in new curls and a silver clasp. She had fixed her hair because she had a fantasy of meeting Hyun Joon in the street by accident and she wanted to look pretty for him. Although she did not think it consciously, she also had an urge to taunt Kun Soo. The book she took with her for the same reason. Now she regretted it.

The bus jounced and rocked. Mi Sook sighed and set her forehead on the glass, watching the furious mass of cars and trucks fighting each other for a space on the expressway.

Below, the asphalt rushed and rushed. It made her dizzy and she pulled her face away, rubbed her breath off the glass with the edge of her hand, and looked instead at the mountains beyond Seoul, shrouded in the purple of late afternoon. Then they were on the bridge across the river, the water thick and sludgy down below, then swinging round the heavy pillars of the ancient city gate and on between Seoul's gray towering buildings, their windows gleaming down at her like eyes.

But now the bus had stopped. People were streaming off and on. The man beside her rose. A woman took his place, balancing a giant basket on her knee. Mi Sook jumped up, pushing her way past the basket and the woman's reluctant knees and her loud muttering, but too late, she had missed her stop. She struggled to the door and although it was not so very far to the next stop—she had walked further many times at night—it seemed a long, long way.

The bus groaned to a halt. The door popped and sighed and she fought her way past two men determined to ignore her presence in the world. She hoisted the baby onto her back and set off for the coffee shop.

Mi Sook had walked the streets of Seoul so often that the city seemed to her like an old friend, but today she felt as though she had been thrown down into an entire new world. The sidewalks overflowed. People jostled at her back, men stepped into her as though she wasn't there, shoved her aside. Cars nudged at people trying to cross the road, threatening to run them down, while people dodged and darted between them, sometimes whacking an angry hand down on a passing hood or roof. Fumes rose off the street and buses belched black smoke. Many people walked with scarves or handkerchiefs held across their noses. And yet the exercise affected her the way it always did. Her legs felt loose and comfortable, her body free. She strode along, jostling with the best.

An American GI emerged from the crowd, his head and shoulders sticking ludicrously above it. She could feel his eyes on her and kept her own turned down, but as he passed, she looked up, eyes glancing off his face. He stopped abruptly, turning, but she slipped off through the crowd, a little panicked but with some other strange sensation also beating in her chest. Triumph? Or was it vanity? Her fierce anger with Kun Soo began to lift.

Now she was forced to walk more slowly, caught behind a group of students who ambled down the sidewalk arguing cheerfully with each other and throwing their hands about for emphasis. She looked at the lean neck of the one in front of her, admired the way his head was finely shaped, the way his shoulders moved, his narrow hips. But wait, this was Hyun Joon. These were the students from her coffee shop. She followed them, eyes fixed on Hyun Joon's every move. The insides of her thighs brushed against each other and she seemed to walk encased in fire.

Kun Soo went home planning to destroy the book, but it had vanished. The silver clasp was there. It had slipped down out of Mi Sook's hair when she jumped up. He set his foot on it, and went outside and round the house to see if his mother was in the yard there, or either of the other children, but it was empty.

He came back inside and searched the house, looking carefully at every inch of floor, first the lower half made of cement, then the three steps to the *ondol* floor, and then the *ondol* floor itself. He took the roll of bedding from beside the wall, shook out the quilt, the three gray blankets. He opened the chest of drawers and looked in all of them, and looked behind the chest, and under it, and underneath the pile of odds and ends on top. Then he looked at every inch again, as though looking harder might make the book appear. He looked inside the pots and pans and on the shelf below the sink and in amongst the ornamental gourds drying on the makeshift shelves above. He looked in his mother's basket and in the coal bin. He pulled the coats down from their hooks beside the door and shook them one by one. No book. It puzzled him. When he ran out the door behind Mi Sook the book had been lying right there against the wall where he had flung it. His mother had already gone off with the children and it was not likely that a thief would come and steal a book. And yet the book had disappeared as though the air had carried it away.

He thought about this disappearing book all day. If he had succeeded in destroying it he would not have given it one thought but now that it had vanished he found it lodged inside his head, its pages turning one by one, the characters black on the white pages and the pictures bright and colorful. He remembered one picture clearly: at the bottom was a rabbit riding under water on a turtle's back, while at the top a bearded man who seemed to be a king watched them from a dragon couch.

Kun Soo himself had never had a book like that, and after a while he found a sort of envy growing in his head. By rights this book belonged to him, and now he wanted it. It was a handsome book, the sort of book a man would be proud to give to his son as a gift. He imagined himself presenting such a book to Dae Young, maybe for his seventh birthday. "Here is a gift for you," he would say, and the boy's eyes would grow big and shine bright black.

Later in the day, he imagined his son sitting with his legs crossed and the book open in his lap, reading with his finger moving character to character the way Mi Sook's had moved. When his friends came to the door carrying bottles of beer and packs of *hwato* cards, he would say to them, "Sst, sst. Can you not see my son is reading his book? We must not disturb him." And the men would look at Dae Young with respect, and at Kun Soo also.

By the time he finished work that day, Kun Soo had resolved that he would teach his son to read. He did not go to the wine shop but came directly home. His little daughter Li Na, who was almost four years old, turned and dipped her head at him from where she stood on tiptoe, splashing something in the sink. She said nothing though and did not run to welcome him.

Kun Soo ignored her. "Where is my son?" he asked his mother, who was squatting on the cement section of the floor with her decorative gourds spread out around her. The old woman shrugged. She did not know. She picked up a rag of cloth and polished on a gourd with a long hooked neck that she was preparing to take down to the market stall to sell.

His son was squatting in the yard behind the house. When he saw his father he jumped up with his arms behind his back and his knees flexed, ready to flee. But Kun Soo made his voice kind and soon Dae Young brought out the book with pictures from behind his back. "*Ama* says if I can learn to read I will know many things."

Then Kun Soo felt a softness in his heart like the softness of a ripe peach in the sun. All that evening until long shadows swallowed up the yard he labored to teach his son to read, but the words did not seem right and many of the characters he had never seen. The boy lost interest and began to draw patterns with his finger on the ground, and at last Kun Soo said, "That is all for now. Tomorrow we will have another lesson." But when tomorrow came he did not do it and the boy did not ask him. Instead, he squatted in the yard with the book and a stick, scratching into the dirt the round and square and angled patterns of the words. When his little sister Li Na came to see, he sat down with his legs stuck out in front, and settling her between his knees, made up stories for the pictures as she turned each page.

That night Kun Soo did not come home for dinner but went off to the wine shop, where he drank a good deal of wine and sat with his elbows on the wooden table and his knees splayed out and did not respond to the greetings of the other men. At first he was ashamed because he could not read all the characters in his son's book and lacked the skill to teach him how to read. Then he was angry because Mi Sook had tricked him into revealing this before his son. But then he told himself he was a lucky man to have a wife like Mi Sook who understood the importance of an education. He would bring her back home from the coffee shop and have her teach his son to read. He would work even harder to make money and stop throwing what he had away on wine and games of *hwato*. He would save. He would send his son to university.

He knew what it was like to go to school because he had gone himself for several years. He remembered carrying a satchel made of imitation leather like thick cardboard. It was dark blue with metal clasps. He remembered walking with it on his back down a long road, holding it on his lap while he bounced for what seemed like hours on a bus, then hoisting it up onto his back again and carrying it through the wide gate set in the thick stone wall around the school, and down a path, and down a corridor with his shoes making a clatter on the shiny wooden floor, to room 3-5, where he set it on the floor beside the desk he shared with his best friend. The chairs had square wood backs and square wood seats and were uncomfortable for him because he did not sit on chairs at home but only on the floor.

The chalkboard he remembered as enormous. It was a dull black color and the teacher, a man with heavy glasses that made him monster-eyed, filled it every day with characters like the ones in Dae Young's book and pointed at them with a stick.

"Repeat with me," he said, and all the children chanted in a loud, monotonous voice. Other classes did the same and sometimes it seemed to Kun Soo that the whole school had a bellyache, moaning and groaning through the long hot afternoon. The chalky smell of the characters made the inside of his head grow heavy, but when he put it on his desk to rest it for a while, the teacher came creeping with his stick and clipped him across the back of the neck. Then he jerked upright with his neck stinging and his face hot because the other children laughed, and eventually he learned to rest the inside of his head while keeping the outside of it upright on his shoulders.

At the end of each day he bowed to the teacher with the other students, slung his satchel on his back, and clattered down the shiny corridor and down the path and through the gate, and nothing he had learned stayed in his head. So when the North Koreans shot his father, he was sorry for his father because he was dead, and for his mother because she cried and wailed all day and all night too, but he was happy that the war had closed the school.

Thinking about all this now, he understood that while he himself had not learned well at school because the inside of his head was heavy, his son's head was not like his. He had the same face as his father, but the inside of his head was quick and light. Kun Soo was proud. It was a smart son he had got himself.

By the time she closed the door behind the helper and locked the coffee shop that night Mi Sook had a plan. The next day she complained that she was ill and the helper sent out for her sister to help her in the shop. The two girls took Tae Hee by her hands and, laughing, swung her out into the shop to spend the day with them. Mi Sook stayed in the back room, creeping out from time to time to peer through the swinging doors into the shop.

Hyun Joon came as usual and after a long time Mi Sook saw him get up and leave. She spun away, snatched open the back door, and running down the lane and up an alley, came out behind him on the road. She had no plan except to see where he would go, what he would do, acting from the instinct of a woman who has become obsessed with a man and wants to know everything about him.

Walking casually, hands swinging at his sides as though he was thinking or just relaxing on a pleasant afternoon, Hyun Joon went into a park, where he sauntered back and forth, looking at the children flying kites and feeding carp. An idea came to Mi Sook. Circling quickly to the other side of the park, she came strolling back, looking up at the kites, looking down at the children playing on the lawns, but all the time with one eye out for Hyun Joon. And there he was, sauntering toward her with his face turned up toward the sky.

It was an easy matter to bump lightly into him and pretend surprise. "Why Hyun Joon, what are you doing here? You startled me." She made her voice light and confident but inside she was shaking violently. What if he should brush her aside?

"Why, it's Mi Sook," Hyun Joon said pleasantly. "This is a

surprise. I almost did not recognize you without your yellow apron. How nice you look."

"It is my day off."

"Then I am fortunate."

Mi Sook acted very gay then, chattering about how she loved to come and walk here in the park on her day off.

"This park is also a favorite place of mine to walk," said Hyun Joon. "Strange that I should never have bumped into you here before."

They both laughed at his joke and Mi Sook stopped being so nervous.

Then Hyun Joon said, "Why don't we walk together, little sister?" which was exactly what Mi Sook was hoping he would say.

It was getting late in the afternoon by now so the time they spent together in the park was not so long. Mi Sook, though, could not remember when she had spent such a happy time. Hyun Joon was kind and talked to her about the sculptures surrounding the pond and about the patterns the kites make bobbing on their strings.

"Look at that one, little sister. Look at that dragon in the sky. Maybe he will bring us luck."

"Us," said Mi Sook to herself. She turned her face up to him and laughed, shivering in the small hairs of her neck.

"Are you practicing reading the book I gave you, little sister?"

Mi Sook opened her mouth to tell him what had happened to the book but some instinct warned her not to. "Oh yes. I am getting very good."

He smiled. "Let us see how good you are." And he led her to the center of the park, where there was a kiosk. Here he bought two yogurt fruit sodas and a newspaper. "Come, we will sit down on this bench and you will read to me."

She could only read a little so he began to coach her. It was arduous and Mi Sook did not understand the things about other countries and business matters and politics that he had her read, but it was pleasant to sit in the day's last sun with Hyun Joon's head bent over her, his arm brushing against hers. To someone passing they must have looked like two lovers out for a little fresh air on their day off.

When the sun turned brilliant saffron, and then gold, then red, and began its quick slide down the arching western sky, Hyun Joon folded up the newspaper and they sat together on the bench watching its reflections on the clouds until it was completely gone and the evening was warm and glowing with its afterlight.

Other couples were sitting on benches too, or strolling together on the hard-packed dirt of the trails and walkways. Some were holding hands. Inside Mi Sook's head came a picture of herself and Hyun Joon strolling past the carp pool, looking down at the flashing colors of the fish. She bent a little low and stumbled. Hyun Joon put his arm around her waist and pulled her back. They stood like that a while, watching the fish, and then they turned and walked again, and came back to this seat, and sat together, Hyun Joon's arm still around her waist.

The feeling of his arm was so warm and real in her imagination that Mi Sook turned to look. But no, Hyun Joon's arms were crossed against his chest, his legs stuck out in front, no part of his body touching hers. And yet he sat a little slouched, as though he was at ease with her. She smiled a small smile to herself. They sat in silence, looking at the sky.

"I must see you home," said Hyun Joon when the lights came on across the park, drawing the moths into their evening dance. They rose and strolled out of the park together—like a married couple, Mi Sook told herself—and through the streets of Seoul with lights coming on in the shop windows all around them and the streetlights sparkling overhead.

In the windows elegant clothes and ornaments of all sorts were carefully arranged. They stopped before a jeweler's window, admiring the display: a small black gong with a pair of sky-blue tassels standing on a glossy yellow rack, an embossed silver incense burner, a pair of celadon vases in delicate pale green with shattered-eggshell surfaces, a red-quilted box with gleaming relaxation balls.

In the center of the display, set on a small rotating platform padded with black velvet, was an elegant orange gourd. Its neck was long, curving like a seahorse and studded with a mane of tiny red and black and yellow feathers. Its base, swollen like the belly of a pregnant woman, was engraved around with golden characters saying *Wealth* and *Many Sons*. At a different spot on each character was a faceted red stone. As the platform turned, the light flowed down the shining curve of neck as one by one the golden characters appeared, each with a red fire glittering at its heart.

Mi Sook sighed. "How lovely."

Hyun Joon examined it. "A good gift for a man to give his sweetheart, would you say?"

Mi Sook felt a pulsing in her throat, a lightness in her head. "A good gift indeed," she said, and laughed, pretending not to take him seriously, although the implication of his words could not be mistaken.

He turned away, a thoughtful expression on his face. Mi Sook turned and walked beside him silently, giving him an opportunity to speak. But he too walked in silence and she was touched by this sudden shyness on his part. She led him to the back door of the shop and gravely said good night, expecting that now surely he would ask to come inside with her.

"Good night, Mi Sook," he said. "I have had a pleasant time. Good night." And he smiled again and turned and walked away around the corner of the lane without once looking back.

Mi Sook was disappointed and went inside with her stomach curling up inside her, but when she had eaten a bowl of noodles she felt better and told herself that she was very lucky to have found such an honorable man. She lay down on her quilt and pulled the blanket round her, thinking of the many walks they would have together and of the day when he would come alone to the back door of the shop and ask for her.

That night she dreamed Kun Soo had died. She did not know how but she saw him lying in his coffin with a white shroud wrapped around him. There were many people making a big wailing but she stood by herself looking down at him and she could feel herself smiling.

She woke slowly, with a sensation of relief, as though some enormous weight had been lifted off her head. Sunlight shone through the high small window of her room, making a golden banner above her head, and she lay looking up at it, moving her body slightly against the soft warmth of the bedding. It was several minutes before the dream came back to her and when it did it seemed almost to be true. She carried it with her into the day, a little frightened but walking with light feet.

That day Kun Soo arrived early at the fish warehouse, planning to make a detour through Seoul, where he would go to the coffee shop and tell Mi Sook to come home and teach his son. It was not such a great detour but he helped the workers load the truck in order to make a little extra time. Some of the boxes were not well packed and when he heaved them onto his shoulder or his head the bloody slime oozed down onto his hair and shirt. He looked down at himself, clicking his tongue. He wanted to go home for clean clothes but did not want to waste the time he had gained by coming early, so he washed himself as best he could under the hose used to keep the warehouse floor sprayed down, then climbed into the truck and slammed the door.

Now he was wet and uncomfortable but the day was warm and soon the wind blowing through the truck's open window dried his shirt. He was well ahead of schedule and soon in good spirits, proud and a little tearful about what he was going to do for this smart son of his, how he would make him into a well-educated man, the first one in his family.

In his mind he saw Dae Young grown into a man wearing a business suit. He sat in a chair with wheels behind a desk in an office of his own. A secretary in high-heeled shoes tapped politely at the door and brought him coffee and a pack of cigarettes. He leaned back in the chair and stretched out his legs while she lit his cigarette, using a silver lighter with the company emblem on its side. Then she went out and shut the door where, painted on the glass in large gold letters, was his son's name and the title of his job. He was boss of all the company.

Kun Soo smiled, tapping his hand against the steering wheel. With a son like this he would not need to work in his old age. He would live with him in a big house with *ondol* floors from wall to wall in every room and tiling on the roof. One room would be for him. All winter he would sit on the warm floor and smoke a pipe and watch movies on the television. Sometimes he would play a little *hwato* with his friends and his daughter-in-law would bring them seaweed soup with sliced beef and *dofu* and bowls of rice. In the summer he would sit outside in a canvas chair, smoking his pipe and drinking sweetened rice water, watching his many grandsons playing in the yard.

In Seoul, he parked the truck and came whistling up the sidewalk toward the coffee shop. He stopped to look through the window for a moment at the students sitting with their newspapers and coffee, opening and closing their mouths at each other, making emphasis with their fingers on the table. He looked scornfully at them, but then an emotion that was almost envy welled up in him and he did not go inside.

Instead, he leaned his back against a cherry tree outside the shop, and lighting up a cigarette, he watched them, the sole of one sneaker on the instep of the other. One day, he told himself, his son would sit here in this window too. He would read the newspapers and have opinions, and the other students would listen to him with respect, nodding at each other and repeating what he said.

Look now, here came Mi Sook, smiling in her bright red lips and flowered apron. She carried a cup of coffee on a tray and set it on a table. One of the students spoke to her and she answered him confidently.

Kun Soo felt a wavering inside him. He had come here to take her home to teach his son, expecting obedience because she was his wife. Now he remembered what sort of wife she was, not like his first but very independent in the modern way. Why, when his son was born and he called her by her new name, Dae Young's Mother, she rejected it, insisting that he call her only Mi Sook. She had always been a great trouble to him as a wife because she did not behave like one. She would not obey him, she ran away, the baby on her back, and he could not overlook the possibility that she would not want to come with him today. But still, as he watched the way she spoke so confidently to the students, he felt a sort of pride. If his son was to become a student, then it was good to have a wife who could talk to him with confidence like that. When he told her of his plans for the education of this son she would come home willingly. After all, what is a job in a coffee shop compared to the education of a son? Yet still he hesitated to go in.

But what was this? A student had his wife's wrist in his hand. He was pulling her toward him. Now he had his arm around her waist and she was not resisting. Her head bowed down to listen to his words. She laughed.

Kun Soo felt the old familiar swelling in his head. He felt the scar throb on his cheek. He dropped his cigarette and ground it underneath his heel.

Inside the shop, the students were helping Hyun Joon celebrate. He had had a letter in that morning's mail telling him he had won a scholarship to study engineering at a university called Purdue. Mi Sook had never heard of it but she understood it must be an important university because the other students were slapping Hyun Joon on the shoulders and congratulating him and he was smiling broadly with white teeth and talking a great deal.

When Mi Sook brought his coffee, he said, "Congratulate me, little sister, because today is a great celebration for me." And he took her by the wrist, pulling her toward him.

Mi Sook blushed and he put his other hand around her waist and drew her close. The students cheered and Mi Sook felt her whole body tingle. It was just like on a television show.

But then the very bad thing happened. She felt herself seized by the shoulders from behind and there was Kun Soo. Even before she saw his face she recognized the smell. He had fish slime in his hair and bloodstains running down his shirt and his eyes were bursting from his head with rage.

"What are you doing here?" she said.

"You will come home with me at once," he told her, keeping his voice low.

She pulled away. "It is not yet my day off."

Kun Soo forgot about the education of his son. He put his face up close to hers. "So now I see the reason for all the little pots of color for your face, the fancy blouses and the curled-up hair. You say to me, 'I need them for my job. How can I work in a coffee shop in rags?' Your job, you say. What good is it? Your wage is not enough to buy blood for a louse. And yet do you bring it home to feed your children? No. All you want to do is flaunt yourself before the students from the university who sit here all day frittering away their time, setting bold eyes on my wife's painted face. But I have caught you at it now. You will come home with me at once."

She stood there with her feet set and her jaw gone hard and stubborn. "I will not come."

He pulled back his fist and punched her in the face and sent her stumbling back against a table, making all the coffee cups fly out onto the floor. She saw him reach for her again but at the same time all the students rose up in a body and grabbed him by the arms, holding him back. He thrashed and twisted and almost freed himself—because he was a laborer and very strong—but there were too many of them and no matter how he kicked and lunged and struggled he could not get free. All this time he was shouting and yelling, calling her whore and cursing her, abusing the students until they tired of him and dragged him backwards through the shop and flung him in the street and locked the door.

He seized the handle and struggled with it, making a great rattle. Then he came and peered in through the window, beating his fists against the glass until Mi Sook was afraid he would break through. The students ignored him. They picked up the fallen coffee cups and straightened up the chairs and tables. Then they sat down with their backs to the window. "Sorry to bring you trouble, little sister," Hyun Joon called to Mi Sook, who was leaning against the counter with her head throbbing from the punch Kun Soo had given her. "If you will bring me the mop I will show my apologies by cleaning up the spilled coffee for you."

As she turned to go into the back of the shop, Mi Sook saw Kun Soo turn also and go off down the street. That was a great relief, so she brought the mop and stood holding her face and even laughing a little at Hyun Joon's clumsy efforts to clean up the coffee. Obviously he had never done any work of this sort before.

But Mi Sook had forgotten the back door of the shop. She thought Kun Soo, having let his rage erupt, had gone away. Not so. He burst in from the lane, and rushing from behind the counter, went directly for Hyun Joon.

Hyun Joon saw him just in time to swing the mop, catching him across the face with the soggy rags and knocking him to the floor. Then the whole thing started up again. By the time Kun Soo, badly bruised and cursing like a storm drain, was once more tossed into the street, every table in the coffee shop had been overturned.

WITH THE RED BLOOD STINGING IN HIS HEAD, Kun Soo came racing through the streets of Seoul, the fish truck swinging like an angry dragon's tail behind him. Out onto the highway he came, hump-shouldered and clench-toothed, hands frantic at the steering wheel, driving as though a fiend were in pursuit. But then he found himself boxed in between a tractor-trailer to the right and a military jeep in front. He leaned into the horn but the khaki flap of the jeep looked back impassively at him and went on with its speed unchanged. He lifted his foot off the accelerator and pressed lightly on the brake, intending to drop back and pass the tractor-trailer in the inner lane, but as he slowed, the suction from the huge truck caught him and he veered into it, clipping his front fender. He spun off to the side and overturned.

That night Kun Soo took his rage off to the wine shop, where he sat in his usual place at the long table running down the center of the room, calling for wine and complaining to his friends and pitying himself. Was he not, after all, a poor man? And did he not have a son to feed, also two daughters and an old mother? What good was a wife to him who spent all his money on books with stories and sat reading them while others worked? And what business had she bringing home advice on what to do about the education of his son? Was he not a responsible father? Did he not labor seven days a week, climbing onto roofs and hauling bricks and stones and tiles, breaking his back beneath great loads of lumber for construction sites? And after that did he go home and rest? Did he not then exhaust himself with driving trucks, hauling boxes on and off, dripping the juice of fishes in his hair and down his back? Did he not come home stinking after that?

And what thanks did he get from this most useless wife who did nothing but smear color on her face and carry coffee to the tables of wealthy students who sat all day on their backsides reading books and flapping their tongues at each other, looking boldly up into her face, and when she turned, tipping their heads and closing one eye at the way her body moved, and then, having taken away her little bit of money in exchange for their old books, shaming her in a public shop? What sort of men were these? If they wanted her body, why did they not act like men and pay her for it? It would be more use to him. Instead they seduced her in the window of a shop.

When he had said all this, Kun Soo fell silent for a while, thinking about it, and then he called for more wine and cried because he had wanted to make his lovely wife into a whore. And after that he flung his arm up in the air and said, as though addressing her, "Go then, if a whore is what you want to be. But don't bring home your dirty money here. Go with students if you want. You will not find one man among them all. You will come back crying to your husband to show you how a real man moves inside a woman."

Peering about him in a truculent manner at the other men, he said first to this one, then to that, "You! Tell me! What good to me is this beautiful young wife? I give her to you."

His face grew sly and narrow. "But she will not have you. No, she will not have a good hardworking man. She will have students who do nothing for themselves all day but flap their tongues. She is too foolish to know that these are dangerous people. Today they laugh and seduce her in the window of the coffee shop and tomorrow they tie headbands on their foreheads and riot in the streets. For their trouble may they get their heads broken by the truncheons of police, may they have their throats burned out by tear gas, may they be dragged to jail and have their fingers smashed, their genitals attacked, may they be left to rot, because they teach my lovely little Mi Sook how to misbehave. They teach her to be a bad wife and deceive her husband."

Then Kun Soo remembered his first wife, who had worn out and died, and he fell to moaning after her because she had been a good wife. He tilted sideways on the wooden bench and farted loudly.

"She was old and ugly," he told the men, who by now were leaning on their arms and hiccuping, "and she bore me only daughters and one toadlike son with no brain in his head, but when I came into my house she brought me tea, and all the money that she made down at the market stall she carried home to me, and put it in my hand, and never wasted it on books, forgetting she was ignorant, and never was seduced by students with their clever words and clever hands and leering eyes, and never made her husband so upset he wrecked the truck that he was paid to drive and made him lose his job and lose his face, and what will I do now? I cannot pay to fix the truck and also feed my family. My family is going to starve."

The wine bowl slipped from Kun Soo's hand and rolled across the floor. He twisted round to look at it, shouting to the owner of the shop to come and pick it up, but the woman came in her apron from the back room and scolded him.

"No more wine for you today. You owe me money from last week and the week before and now you are making a disturbance in my shop."

She stooped down with one hand against her back and picked up the fallen bowl. "Enough," she said and went back to the kitchen with it, muttering.

Kun Soo set his hands flat on the table and beat his head between them, wailing in a loud voice for his first wife and for the bitterness of his poverty. Then he fell asleep, tilting sideways, and did not wake when he slid down onto the floor beneath the table.

His friends moved their feet to give him room, and yawned and belched and scratched themselves and lit more cigarettes, tilting their heads and blowing smoke up in the air and telling each other that Kun Soo was a fool. If they could get a wife as young and beautiful as Mi Sook they would never weep for some dead crone. And they leered and made descriptions to each other of the great advantages they would draw from having such a wife.

Then the false dawn was in the sky and the men threw down their cigarette butts on the floor and went off, singing and disgruntled, to punish their own wives for Mi Sook's loveliness.

Kun Soo did not wake until the owner of the wine shop came pushing at him with her broom and saying, "Aiee, how is an honest woman to run a business with all this wailing in the night and drunkenness and sleeping on her floor?" And she rattled the sharp bristles of the broom against his head.

Kun Soo rose and held tightly to the table, bowing and making his apologies. He went outside and peed against the wall, blinking in the light. His stomach heaved and his head spun, and he came home along the streets supporting himself on fences. Twice he had to stop to vomit in the drain.

That day he went to work with no good sleep at all. When he climbed the ladder and set one foot against the first beam of the roof, he slipped because his brains were jumping in his head, the ladder shot from underneath his other foot, and he was tilting back and falling, with one arm through the rungs and four heads in a row along the roof peering down at him with shouting falling from their mouths.

When he came back to himself, he was lying in the dust beside the front wall of the half-built house, confused because he could not move his legs. His workmates crouched around him, smoking and offering opinions to each other. One by one they felt his legs, fingers probing up one side and down the other. And one by one they shook their heads. His legs were fine. Not broken. Nothing wrong. But still he lay there on the ground, and still his legs refused to move.

Impatience took him. This was Mi Sook's fault. He would beat her well for it when his legs began to move again. "Heh," he said in a rough, disgruntled voice, "I cannot lie here on my back all day," and set both hands against the ground and pushed as though to raise himself.

Now he thought that he was walking home, but then he saw the sun looking straight down at him and the stone fences going by close at each side of his head. He saw his feet bob up and down in front and understood that he was being carried. Three men were on each side and they were carrying him on a board like a dead man to his burial. Behind him he could hear the voices of more men talking to each other. So. His workmates were carrying him home. He submitted to this. What else could he do?

Six or seven little boys came skipping and running toward him. They stopped to stare and then ran on. He heard their shrill voices going off into the distance back behind. One of them, though, turned and ran along beside the men in a kind of skipping dance, legs spread wide, straddling the storm drain along the right edge of the alleyway. He kept his head turned down, moving it from side to side, watching his feet to keep himself from falling in the drain.

Kun Soo let his head drop to the side and watched him, an

agile boy with good strong legs, the way legs are meant to be. He had a boy like this himself.

A dog barked up ahead, a skinny yellow thing with its tail wagging and its feet planted on the ground. One of the men made shooing motions with his hands and shouted. The dog backed off a step, curled down its tail, and went on barking. The man took a stamping step, hissing, and the dog rolled up its lips on each side of its mouth and snarled, the fur rising in a ridge along its back. The procession stopped and the men set down the board with Kun Soo on the ground.

The boy on the drain, not noticing that they had stopped, went dancing on ahead and the dog turned its head and looked at him. At once the men leaped on it but the dog slipped out of their arms and fled before them up the alleyway, legs locking and unlocking, haunches low, voice going on ahead in a high wailing loop of fright.

The men picked up the board again and when they caught up with the little boy he fell in with them, walking close on Kun Soo's right.

Kun Soo saw now that this was his own son. "Dae Young?" he said, and his voice echoed loudly in his head.

"*Apba*, are you going to die?"

Kun Soo felt self-pity well in him. He looked at this son of his, who was only six years old, and admired his strength and his straight back and the way his arms moved back and forth as he walked. He was a handsome boy, his face a perfect image of what his own used to be before the scar.

Shame came to join self-pity in his head. He thought of

how this son would have to go to storekeepers and street vendors to beg for food on credit, telling this one and that, "My
father lies on his back all day because his legs won't work." He
thought of the boy's grandmother, of the thinness of her arms,
of her stooped back, the way the bones of her face seemed as
though they would grow right through the flesh, the way she
labored constantly in her old age to raise this second family of
his and keep them fed. What if his legs should never work
again? Where would she get money to buy vegetables to fill
her kimchi pots? Where would she get food to feed a pair of
little girls and a hungry boy as well? He thought about the
wage Mi Sook earned at the coffee shop, dismissing it. "Dae
Young, my son," he said, "you must be responsible."

The boy looked down at him with solemn eyes.

But now here came Mi Sook in her jeans, taking long steps
like a man, the baby strapped against her back. The men set
down the board again and squatted on the ground, sucking at
their teeth and watching her approach with sidelong faces.
They feared this woman—for her beauty, and for the way she
looked into their eyes with no humility. Every one of them
would have liked to have her but not one would dare. Instead
they cringed and afterwards slapped their thighs and told each
other what they would do to her if Kun Soo were not a friend.

Dae Young ran to meet his mother, snatching at her flying
shirttail, crying, "*Ama! Ama! Apba* cannot walk. *Apba* cannot
walk."

Mi Sook brushed him aside and came running to crouch
beside Kun Soo where he lay with his eyes tight shut on the

board. He had shut his eyes because when he saw her coming down between the two toes of his dusty sneakers, he felt fury crowding up behind the shame inside his head. So many times she had come rushing up to him like this, with her face angry and the baby flapping its arms out on her back, and he a working man with no crime on his soul. So his friends made a little noise when they came to crouch down in a circle on the floor to play a game of *hwato* with their wages in their hands. So they shouted a little, rattled the plastic cards and slapped down coins and sometimes, on a payday only, paper money. So they made a little mess, a little dust, some *soju* bottles to clean up. It was nothing. A working man deserved a little relaxation with his friends. And he deserved his wife's respect before his friends as well. When Mi Sook came striding, saying, "What is this? Gambling again?" he would stand up with his arm pointing to the door and order her away.

His mother, a traditional woman who understood the needs of a man, would take his children off to spend the evening with a neighbor's wife when his friends came to the house. But Mi Sook! She stood with her legs apart and anger sitting on her face, defying him. What could he do before his friends but knock her down? A man could not lose face before his friends.

But now Mi Sook was shaking him. "Husband!" she said urgently. "Open up your eyes."

She would not leave him alone, pestering him and asking questions, clicking her tongue and poking at his legs, his work-mates now in a tumult at her back, coming close and breathing on her hair and telling his sad tale and offering advice.

And still she pestered him. "Here I have come home as you ordered me and now what do I find? You have wrecked the fish truck. You have lost your job. You have fallen off the roof. Now you will not even open up your eyes and speak to me. What sort of husband have I got?"

He could bear no more. He flung his arm out and she tumbled backwards with the baby screaming and pushing its arms out underneath her. Dae Young burst into tears and pulled his mother's arm, but she shook him off, and rising up above her husband, worked the spittle in her mouth and spat onto the ground beside his head. Then she turned, Dae Young once more snatching at her shirt, and strode away with angry steps.

Kun Soo watched her go away between his toes and he was sad now for his son because he would not get an education after all, and because it was his mother's fault. The men also watched her go, and when she disappeared over the curving hump of alleyway, they crouched down and lit more cigarettes, tilting their heads from side to side and making wide eyes at each other.

Kun Soo closed his eyes and felt the hard, rough board beneath his head, and saw the two bright burning circles of the sun, and opening his mouth as wide as it would go, he called down curses on his worthless wife.

At last the men carrying Kun Soo on the board came to his house. But when they headed toward the door with him he became agitated, begging them in a loud imploring voice not to take him inside because his wife was there and she would bring him more bad luck.

"No, no, do not take me in," he cried. "Do not take me in. Do you want to carry me to my death? I beg you—no, I order you—do not take me into that place."

His mother, agitated on the front veranda, called, "Nonsense, nonsense. Bring him in. Bring him in."

The men ignored Kun Soo's beseeching and obeyed her, but as they took him through the door, he pushed out both arms and held them stiffly, preventing them from going through. Mi Sook, with Li Na clinging to her leg and the baby still on her back, appeared between his feet. She was crying now, the baby also, and shouting at the men to bring him in. He heard his mother wailing at his head, the baby screeching on its mother's back, his son's voice pleading, "*Apba, Apba*, please," although he could not see him, the commotion of neighbors behind him in the yard.

One of the men carrying the board turned down his head from just inside the door and cursed him, but still Kun Soo would not relax his arms, and at last the men backed out of the doorway and took him to the storage shed behind the house, where they rolled him off the board onto the hard-packed dirt floor. They stood with the board propped between them, discussing what they should do next, but Kun Soo dismissed them, and one by one, with a shrug or a tilt of the head, they shuffled out the door.

Now Mi Sook came running in, fear behind her angry face. "What are you doing here on the hard floor of this dirty shed? Here is no place for an injured man. Let me look at your legs. Yes, I will look. No, do not shout at me. No, do not push me away. What good will that do you? Will you lie here shouting on the ground all night while the rats come to chew on you? You must come into the house. Yes, you must come inside."

But he cursed her, and the fate that had brought her to his house, shouting louder and louder until her anger jumped out and shouted back at him, berating him for his carelessness and his stupidity.

She caught herself. "Come now, I am sorry to be angry with you. It was not your fault, no, not your fault. Let me help you now. Am I not your wife? I will help you and tomorrow you will be better. You *must* be better. If you are not better you cannot go to work, and what will happen to us then? Here, let me—"

But when she came close, Kun Soo lifted up his closed fist

and hit her so hard on the side of the head that the sound of it was like the sound of a log hammer struck against a temple bell. "Stop your talking, woman. Go away."

Mi Sook set her hand against her head and left him raging on the ground.

All day he lay there, stubbornly refusing help. His mother brought a doctor but Kun Soo shouted at him. "What right have you to come? I am a poor man with no money to waste on doctors. Can you not see there is nothing wrong with me? Do you see blood? There is no blood. See, you prod me and there is no pain. Of what use is your medicine when what is wrong with me is nothing but the evil my wife has brought down on my head? Look, I try to move my legs, they will not move. And yet there is no pain. No, I will not come in your ambulance. No, I will not come to your hospital. I am a healthy man, and only forty-three years old. Never have I been subject to a doctor. I will set my mind against this thing and in one day I will overcome it. Tomorrow I will go to work. I do not want your sad face looking down at me, or your cold fingers creeping on my skin. Go away."

He shouted at his old mother when she offered water. He took the bowl of food she brought and threw it at the wall. He shouted when she begged from him a little money.

"Let me buy at least one mosquito coil for you," she said.

"Be quiet, woman. What money do I have to waste on mosquito coils? All I have must be set carefully aside for food unless you want to starve before my legs begin to work again."

Later, Dae Young came to the door but his father's anger in the shed was like an untamed animal and he crept fearfully away and squatted against the wall of the house, listening to his mother and his little sisters cry inside.

By nighttime, Kun Soo was exhausted from his rage but he refused to let his mother so much as spread a blanket over him. All through that first night he lay alone on the hard ground of the storage shed, wrestling with his injury. He was not afraid, although his anger now was tinged with something between fear and self-pity, something self-destructive.

In the morning Mi Sook came to the door and knocked, calling to him. He did not respond so she pushed it open and stood looking down at him. He lay on his back as he had lain on the board when he was carried home, but now his arms were flung out from his sides and his jaw had fallen down. Mi Sook caught her breath because she thought he had died in the night, but the slight sound awakened him. His jaw shuddered and his teeth clacked shut against each other. His eyes rolled up in his head as though in a fit but then they settled on Mi Sook standing in the door and narrowed. His lips drew back into a snarl.

"Grannie," Mi Sook said when she went back into the house, "I will go back to work now. I must support my children because my husband has made up his mind to die."

For three days and nights Kun Soo lay on the ground and raged. He ate nothing in that time and drank no water. If he slept he had no memory of either drifting off or waking.

During these days Dae Young squatted in the dust outside the shed and his grandmother went back and forth, moaning to herself, with his sister Li Na clinging to her skirt.

It seemed to the old woman that she went a thousand times each day to listen at the door while Kun Soo raved and cursed his wife, his luck, his life, his poverty, his useless legs, and a thousand times again at night to listen to him curse and slap at the mosquitoes plaguing him. He would not let her in the shed and when neighbors or workmates came to stick their heads around the door, he spat and cursed until they went away, and soon they did not come. It seemed to the old woman that he was weakening and she did not know if that was good or bad. If he weakened he might sleep and then recover. On the other hand, he might die.

On the fourth day, the shed was silent when she came early in the morning and so she crept inside. Kun Soo's face was white and puffy, the scar across his cheek like something buried in the flesh, his eyes swollen shut where mosquitoes had bitten him. "Ah, my son, what foolishness," his mother sighed, and this time he rolled his head toward her and didn't shout.

Dae Young came creeping in behind his grandmother and Kun Soo peered at him through swollen lids. "My mother, who is with you now?"

Dae Young looked up at his grandmother before he spoke. "I am your son," he said.

Kun Soo's head jerked back. "What is this you do to me, my mother?" he whined. "Are you a conjurer, to bring me back my vanished son? Or is this a ghost?"

138

"But *Apba*, I am not a ghost. See, I am touching you."

Kun Soo twisted his arm away, trying to back off. "What is this, my mother? What does it mean?"

The old woman tried to explain that this was not his first son but his second, the child of Mi Sook, but Kun Soo threw his head from side to side, crying loudly, "Go away."

For a while his mother tried to reason with him but he grew more and more upset and at last she took Dae Young by the shoulder and led him out into the yard.

"Why does he say I am a ghost?" Dae Young asked. "And who is this other son?"

"Hush, child, hush. He is confused because he is sick from the mosquitoes biting him. We must ask Mr. Hong to let us have some coils on account."

"But why won't *Apba* come inside the house? And why is he so angry? Grannie, is he going to die?"

But his grandmother just said, "Hush," in a worried voice. "Come child, we will go and talk to Mr. Hong about mosquito coils."

The old woman pushed open the door of the general store and she and Dae Young went inside. The store had a counter at the far end and four rows of shelves in front running lengthwise down the shop so the owner could watch everything without having to come out from behind the counter. In the middle of the last shelf on the right, the old woman found one box of six mosquito coils, the last box left. She took it to the counter, asking Mr. Hong for credit. But Mr. Hong had heard about Kun Soo falling off the roof and was afraid that he would not be paid. "I am a poor man," he said, turning up his hands. "I want to give you credit, Grannie, believe me, but already you owe me and I cannot give you any more."

"Mr. Hong, I beg you, just one coil out of the box. I swear you will be paid, and very soon. This is just a temporary thing. My son is ill and bothered by mosquitoes but soon he will be well and he will come himself and pay you everything we owe."

But Mr. Hong refused and the argument went back and forth.

Meanwhile, Dae Young was left standing at the empty shelf. Below it, on the next shelf down, was a stack of flat, plastic-wrapped packages. The picture on the top one showed a dim figure underneath a net and on top of the net, trying to get in, an enormous mosquito. He looked at it while his grandmother pleaded with Mr. Hong.

At last she gave up and turned to go, calling to him.

"Coming, Grannie," he said, but didn't move. The mosquito was crawling on the net and the man was inside looking at it, but it could not get to him. The man's eyes were clear and dark, not swollen at all.

"Come, child, come at once."

"Coming, Grannie." And this time he came, running to catch up. "Look," he said behind her.

The old woman ignored him. She slapped her rubber shoes along the road and he knew by this that she was upset. He trotted on behind, waiting for her to calm herself, and by the time they turned the corner to their alleyway her feet were quieter and she had slowed her pace. Now he came up beside her, holding out the package with the picture of the man and the mosquito. "Grannie, look."

The old woman stopped. She turned to Dae Young with a red face and rapped her knuckles up against his head. "Ah, what have you done? This is a bad thing."

"But Grannie." Dae Young held out the package to her but she refused it.

"No, I will not have it. You must go back at once and bow low to Mr. Hong and beg for his forgiveness."

Dae Young stood stubbornly. "*Apba* will pay for it when he is better."

"No." She turned and began to go back toward the shop, but her steps were slow and her body moved as though she were pushing against a wind.

At last she stopped. "All right, then. When your father is better, though, it is you who must ask him for the money and you who must pay Mr. Hong."

"Grannie, I will do it." And Dae Young strode determinedly home, the mosquito net tucked underneath his arm.

When they arrived at the shed, Kun Soo was lying quite still with the back of one hand across his eyes. "*Apba?*" Dae Young whispered at the door and when there was no sound he came boldly to his father, who moved his hand aside, revealing red welts all across his puffy face. They were on his neck too, and his naked forearms.

"Ah, my son," he said, "have you come back then?"

"I have come back, *Apba*. And see what I have here? It will keep the mosquitoes off you."

"Who is that behind you?"

"It is Grannie only."

"Tell her to go away. I will not go inside the house."

"She has come to help with the mosquito net."

Between them Dae Young and his grandmother fetched the wooden ladder from where it stood propped against the wall and set it up beside Kun Soo. Dae Young climbed up and tied the apex of the net to the rafter above Kun Soo's head, while his grandmother spread it around him like a tent. When it was done, Kun Soo said, "My son, who is that with you now?"

"Still Grannie, *Apba*."

"Tell her to go away."

Later Kun Soo said, "Look there. Who is that?"

"See *Apba*, only me."

"No. Behind you. Who is that?"

Dae Young turned to look. "No one, *Apba*. Only me."

All that day Dae Young sat with his father. Sometimes he thought Kun Soo was asleep but then he would cry out, "Who is that? You there, who is that?" and after a while it seemed to Dae Young that the room was full of people that he could not see.

Toward evening Kun Soo made a noise in his throat and Dae Young lifted up the edge of the mosquito net and looked at him. Then he went to a ledge at the far end of the shed, where he took down a chipped glass bottle that had once been used for storing kimchi. This he maneuvered into position beside his father's leg, and when Kun Soo was done, Dae Young carried the steaming bottle through the door and in through the outhouse door beside it, nudging it open with his knee. In a few moments he brought the bottle back, carefully rinsed, and set it on the ground beside his father.

Kun Soo looked behind him at the door. "Who is that came in with you?"

"No one, *Apba*. Only me."

That night Dae Young took the blanket his father had refused, and rolling himself up in it, lay down on the ground to sleep. When the mosquitoes came for him with their tiny screaming voices, he lifted up the flap of the mosquito net and laid his head down on his father's arm.

The fifth day came and went, and then the sixth, the seventh. Kun Soo was quiet all the time now and seemed to have trouble moving his neck. He moved his arms less too and still refused to eat, to drink, to come inside the house. Now, though, he insisted that Dae Young stay beside him and the boy spent all day at his side and all night with him under the mosquito net, leaving the shed only to eat and, twice a day, to empty and rinse the bottle. And every time he left and came again Kun Soo asked who he had brought with him and talked to people Dae Young couldn't see.

On the morning of the eighth day Kun Soo's flow was very small, a dark yellow-brown color and evil smelling. That evening he had none to give and none again on the morning of the ninth day. On the evening of that day he said, "Put away the jar."

On the tenth day the sky began to lower and soon it hung so low it seemed that any moment it would fall. That night it did, exploding on the roof above Dae Young's head with such force that he leaped out of sleep with his heart pounding in his chest. But after all it was just a storm and because he could not sleep now he went to stand beside the window, watching the water slide down off the roof, falling from the eaves like a glistening solid wall. Then the wind blew water in his face and he went back to sit on the blanket beside his father with his knees held in his arms, listening to the thunder on the roof and watching the shadow of his father like a ghost behind the white mosquito net. He seemed to be asleep.

Kun Soo, though, was not asleep. The crashing on the roof had woken him too and he felt a panic of frustration rising in his chest because now he could not move his arms at all, and to move his neck took all his concentrated effort. Beside him, outside the net, he could see his son's face turned to look at him and for the first time he asked for help. "Run quickly for Grannie," he said, but the boy did not hear and although it seemed to Kun Soo that he had spoken, he could not tell if he had made a sound or not. He tried again, and yet again, making his voice louder each time, but if he made a sound at all his words were beaten down and drowned by the crashing of the rain and the sound of water rushing.

There was fear in him now, like a deep abyss, and yet there

was a sense in which he loved the melodrama, pitying himself and watching himself at the same time, wanting the crash and racket of the storm to last forever because he knew that when it was done silence was waiting at the end.

That night Kun Soo saw the dead of his family. Here was his oldest brother with one leg blown off, his other brother with a rotten purple face, his father come to visit him. He looked for the hole in his father's head the way his mother always spoke of him but found that all this time she had been mistaken about how he died. It was not his head the North Koreans blew apart but his chest. Nothing was left of it and Kun Soo could see clear through him to the other side.

Here now came his first wife weeping with bruises on her face. He cried out to her for her forgiveness but she kept her face turned down and wept.

He looked for his five daughters because although he never spoke of them he was puzzled that they never came to visit him and had convinced himself that they were dead. He wanted to chide them, "Did you not know your mother wept for you? Why did you not come? Each New Year she looked for you, each birthday, each Moon Festival. Why did you not come?" But his daughters were not there.

There were others, though, many of them, and these he understood to be his ancestors. Some he seemed to know but most were strangers to him. They came jostling through the walls as though they had been waiting for him in the yard and the fury of the storm had driven them inside. They came in ones and twos and groups and soon were far more than the shed could hold but still they came, milling around him, talking to each other and to him, sometimes making gestures toward him with their hands, although none seemed either to condemn him or to welcome him, and the sound of their voices was the sound of the storm.

Some were vaporous, their faces indistinct, others seemed as solid as he was himself. Men came in high-crowned horsehair hats and shoes with turned-up toes, women with their hair rolled at the back in buns, children running naked with the skins of their bellies drawn tight against their spines. Here was a very fat young woman walking in a strange rolling fashion side to side, and here a young man with blazing eyes who reminded Kun Soo of himself. They wept and laughed and bowed low to each other, arguing, discussing earnestly, while others just stood watching him with hungry eyes.

These hungry ones stood closest, brushing up against the net that hung above him like a sheer white shroud. When he looked up, their eyes looked down at him and when he looked down, they looked up at him from between his feet. And all the time the others' voices roared and crashed inside the storm.

One of these hungry ones he thought was his son Joo Yup, but he was an idiot no longer and when Kun Soo looked closely at him he seemed to have a double outline. Kun Soo remembered the apparition that had appeared to him in the body of the White Shaman, the way it had cried, *"Ama, Ama, Ama,"* and he understood that after all it had been an omen.

146

"Joo Yup, my son," he cried, "so you are dead, then. My son, forgive me. I have killed your mother."

Joo Yup made no response, just stood there watching him, and Kun Soo could see that he was a very handsome son. This confused him because he thought his son was beside him on the floor. He tried to call out to the boy beside him but by now Dae Young had grown weary and was curled up, sound asleep. For hours he had sat beside his father, watching his eyes roll in his head and his mouth work as though he were speaking to someone, but there was no one there and the rain drowned everything he said.

Later in his life, in dreams and fantasies, Dae Young will remember strange things from that night. Years from now, when he is a man living in America with his childhood long forgotten, he will hear, from time to time, his father's voice speaking in a language buried in his head. "She has killed me, this woman who is your mother," or, "Pity me, Father, I have done the best I could," or sometimes, "Wife, forgive me, it was a demon that took hold of me." Then Dae Young will start up, looking about and reassuring himself that it is just imagination, that he works too hard, that he needs a rest, to go on a vacation. But then he will remember driving and driving in a white bus full of people keening and wailing and an old woman rocking back and forth. He will remember countryside and mountains, the long boredom of a speech that seems to be a eulogy. He will remember being left alone with a man in long gray robes and a blue-shaved head. He is helping the man, whom he knows to be a Buddhist monk, to spread out a red cloth, securing it at each corner with a rock, and to load onto it bottles with Korean writing, which he understands are beer and wine, and boxes of cigarettes and food. He will remember that he doesn't cry, and an old woman's voice will come inside his head, saying, "Now you must be responsible." Then he will work and work compulsively.

Kun Soo tried time and again to wake this sleeping boy beside him but he could not make him stir and at last turned his attention back to the others gathered in the storage shed. They had drawn away now and stood looking at an old, old man who stood apart from them, hands folded on the knob of his bamboo walking cane. His shoulders stooped and he wore a long white coat and long white baggy pants. A white beard flowed across his chest and his pure white hair was twisted up onto his head in a topknot in the ancient way. Kun Soo did not know his face and yet it had the familiarity of family.

Seeing the respectful way the other people in the room treated this ancient ancestor, Kun Soo understood that he was in charge here, and he beseeched him, alternately blaming and excusing himself. "What have I done," he cried, "but try to give a son to my father to carry on his line? Oh, but what have I done to this poor woman, my good wife of many years? I have driven her to her death and what has she ever done but bear me children? Was it her fault that fate decreed she should not bear a useful son? Was it her fault or that of the gods? Did not the gods decide that my father's line should die away? All I wanted, Grandfather, was to do as a good son should do. But I have meddled with the fates. Forgive me, Grandfather. I have been arrogant and foolish and the gods have sent me this unfaithful wife to torment me and drive me to despair." And so he went on and on.

When Kun Soo had said everything over and over until his throat grew so hoarse he could no longer speak, the old man came forward and stood beside him, looking down through the fine white drop of the mosquito netting with a face full of the wrinkled kindness of extreme old age. He spoke to Kun Soo for a long time, gesturing toward the other spirits, and seemed to make an explanation, while Kun Soo lay watching him, unable to move, and from time to time begging him to come closer, speak louder, because although by now the storm had ceased to crack and shriek, the rain still fell down with a steady roar like a giant waterfall. He knew that what the old man said was critical to his next life. Some lesson was being imparted to him and if he did not follow the instructions closely, he would not rest. He would become one of the vengeful flying spirits that lurk in hedges and underneath the eaves of houses. And there he would be trapped. He would not come back to have another life.

And so he strained to hear this kindly spirit's words, the pressure in his chest growing and growing, until, as dawn spread out gray hands behind the weeping sky, he sat up suddenly, reaching to seize the old man by the shoulders and bring his mouth close to his ear. But as he reached, the old man smiled down at him and turned away.

Something burst in Kun Soo's chest. Blood spurted from his mouth and sprayed across the floor. Then he fell back.

• • •

Dae Young awakened slowly. The rain had eased and now fell with a low whistling sound punctuated by the click of water falling from one corner of the eaves. It was not the whistling or the clicking, though, but the smell that had woken him. He sat up in the half light, feeling shame flood over him because his father had soiled himself in the night.

He crept to tell his grandmother. She was coming through the yard, a black umbrella held above her head. "Grannie," he whispered, "*Apba* has soiled himself."

She threw the umbrella in the air. "Ah, my son is gone!" And ran into the storage shed, crying out in a wavering voice, "My son! My son!"

Dae Young ran after her, fearful that her commotion would wake his father and start his rage again, but his grandmother was rocking on the floor with her apron thrown across her head, wailing and wailing, while his father lay, his head turned to the side, watching with his mouth hung open in astonishment and eyes that did not move. The stench of him filled the air.

Dae Young felt a rising in his throat and, rushing out into the yard, he vomited until he fell down in the mud on hands and knees, and heaved and heaved.

THE STORY OF KUN SOO'S DEATH spread like a ripple from a stone dropped in a pond. So many people came to his funeral, bringing with them offerings of food and money, that for almost a week the tiny house and yard were filled with weeping and wailing, while groups of people gathered in the street to talk and stare and offer gossip to each other and set their hands against the darkened windows of the small white newly polished bus that was the hearse. The pungent smoke of incense and the spicy smell of food drifted from the house, scenting the air for blocks around.

The old woman watched her good friend, Jung Hee's mother, and her daughter, Jung Hee, accepting food and drink from mourners, carrying it to the back of the house, where they set it on folding tables underneath the canvas canopy the funeral director had erected there. She did not go with them. The canopy had been attached to the storage shed where Kun Soo had died and she did not want to look at it. Instead, she stood beside the gate, bowing from time to time to some newly appeared mourner but not joining any of the groups that clustered in the small front yard or alleyway.

Behind her, on the fence, her ornamental gourds were fat and ripening, twisted in the elegant fantastic shapes into which she had trained them, tying some with string to encourage the proper direction of their growth. The vine had grown luxuriant this summer, covered in flowers that were closed now, each one shrouded in its own white petals, because it was almost midday and the sun was fierce. In the evening, when the sun was gone and the moon was gentle in the sky, they would open up their faces, trembling in the soft night breezes like a hedge of ghosts.

The old woman saw many people who were neighbors, many who were friends, and many who were strangers come to see what the commotion was about. They had heard stories about the strange, stubborn death of Kun Soo and about his lovely wife who had brought this misfortune on herself by her repeated infidelities. Even as they stood, they made the stories bigger and more dramatic, introducing new characters and fantastic events, vying with each other, spittle beading at the corners of their mouths.

The old woman understood that this gossip was going on by the way these people put their heads together, opening big eyes and sometimes turning to look at her across their shoulders. They had all been inside to stare at Kun Soo's coffin and to criticize the poverty of the small house. They had walked in the yard, eaten from the bowls of food set out for mourners, stuck nervous heads inside the storage shed to see the stain of blood Kun Soo had coughed across the floor, swearing to each other afterwards that they had felt his spirit touch them on the shoulder or the arm, that when they turned to see the air was not quite clear, that when they turned away again they heard a sob, a moan, death's rattle in an unseen throat.

It all went past her like a dream. Every night for four nights now she had sat in her white clothes beside her son, staring at the darkness, overwhelmed with shame that she, his mother, had outlived him. Now she was exhausted and the people weeping in the house and going to and fro to offer her their sympathies had no more reality than ghosts.

After Kun Soo died she had insisted on doing everything for him herself, accepting no help except to carry him into the house. She would have done that too but he was too heavy for her and she was forced to send Dae Young for the two strong sons of Mrs. Park. Once she was sure they had laid him down with his head toward the north, she had thanked them and dismissed them.

By that time her old friend, Jung Hee's mother, and her daughter had arrived, bringing with them burial clothes and a roll of thin white cotton fabric to use as a shroud. The old woman accepted the clothes and the shroud and sent the children out walking with Jung Hee, but she refused all other help except to let her old friend go off to make arrangements with the undertaker and to send out notice of the death.

Alone, she prepared the perfumed water in which she washed Kun Soo, then dressed him carefully, straightened his legs and head, folded his hands together just below his chest, and wrapped him in his shroud, rolling him from side to side to get it under him. She prepared the ceremonial rice for the messenger from the other world so that he could refresh himself after his long journey to find Kun Soo's spirit, and when she had set it out, knelt down with her palms against her forehead, rocking back and forth and weeping in a loud voice for this the last of her three sons and the most stubborn. By the time her old friend came back she was quiet and composed, and although she mourned deeply after that, there were no more tears left in her for her son, just a heavy sorrow like regret and shame mixed up together.

She sat awake with him all night. The skies crashed as they had the night he died and from time to time a bright light filled the room. Once she turned her face up to the window and saw lightning like a flaming horse racing through the sky, and all night the rain came down, falling and falling as though it would never stop.

That night she mourned not just for Kun Soo but also for her two older sons, who had been no more than children when they were press-ganged with their father early in the war with the North. The oldest had his leg blown off below the knee and for two days and nights lay on the side of a frozen hill while a battle raged about him. From the injury he might have recovered because it was frozen and so would not have been infected, but the rest of him was frozen too and he died of it. When the battle on the hill was done, his fellow soldiers buried him. Her younger son was taken captive with some others. They were made to dig a trench, hands freezing to the metal handles of the shovels, then forced down into it and shot. The old woman was told this by a friend of her younger son. He had been press-ganged at the same time as all the men of their village and was the only one to come back home. When the old woman heard of his return she jumped into her shoes and ran out without a coat. But the boy lay on the floor bundled in his bedding, shaking so hard that when he tried to speak his jaw rattled and the words would not come out. He shook like that for three full days and then his mother sent for Kun Soo's mother and she came again, this time in her coat, and he told her how her sons had died. Neither could be brought home to be buried with their ancestors, which was bad luck enough, but now her youngest son had refused to die in his own house, which was worse.

The next night no rain came, nor the next night, nor the next. These three nights the old woman sat unmoving in the stifling heat with incense filling up her lungs. All she could hear was the sound of Kun Soo's children moaning in their dreams, the breathing of the people who had brought sleeping mats and settled back-to-back and nose-to-nose across her floor, the feet of Mi Sook pacing back and forth on the wooden boards of the veranda, her voice wailing over and over, "What shall I do now? Oh, what shall I do now?"

The old woman did not remember sending word to her of Kun Soo's death but she had appeared on the evening of that day, rushing into the house, half hysterical, her hair flying everywhere. Since then she had done nothing but weep and moan, slapping her hands against her face and frightening the children, coming constantly to the old woman to pull at her arm, demanding, "What shall I do now, Grannie? How will I feed all these children? I make only a small wage and now my husband has died and all these children he has given me will starve to death. Tell me, Grannie, what shall I do now? Oh, what shall I do now?" and the old woman had begun to fear that she would lose her mind.

During that time she felt as if she might even lose her own mind. She could think of nothing she had done in this present life that deserved the punishment that had come down on her: a husband dead, a first son dead, a second, now a third. And not one of them had died at home, not even Kun Soo, who had not been killed by war. How perverse of him to insist on dying in the storage shed when he knew as well as anyone what bad luck it is to bring a man into his house already dead. In his urgency to punish Mi Sook he had surely brought misfortune down on all his family. She feared for her grandchildren, especially for the boy Dae Young, the last of her husband's line, because he had the bad luck of his father's death upon his neck. Because of this, when Mi Sook demanded, "What shall I do now?" the old woman had no answer for her.

On the fifth day, Mr. Bang, the undertaker, came to her and said, "Kun Soo's Mother, today the coffin must be closed," but when she heard him use her name like that, fear took hold of her. When her first son had been born, she had been named for him, but since he and his brother had been killed she had been called Kun Soo's Mother. Now she would have no son for her name. "Go away," she said, and went behind him to the gate to watch him vanish among the mourners milling in the lane.

But then he came again, bowing with his hands crossed on his genitals. "Kun Soo's Mother, it is a great sorrow for you that your son is dead, but the weather is very hot. I must advise you to close the coffin now."

"But what of my son's spirit? What if it has been left behind in the storage shed? If he is not close beside his body, the messenger who comes to lead him to the other world will go away without him. Then he will be lost forever. I beg you, let him have just one more day to find his body."

Mr. Bang led her inside the house to where Kun Soo lay wrapped in his shroud beside a plain deal coffin. At his head the Buddhist monk sat cross-legged in his long gray robe with his hands pressed together and his mouth moving with the prayers he made. On the floor between his knees and Kun Soo's head, sticks of incense burned in brass containers and all around the edges of the *ondol* floor others were set at intervals. Their smoke filled the room, the floral odor of the incense overwhelming any smell that Kun Soo's deteriorating body might have started to produce.

"See how he makes the prayers," said Mr. Bang, gesturing toward the monk. "There is no doubt that all these prayers and the smoke of all this incense rising up to heaven will ensure that Kun Soo finds his way into the other world. You must not fear for his spirit, Kun Soo's Mother. I have been an undertaker for thirty years now, and my father and grandfather before me, and my great-grandfather before that, and I know about such things. Kun Soo's Mother, do not hesitate any longer. Even now it is insanitary and in one more day he will surely stink. It will be very bad for you and very bad for my reputation."

When Mr. Bang put it this way, the old woman saw the wisdom of his words and agreed to have Kun Soo lifted into his coffin and the lid sealed down. Now she was glad of it because she did not want gossips coming to stare at him and sniff and go away, saying, "Oh, that Kun Soo's Mother left him lying in his shroud until he rotted." She thought of the blue-shaved head of the monk bowed over him and felt comforted, also because Mr. Bang's great-grandfather had been an undertaker too.

Now here came Mrs. Park, who lived across the lane with her two strong sons and a telephone as well as an indoor flushing toilet. She held a steaming dish of food and was looking for a place to set it down. And here was Jung Hee's mother taking it. Here were women from the market stall. They came to the old woman with their hands together, looking sorrowful and saying their words of sympathy. Here was Mr. Hong, who ran the general store. He would not get payment now for his mosquito net. Here was Mrs. Won, who ran the beauty shop, Mr. Lee, a local policeman, a group of men from Kun Soo's construction site with their foreman, Mr. Chang, who had already come three times to tell her he was sorry about Kun Soo falling off the roof but it was not his fault. Now he was telling her again.

Here was the owner of the wine shop, also telling her that

it was not her fault, that Kun Soo drank too much, that she had told him ten thousand times a night he should go home and get some sleep but did he pay attention to her? No.

Here now was Mr. Shin, manager of the warehouse whose fish truck Kun Soo had wrecked. He looked sorrowful and guilty too. "Ah, Kun Soo's Mother," he said, "I must make a special offering or I will be a lizard or a worm in my next life. I was angry that Kun Soo wrecked my truck and I fired him, yes. But always I calm down after I am angry and I would have given him his job back. I know he was a good man and trustworthy. He worked hard. He stayed on schedule. Never did I have a complaint that my fish were not delivered on time. Never did I have a complaint that he delivered a short order to my customers. Every box loaded from my warehouse onto his truck was unloaded at the other end. Yes, he was an honest man. Not once did I have any reason to suspect he was selling fish out of my truck to black marketeers along the way. Never one box missing, always the bills of lading balanced evenly. So, you see, it was only my quick temper that fired him. When I had drunk a little beer and calmed down I said to myself, foolish man, what have you done? Where will you find another worker like that Kun Soo? You must accept that sometimes a man will have an accident, no fault of his own. So, I said to myself, you must go to see Kun Soo and make a deal with him. You must tell him that if he will work a little harder for a while to pay for the repairs to the wrecked truck, and also for the temporary rental on another, then he can have his job back. So I have put on my straw hat and my clean shirt and I have come to see him. But now what do I find? Outside my old friend Kun Soo's house is a hearse and all these many people dressed in white and beating on their chests. Ah no, I tell myself, my old friend Kun Soo cannot be dead. So I run into the house, forgetting even to step out of my shoes, and sure enough, there lies Kun Soo's coffin and at its head a monk making his mutterings. Ah, Kun Soo's Mother, it is a sad day for you and all your family." And so he went on and on, adding to the turmoil and commotion.

Behind him the old woman could see Mi Sook, tears wet on her face, going back and forth between the guests, weeping and accepting food, which she handed on to Jung Hee's mother, and money, which she tucked inside her blouse. Following Mi Sook as though she wanted to speak with her but could not make her mind up to it was a woman whose round fat face seemed to be familiar. Except for a string of jade beads, which even from here the old woman could tell were quite expensive, and a large black eelskin purse hooked around her forearm, she was dressed all in white like an official mourner, her long loose skirt and long loose jacket designed to hide a body round and fat with flesh. The old woman watched her, puzzling on her identity, until she vanished inside the house. The old woman wanted to follow her but Mr. Shin was still making his long speech of apology and she was obliged to hear it out.

A clump of children who had been shoving at each other on the front veranda followed the stranger inside. Many children were here, some mourners' children, some Kun Soo's children's friends, some whom the old woman had never seen before. They crept in and out between the adults' legs with their eyes big in their heads, daring each other to go inside to see the coffin or into the storage shed to see where Kun Soo had coughed his blood. Now the ones who had just gathered courage to go inside the house came running out again. They jumped off the veranda, and squeezing in and out between the adults, ran into the alleyway, where their shrill voices screeched and laughed behind the fence.

At last Mr. Shin's flow of words ran out. He bowed, and bowed again, and turned away in search of food. But behind him came another, and another, a friend, a workmate, one of the men who used to squat with Kun Soo on the *ondol* floor and rattle *hwato* cards. They all must make their speech and they must all be listened to.

When next the old woman looked for her, the stranger who had been following Mi Sook was sitting on the edge of the veranda with the baby Tae Hee on her knee and Kun Soo's other children standing on each side of her. Tae Hee was playing with her jade necklace and she had one arm around Li Na, who was crying in the silent helpless way she had cried ever since her father came home on the board. This stranger pressed the little girl's head against her full breast like a sympathetic mother while she spoke to Dae Young with a face alternately sad and happy, and Dae Young tilted his head toward her, paying close attention to her words. From time to time she brought out candy from her eelskin purse, calming the children with it while she talked and talked.

The old woman watched them, puzzling to herself. This woman's face seemed so kind and so familiar that she wanted to embrace her, and yet she could not remember ever having met her. She went toward her, curious to hear what she was saying to her grandson that he took so seriously. Because of the moving crush of people, the strange woman did not notice her approach and when the old woman got very close she heard her say to Dae Young, "So you can call me Auntie but really I am your sister."

The old woman's hands began to shake because she realized that this was Eun Hye, the oldest daughter of Kun Soo's first wife. She had not recognized her because she had grown stout, and her face, which once was thin and nervous, was now round and fully fleshed and full of solid confidence.

Eun Hye looked up and saw her. She set the baby down and rose to make her bow. "Hello, Grandmother," she said. "I am sorry for my father's death."

The old woman seized her hand. "Ah, my own Eun Hye." She drew her across the yard and out into the alleyway, where she embraced her. "But you must go away at once, my child. Your father's new wife does not know about you. She only knows about Joo Yup. Your father never told her about his daughters."

Eun Hye patted the old woman's hand. "All this I know already. My friends who live here have told me everything. I was so angry with my father that I could not come to the funeral of my own mother but now I have accepted it and I am sad for you that your last son is dead."

162

"But if you knew all this why did you come? It will only make trouble at your father's funeral."

"But I have come to help. I want to make an offer to his wife."

"To Mi Sook? No, I do not want you to."

"I must, Grandmother. I must. I want to help her with these children. With my father dead she will not be able to support them, but I have married a businessman in Pusan who has sufficient money, an exporter of seaweeds and a clockmaker as well. Are these little children not my half-brother and half-sisters? Should I not help?"

"Eun Hye, this is very generous of you, especially as the mother of these children took your own mother's place. Yes, it is very generous. But you are not obliged. Surely by now you have children of your own to spend your money on."

"No, Grandmother, I have been unlucky. I have had an illness and had to have an operation. Now I cannot have children of my own. That is why, when I heard my father died—"

"But do you mean you want to take these children home with you and *keep* them? I thought you had come to offer money for their support. This is a different matter entirely."

"I want to adopt them, Grandmother."

The old woman bunched her mouth together. "When Mi Sook discovered that her husband had had a first wife and a son she was so angry that I think if she had had some way to support herself and all her children she would have taken them and gone. I think she will be even more angry when she finds out her husband also had five daughters that he hid from her. I do not think she will agree to let you adopt her children."

"But Grandmother, don't you see it will be a good thing for her? How can she pay for all these children? What is her job? I am told she is just a coffee shop girl. That money is nothing. Nothing. And you are too old now to go out to work. If you rely on Mi Sook to support you everyone will starve. And no man will have her with all these children. She will never find another husband."

"All this I know, Eun Hye, and I think myself it is a good solution for you to adopt the children. You seem to have become a good woman and if you are as prosperous as you say then it would be an excellent thing."

"Excellent indeed, Grandmother. If we do this, my husband will have children, Mi Sook will find another husband, and you will come to live with us. Of course you will. We will take care of you very well. It is a perfect plan."

So they discussed the matter back and forth and there was perfect agreement between them that everyone would benefit from the arrangement. However, the old woman knew that Mi Sook would be hard to convince. "We must take this slowly with her, Eun Hye. At first she will be angry and upset so we must take her a little at a time and let her get used to the idea gradually."

"Of course, Grandmother, of course."

"You must let me speak to her first. Promise you will say nothing until I have spoken privately with her."

But Eun Hye was not paying attention. She was watching

Mi Sook, who had just come out into the lane with a handkerchief to her eyes. When she saw the old woman standing there she came up with her face swollen from weeping. "What am I to do now, Grannie?" she said. "Tell me, what am I to do? I did not think that he would die. I went back to the coffee shop not thinking he would die. Oh, it was cruel of him to die and leave us all like this." And she burst out into tears again.

"Don't cry, Mi Sook," Eun Hye said. "I have come to help you."

Mi Sook looked up at her in puzzlement. "Why should you help me? I do not even know you."

Just then the three children came pushing through the crowd looking for their new Aunt Eun Hye. Li Na wrapped one arm around her leg, looking timidly up at her mother because she had grown afraid of her these last few days. Dae Young stood between his mother and Eun Hye as though he could not decide with which his allegiance should lie, but Tae Hee ignored her mother entirely. She liked this aunt who gave her candies and held her on her lap, speaking comfortingly. "Up, Auntie," she said, holding up her baby arms.

"Auntie? What is this? You are not my children's aunt."

The old woman began to speak but Eun Hye cut her off, speaking excitedly. "No, this is true, but they are my close relatives. They are my own half-brother and half-sisters. You do not know me yet, but I am Eun Hye, the oldest daughter of your dead husband." And while Mi Sook stood staring with big eyes and open mouth, forgetting even to cry, Eun Hye went on to tell her in more detail who she was and also many of the things she had told the old woman.

Several times the old woman tried to interrupt this flood of information but neither Eun Hye nor Mi Sook paid her attention, so at last she just stood helplessly. She could see that Mi Sook was growing angry and wished that Eun Hye would not talk in such an excited voice, that her face was not so round and fat, her stomach also round and fat. She wished she did not look so confident and prosperous. It was clear that Mi Sook did not take to her.

But now she had started on it, Eun Hye was determined to win Mi Sook over. "So you see, Mi Sook, you and I are relatives. I am your stepdaughter. Not everyone is fortunate enough to have grown daughters come to help them when their husband dies."

"Daughters? What, are there more of you then?"

"Four more, two of them twins and then two more, all younger."

Mi Sook turned to the old woman in astonishment. "Five daughters? How can this be?"

The old woman pressed her palms together, holding her hands up before her as though in prayer. "It is the truth, Daughter, although I did not want to tell you in this way."

"Surely you are mistaken."

"How can I be mistaken? Kun Soo is my own son. I was at the celebration of his first wedding. I helped bring those five baby girls into the world, and then the son. I lived with them for many years. I raised the girls while their mother worked down at the market stall, and I hunted that mad wandering boy through all the streets, dragging him home by the arm time after time. How can I be mistaken? It is all the truth. Kun Soo had a wife before you, which you know. He had a son born with no brain, which you know. He also had five daughters who are grown, and I saw no need to distress you any further so I did not tell you about them. Forgive me, Daughter, I acted for the best."

Mi Sook turned back to Eun Hye. "But—"

"It is all true," Eun Hye told her. "All of it. My sisters who are twins have married two of my husband's old school friends and the two younger girls still live with me. We all work together in my husband's business—as I told you, he is a sea-weed-products exporter and also has a clock shop—so your children will have a big family to care for them and a good business to work in when they are older. My husband is right now talking to the builder about drawing up plans for a new wing of the house."

Up till now Eun Hye had not told Mi Sook clearly that she wished to adopt the children, only that she wanted to help, and the thought of some extra money for their support had gone some way toward balancing Mi Sook's anger at this new deception of Kun Soo's. Now it seemed that Eun Hye was planning to take them all to live with her in her husband's house in Pusan. "But I do not want to live in Pusan," she said uneasily. "I have a job in Seoul and that is where my home is."

"Oh, but you can live anywhere you want. Only the children will come to live with me, *Halmoni* also. When the adoption is agreed to—"

"Daughter, listen to me," the old woman interrupted hastily. She had seen Mi Sook's head draw back and her eyes grow tight and narrow and she knew that Eun Hye had made a serious mistake in negotiation by going too fast. "Daughter, listen to me, please."

But Mi Sook ignored her, drawing in her breath to speak. "So," she said in a hard voice, "my husband has deceived me well. He tells me he is the owner of a company and makes me think that he is rich. He dyes his hair and makes me think that he is young. He hides from me a wife of many years, an idiot son. And now I find he has hidden from me five grown daughters, this one older than myself, coming now with a brazen face to take away my children. What else has my husband hidden from me? What else, Grannie?"

"But Daughter, I did tell you about the wife and son."

"But what of this fat-faced woman and all these other daughters? Why did you not tell me of them? What else are you hiding from me, Grannie?" And she took the old woman by the shoulders and shook her until her head bobbed on her neck.

"Here, stop that!" cried Eun Hye, and slinging Tae Hee onto her hip so she could hold her with one arm, she pulled Mi Sook away from the old woman with the other.

Mi Sook turned and grabbed the baby underneath the armpits, screaming, "You will steal my children, will you, you fat thing? Give her to me, I tell you. Let her go!"

Eun Hye, confused and afraid to let Tae Hee go in case she fell, clutched both hands around the baby's waist, crying, "But you don't understand, let me explain, please let me explain."

Seeing the two women wrestling for his little sister, making her scream in fright, Dae Young inserted himself between them, hauling down on Tae Hee's legs and shouting, "Leave her alone, you're hurting her," while Li Na flung herself down in the dust and kicked and screamed, and the old woman, snatching first at Mi Sook then at Eun Hye, cried over and over, "Stop it! Stop it, I tell you! Stop!"

By now the whole funeral party had gathered around to watch the excitement, but when the screams and commotion did not abate and it seemed as though the baby would be torn apart, the two sons of Mrs. Park stepped in. They had muscles in their arms and legs like heavy rope. One seized Mi Sook from behind, the other Eun Hye. At the same time the old woman scooped the baby out from between them and ran into the house.

Eun Hye did not come in the undertaker's bus to Kun Soo's burial because Mi Sook would not allow it. Instead she came behind with some others who had rented another bus. They drove into the countryside until they came to the village where Kun Soo's ancestors were buried, both buses filled three to a double seat, the aisles full too, and people crowded on the steps so that they had to scramble up and flatten themselves against some other person's chest or back to keep from being crushed when the heavy doors folded back. With all these and the crowd that came shuffling and stamping from the fields and houses of the village to swell the group of mourners, there were as many people milling about as had been in the house and yard.

The coffin was taken from the bus and carried to the grave on the shoulders of Mrs. Park's two sons and four of Kun Soo's cousins from the village while the mourners followed on behind, led by the Buddhist monk with Dae Young beside him as chief mourner. They went along a narrow asphalt road, children and dogs running beside, crying out to each other and barking, past the thatch-roofed houses and the storage sheds and piles of hay and bulging sacks with A-frames leaning up against them and a few cows watching them with sympathetic eyes.

The asphalt ended not far behind the village and the mourners turned onto a beaten dirt trail below a hill, then set off across a rising field where the air breathed out the hot sweet smell of dung and long grass clutched at their ankles, leaving burrs in the lower edges of the men's pants and in the long skirts of the women. Crows rose up before them as they went across the field, cracking their wings and making ugly hacking cries, while the children, who at some invisible signal had stopped behind them in a cluster on the trail, called and whistled to the dogs now stalking the procession through the grass, barking invisibly at the excitement of the day, first one and then another leaping to snap at a rising crow, rushing briefly after it with upturned head and open grinning mouth, then vanishing once more inside the grass, dark backs rising and falling through the pale rustling grass like porpoises through ocean. And the villagers, most of whom had never seen Kun Soo, some of whom had known him as a child but had given him no thought for many years, treated his return as occasion for a ceremony. A great deal of racket and commotion went along with this. Some waved flags, some swung cans with incense burning in them, some rang bells, and everybody howled and wailed and sang in anguished voices while the Buddhist monk gave out his invocations in a loud, monotonous lament. Mi Sook was swept up in it, and even the old woman, who had not wept aloud since the afternoon she had spent alone with her dead son. Both joined in the wailing, giving out loud shrill mourning cries and swaying back and forth.

On the way home, Mi Sook was still weeping so intently that she did not notice Eun Hye climb up into the undertaker's bus. By the time she realized who it was beside her it was too late, the bus was already coughing down the road in a cloud of fumes and dust.

Eun Hye spent the journey home talking to Mi Sook's downturned head, talking and talking about the advantages to everyone of this proposed adoption, pleading and pleading with her to agree to the arrangement. "They will be happy, I give you my assurance. Why, already they have taken to me. Have you not seen that? And they will like my husband too. He is a kind and generous man who longs only for some children to make his happiness complete."

This description of Eun Hye's husband made Mi Sook

envious. She turned to her, speaking abruptly. "Why should he love them? They are not his bloodline."

"No, but they are my half-brother and half-sisters and he will love them on account of me. When I heard my father died—"

"When you heard your father died, you came running to steal my children from me," Mi Sook said bitterly, turning her head to look out the window of the bus.

"No, no, I do not mean to steal your children. But now it will be very difficult for you. How can you take care of these three children? With them on your back, how will you ever find another husband? No one will marry you if you are weighted down with the children of another man. It will be very hard for you."

Mi Sook said nothing, staring out the window, so Eun Hye went on with more confidence. "Although we have never met before, you are my stepmother." She gave a little laugh. "It is strange to have a mother younger than myself. But we can do a good thing here for each other. I need to have children and you need to be free of them."

In the window Mi Sook could see Eun Hye's round, anxious face behind her, and she relented a little. "Well, at least you have come to your father's funeral, which is more than any of your sisters have done for him all these years, never coming to visit him at all."

"They were afraid of him."

"What, did none of you love your father?"

"How could we love him? How could any of us love him? He hated us all."

Mi Sook's head came round. "Hated you? Why?"

"For being girls. Always he would berate my poor mother for giving him only girls. When my brother was born, at first he was happy, but then he was even angrier than before because he was ugly like a toad and queer in the head. He beat my mother after that, and sometimes he beat us too, his own children, because we were only girls."

Mi Sook, looking into Eun Hye's face, saw that what she said was true. She turned away and was quiet for a long time, resting her forehead on the window of the bus and thinking about what she had tried not to think about before: how Kun Soo cared only for Dae Young, how he brushed his little girls aside, and how they never climbed up on his knee or clung against his leg or ran to meet him at the door when he came home from work because he had taught them not to love him. Now she recognized that Kun Soo had treated her daughters in the same way he must have treated Eun Hye and her sisters. He had not yet begun to beat them when he died, but he had beaten her, and would have demanded a divorce from her just as he did from Eun Hye's mother if Dae Young had turned out not to be a suitable son. She thought of how *Madame* had warned her, saying, "From his wife a man hides many things, but many more are hidden from the wife who first was mistress." *Madame* was right. Kun Soo had hidden many things from her. And Mi Sook began to think that maybe Eun Hye was not, after all, a selfish greedy woman as she had judged her.

When they arrived home, Eun Hye blocked Mi Sook

from getting off the bus. "So, do we have an agreement?" she insisted. "Will you send the children home with me?"

"I will think about it."

"I will come to see you in the morning, then."

All that night Mi Sook paced up and down the wooden boards of the veranda, staring into the darkness and trying to come to a decision, but the shock of everything she had learned was too much for her and she could not reason clearly with herself. First she thought that Eun Hye's offer was the solution to her problem and then she thought of how Eun Hye was rich and could easily give her money to support the children—should she not do this for her own father's children?—but no, she was only interested in stealing them away. Then she thought of Eun Hye's husband, of what a good man he must be to take on a stranger's children in this way, but then she thought that Eun Hye planned to steal away her children as revenge because she had taken her mother's place. Later she remembered the gifts of money still tucked inside her blouse, and squatting down in the moonlight, she counted the notes out onto the veranda, setting aside an amount for Mr. Bang the undertaker. Then, swinging back onto her heels with the remainder spread in a fan between her fingers, she sucked her breath between her teeth, assessing rice and vegetables, electric bills, a little fish for health. This much would last—how long? The children ate more every day.

She patted the fan of notes on the board between her feet,

making it into a neat stack. Surely in her mother-in-law's frugal hands it would last long enough for her to figure out some way to make more than she was making at the coffee shop. But then she thought about how the children would need new clothes every year and how they would need books and pencils to take to school, because they must have an education if they were going to make a decent living.

After that she remembered the kindness in Eun Hye's round fat face reflected in the window of the bus, and thought about the seaweed-exporting business and the clock shop in Pusan, and how easy it would be for the children to work there when they were grown. Why, with a business like that they would hardly even need an education. They would all grow fat and wealthy like Eun Hye. But then she thought of how she would hardly see them anymore, and maybe never, and she wanted to keep them with her, because doesn't every woman want her children with her?

She thought about how Eun Hye said, and Kun Soo's mother also, that she would not get another husband with three children on her back, and she knew that it was true. And yet she could not make herself believe it. Hyun Joon, after all, had held her little daughter on his knee and played with her the way a father would. Maybe he . . . But no, she would rather be like *Madame* and have a business of her own so that her children would work with her instead of with Eun Hye. But still her heart asked, What about Hyun Joon?

She looked down at the little pile of notes. What if she should use it to start a business of her own? It was not enough, but it could be a place to start. She could save and add to it. But how could she save if she had children always with their mouths open for food? She had no option but to give them to Eun Hye, at least temporarily. Yes, temporarily. That was the answer. Eun Hye would take care of them while she set up a business for herself, and when it was done, she would take them back. But no, Eun Hye was talking about adoption. She wanted children of her own. If she took them she would not give them back. No, they must not go with her. But now she asked herself again: How will I feed and clothe them?

Thus Mi Sook went back and forth all night, and by the time the sky grew light, she was fully resolved: she would give her children to Eun Hye.

When Eun Hye came to the gate Mi Sook went out to meet her with Dae Young at her side.

"Have you decided?" Eun Hye asked.

"I have decided."

"Is it to be yes?"

Just then the two little girls came running out of the house, calling, "Auntie! Auntie!" Eun Hye swept Tae Hee up onto her hip and with one hand pressed Li Na's head against her thigh.

Mi Sook looked at her two daughters looking back at her—Tae Hee with her head on Eun Hye's shoulder, chubby hands locked around her neck, Li Na with one arm so tight around Eun Hye's solid leg that the whole leg was inside her arm—and a strange trembling came over her. She set her hand on Dae Young's neck, remembering how, after all his duties at the funeral were done, he came not to her but to Eun Hye and laid his head down on her lap.

"Is it to be yes?" Eun Hye asked again, smiling at her.

Mi Sook opened her mouth to say "Yes" but "No" came out instead.

Eun Hye's mouth went on smiling. She looked into Mi Sook's face as though to ask again, but then her eyes filled up with tears and a red flush crept around her neck and up onto her cheeks. She set the baby down, unwound Li Na's clutching arm from round her leg, and from her eelskin purse took out a pen and a small spiral pad.

"Here are my address and phone number. Please call me when you change your mind."

She tore off the piece of paper, holding it out to Mi Sook, but Mi Sook turned away and so Eun Hye tucked it into the pocket of Dae Young's jeans. "Be sure to keep this safe," she said, and then she bent and touched each child on the head and turned and walked away, holding herself very straight, while they stood watching her without a sound.

Later that week, the old woman would pin Dae Young's jeans out on the wire clothesline strung behind the house, turning out the pockets to help them dry more quickly. A folded scrap of paper would fall onto the ground and she would pick it up, carefully spreading it out to see what was written there, but there would only be a smudge of ink.

One by one the old woman pulled the heavy lids off the kimchi pots buried in the yard. The smell of garlic and hot pepper rose out of them, pungent in the cold gray dawn. She peered inside the biggest—a quarter full maybe—and rocked back on her heels, frowning down into the big jar, estimating. A week, ten days at most, and no money left to buy more food unless Mi Sook came back from the coffee shop before it was too late.

But who could know when she would come? Or whether she would come at all? Or if she did, what small pittance she would bring with her? One thing was certain: it would not be near enough to feed three hungry children and an old decrepit grandmother. By the time she paid her bus fare, it would be hardly worth the bringing back at all. Still, even a few coins would help, and the old woman waited anxiously each day for Mi Sook to come home. If she did not come this week there would be no money even to pay the charges for electricity.

She grunted, and taking up a metal bowl from the ground beside her, and a long-handled ladle made out of a gourd, she plunged one arm down inside the jar, bringing up dripping stalks and leaves of the pickled cabbage in a calculating way. When the bowl was about half full she shook the ladle over the jar, watching the drops of fiery fluid fall down into it, preserving every drop. Then she set the lid back on, and with the metal bowl and ladle in her hands, rose slowly to a crouch, paused as though gathering strength, then with a single heavy movement came up to her feet, the effort wrenching out of her a low hard groan, as of accomplishment.

Slowly, bent against the frozen wind like a conspirator, she carried the kimchi through the yard and around the corner of the house to the front door. Half turning to push it open with her elbow, she slipped off her rubber shoes inside the door and stepped into a pair of house slippers. Still in her padded cotton coat, she carried the bowl and ladle to the counter, where she plugged in the hotplate and busied herself warming water, measuring out a careful ration of the pickled cabbage to make kimchi soup.

She stood there stirring at the soup with a long pair of cooking chopsticks until small bubbles began to form below the surface, then set the pan down on the counter with two small white ceramic bowls beside it. From the corner of the room she got the little lacquered table with the curving legs and set that on the counter too.

Turning, she looked toward the other end of the house where her two granddaughters still slept on the bedding spread out across the surface of the *ondol* floor. Thin gray light seeped down across them from the window, creeping amongst the hills and valleys of the tumbled blankets like an early morning fog, making the varnished paper surface of the floor glow like yellow fire.

Through her slippers, the old woman could feel the rising chill of the cement. She looked across to the door below which a crack of light could be seen, the rag she used to block drafts pushed out into the room. She went across and pressed the rag back into place with the toe of her padded slipper. She looked at the coats and jackets hunched against the wall as though trying to keep warm, at the children's sneakers huddled against Kun Soo's padded boots, at her own boat-shaped rubber shoes. She looked again at Kun Soo's boots, then at his coat, and sighed.

Turning away, she went toward the *ondol* floor where she stepped first on one heel, then the other. Her slippers had been stepped on like this so many times that the backs had been squashed flat and they came off easily. She slid them neatly into the row of other slippers, and setting one hand on her right knee, hoisted herself up the three steps, then slowly bent her knees and crouched down beside the sleeping children.

The baby Tae Hee lay on her back, arms flung out as though sleep had sprung at her in a surprise attack and knocked her to the floor. Her sister Li Na was curled up in a ball. Long hairs straggled on the quilt where she had rubbed at that sore spot on her head during the night and more hair had fallen out. The old woman leaned over her, examining the spot. The hair was getting very thin there, and the skin looked angry and inflamed.

Something was growing on the child's head. She had shown it to the old women who were her friends and they had pulled their faces down and recommended this and that to dress it with, but nothing helped. The sore was growing and the little girl should see a doctor, but there was no money for a doctor.

The old woman whispered softly to the children but they went on sleeping and she settled back onto her heels, waiting patiently, watching the baby's mouth make little sucking motions at the air. After a while, she leaned back and to one side, setting her hand against the surface of the floor. It was barely warm and she could tell that it was cooling rapidly, the small supply of coal Dae Young had shoveled under it last night burned down to nothing. She looked down at the floor, moving her fingers gently on its glossy surface. Kun Soo had built that floor, back when they were happy. It was not designed like any he had seen but conjured from his own imagination. He told her once it used to make him proud each time he lay on it, that sometimes, before he fell asleep, he dreamed of becoming a house designer. As time passed, though, and he became hard-pressed, he never spoke about such things.

But she must not think of that. She rose again, and stepping back into her padded slippers, went to the coal box in the corner, where she stood, one hand on the shovel, looking down into the box in much the same way she had looked down earlier into the kimchi pots. She went back and lifted up the metal hatch in the side of the *ondol* floor, dropping it down so that its handle rested against the cement floor of the lower room. She peered in at the few coals still glowing underneath.

The draft from the open hatch made them glow brighter and the old woman felt the rush of air against her cheek as it was drawn in across the coals and on across the stone underlayer of the sleeping platform on its journey toward the vent at its far end. The smoke made her eyes sting and she turned her head aside to wipe her eyes with the corner of her hand.

Closing the hatch, she went once more to the kitchen area, where she set a lid on the pan of kimchi soup. She took a larger pan, maneuvered it into the sink, and twisted the handle of the single faucet, watching the water run down into it. When it was about half full, she hoisted it out and set it to heat on the burner. Then she went outside again, shoulders hunched against the bitter wind, and stood in the shelter of the garden wall, looking up and down the alleyway, watching for Dae Young to come home.

When she had woken that morning his sneakers were already missing, and his coat gone from its hook beside the door, so she knew he was off looking for supplies to bring back to his family. Perhaps when he came home today his jacket would be bulging out with coal, his pockets stuffed with food. She dreamed about what he might bring: perhaps a couple of crisp fat pears, some apples, a pocketful of rice, a head of fish, a giant radish or a curly cabbage. If he were lucky there might be a sheet of dried squid for the children to chew on, a cigarette or two for her.

She took from her jacket pocket a half cigarette and an almost empty box of matches and stood smoking. She thought about her grandson. He was in his sixth year now, a healthy boy, smart and very handsome as his father used to be, also his grandfather before him. Now that her son was dead, this child was head of the family, and head of her. While her son lived, he was head. He honored his mother, but he was her head. Now this little boy assumed his place. Every day the old woman told him he must learn to take care of his sisters. She told him she was an old, old woman, and soon would go to live among her ancestors the way his father did. He must take responsibility.

She told herself there was no shame in her grandson being forced to beg to keep his sisters and his ancient grandmother alive. It was the family's bad luck and nothing could be done. But her heart was heavy because she knew that the shame was not in the begging but that her grandson had become a thief. He had not told her so, making up stories of this kind man, this generous old woman, but she knew that it was true. If things went on like this he would become one of the children who ran all day in the streets, sneaking and darting, slipping over fences, into the back entrances of stores, under market stalls, where they stole from the boxes of fruit and vegetables waiting to be sold. The day would surely come when a market steward would take Dae Young's ear between thumb and forefinger and call for the police. Then he would be brought home with sirens wailing to broadcast his disgrace. Her neighbors would see and they would tell it to their friends, first to this one, then to that, and soon all the town would look at her with pity and with condescension. In her old age she would lose all her face.

The old woman pinched the glowing end of her cigarette between forefinger and thumb and stored it in her pocket. She could make one cigarette last all day if she was careful. She shivered, slapping her hands against her arms and stamping her feet. Perhaps in her next life she would have a son who was rich, or at least did not fall off a roof and die, leaving his old mother with three small children and no money.

A voice called behind her and she went back into the house. The little girls had woken and were hungry. She poured the steaming soup into the two bowls and set them on the lacquered serving table. From the wide-mouthed glass jar at the corner of the counter, she took two pairs of chopsticks and two spoons and set them on the table too. Then she carried the table across the room, walking carefully.

The children sat on their heels and ate the soup while their grandmother shook out the blankets and spread them one on top of the other on the cotton quilt. Then she rolled them together into a long bundle and set the bundle up against the wall. The children asked for rice but their grandmother made her mouth tight and they did not ask again.

When they had finished eating, she stacked everything on the lacquered table and took it back to the kitchen area, where she washed the bowls and spoons and chopsticks over the sink with a little of the water she had warmed. Twitching the electric cord out of the wall, she lifted the heavy pan and set it on the floor, and with her hand turned downward, beckoned to the girls.

They came obediently and splashed water on their hands

and faces, rubbing them dry on a small towel their grandmother handed to them, and when they were done, spread out
across the counter to dry. The girls sat down together on the
floor and pulled on sneakers, then stood with arms held out
for their grandmother to bundle them into padded coats.

She led them outside to the storage shed. Both doors were
shut. Her glance fell on the right-hand door and for a moment
she saw Kun Soo behind it, cursing and dying on the ground.
She had not been once inside that door since then. It seemed
very long ago.

The little girls were pushing at the other door. It opened
grudgingly and one by one they pulled down their padded over-
alls and squatted above the toilet while the old woman knelt in
front of them, saying, "Hurry, hurry," because it was too cold to
be sitting here half exposed on this frozen morning. The children leaned their heads against her chest and strained, teeth
clattering in their heads.

Done, they stood out in the yard hitching up their pants
and pulling at each other's straps and snaps while the old
woman smashed the frozen surface water in the yellow trash
can beside the toilet and scooped water down into the bowl.
The door groaned and stuck half open when she backed away
and she jerked the handle, scraping it across the cement slab
until it was completely shut because she did not want the children frightened by a rat when they came out here alone. The
haunted storage room next door was bad enough.

"Come now, take Baby's hand," she said to Li Na and they
each took one of Tae Hee's hands, leading her between them

from the yard and down the narrow, sharply sloping alleyway.

She told the children, "Walk quickly, the exercise will make you warm," and, "Be careful, don't slip on the ice and fall into the drain."

They asked, "Who are we going to see?" and their grandmother told them Jung Hee's mother, her best friend.

The children brightened then, saying perhaps Jung Hee's mother would offer them some of the candy she made to sell down at the market. The old woman tipped her head from side to side and told them if they wanted candy they must be good and not whine about walking such a distance in the cold. She did not tell them she was going to visit her old friend because Jung Hee's mother was very wise. She did not tell them she was going to ask her friend for some advice.

As she walked, the old woman thought about Mi Sook. Before Kun Soo died, she used to take the baby to work with her in Seoul, strapped against her back, and come home on her days off to tell all the flattering things the students in the coffee shop had said about her baby daughter. But now, with her husband dead, she seemed to have lost interest in her children. At Kun Soo's funeral she had seemed to be a little mad, walking up and down and talking to herself all day and all night too. When everything was done and Eun Hye had gone away, she had sat on the edge of the veranda for a long time with the baby in her arms. Then she brought her inside and handed her to her grandmother. "I will go to the coffee shop now," she said.

Since then she had not been home at all and the baby had

become another mouth to feed, another weight to carry on the back of an old woman.

And yet, perhaps it was the wisest way for her. If, after all, Mi Sook had resolved to leave Kun Soo's children behind her, there was no point in dragging out the separation. The girl was very beautiful and still young. She needed a husband and no doubt would find one easily. Not with children, though. No man would take another's children. The old woman had seen this sort of thing happen before. Mi Sook would meet another man. She would say nothing of her children. He would marry her and then she would either be wise and forget her children or foolish and tell him and he would be angry and beat her and she would be forced to forget them anyway.

The old woman gathered up her phlegm and spat onto the yellowish swirled ice at the bottom of the storm drain. It was a hard decision Mi Sook had to make, and she could not blame the girl. It was the way things had always been.

Once though, such decisions had not been so difficult to make. Once, when there was a wealthy head man in each village, the poor widowed mother could take her child and leave it at the side gate of his compound. This was called the orphan's gate and the head man was obliged to take the child and raise it as his own. It meant that the child was no longer his mother's son, but at least she could watch him grow, and if she were fortunate he would visit her sometimes when her new husband was not home, even take care of her when he became a man and she was old and widowed once again.

These days, though, there were no head men. The old customs were all dead. The Catholics had come into Korea with their orphanages, taking the head man's place, and once a child went into the orphanage there was no telling if his family would set eyes on him again. He would be treated kindly and fed and dressed in decent clothes and taught to read and write if he was old enough, all of which was good. But he could also be adopted by any sort of foreigner and taken to the far ends of the earth.

They rounded a corner and the children screwed their noses up and sniffed the air. "*Appa,*" said the little one, and she was right. It was the same smell Kun Soo used to bring home on his clothes and in his hair when he drove the fish trucks to and from the waterfront, carrying his loads of fish. The old woman sucked in the smell of her dead son through her front teeth and the little girls laughed and imitated her.

She sighed. It had been good work for him. He was away sometimes for days on end, but the money he brought home was good enough. They said he had been drinking when he wrecked that truck, although he swore upon his ancestors it was not so. She shrugged contemplatively. Drunk. Not drunk. It was all the same—he lost the work. And it was drink, no doubt of it, that had caused him to fall off the roof.

The old woman did not know why her son had blamed Mi Sook for it all but she suspected that something had happened in Seoul that day between him and his wife and that he did not wreck the truck from drunkenness, as Mr. Shin had claimed, but because he was in one of his red rages. In that he was like his father, the old woman's husband. He had been a man of rages too, and had beaten her many times. But then he went to fight the North Koreans and they shot him dead. Since then no one had beaten her.

She thought about Kun Soo's first wife, how he had raged at her. Poor woman, she did not deserve the beatings he had given her. She had liked that first wife, a gentle woman who had honored her. When the old woman had turned sixty she had made a good party for her with much bowing and wine and fruit and plates of rice cakes. Even some drummers came, and a man to take her photograph. The photograph turned out too dark to see but still the party was a good one. Yes, that wife had been a worthy woman. But she had been unlucky with her children. Five girls, eh! Such bad luck. Then came that boy with no brain in his head and a body like a goblin.

It was after that strange child was born that her son became a man of rages like his father. His eyes would bulge out in his head and he would scream and smash his fist against the wall and beat his wife. As soon as one bruise on her face was healed, another took its place, and sometimes sooner. At those times the old woman would go outside and smoke and think about the way the North Koreans shot her husband. No matter how much anger a man has inside him, it cannot protect him against a bullet in the head.

She never knew where in his body her husband had been shot, so she did not know if it was in the head or not, but sometimes she would stand outside and smoke and imagine it that way. She would see him in his soldier's uniform, standing on a cliff, screaming and shaking his fist at an enemy he could not see. And then—*ping!*—out of nowhere came the bullet. His head exploded in a spray of blood and his body leaned forward over emptiness and then spun slowly down with his anger spinning out of it, making a red spiral through the air.

Kun Soo also had that red anger in his head after the goblin child was born. He never hit him, and his sisters not so very often, but his wife, poor woman! As though it was her fault to have a son like that, lurching about the streets with his hands flapping off his wrists and the tongue lolling from his head. Eh! No. It was fate that put him in the world, and fate that took him back.

It happened on the day his mother died. He waited for her at the market stall and when she didn't come wandered off into the town in search of her. His grandmother went hunting after him, up one curving lane and down another, rapping at strangers' doors, clanging on their gate bells, peering into storefronts. And then at last, when the sky was drawing down toward the earth, she found him far from home, standing with his toes stuck out into the air beyond the sea wall, watching the gleaming orange tide rise across the mud flats. The tide was still far out, the stones of the sea wall higher than a house, an office building, and it occurred to her that he would jump. She called to him but no response and for a long time stood there silently behind him, waiting to see what he would do. But he did nothing, just stood there rocking side to side, hands limp and hanging down, watching the sea advance.

When the sun was just an afterglow across the sky, the old woman heard the sigh and slap of water high against the sea wall. She called again. Still no response. She scrambled down into the thick mud of the ditch and up the other side, loudly calling Joo Yup's name. She was angry with him now—he was not so stupid that he did not know his own name—and came behind him, reaching out. And then he was in the water, vanishing and gone, with no struggle and his empty smile turned up to her as though in thanks.

The old woman shivered at the memory and half turned, glancing back across her shoulder as though the goblin child might come lurching down the street behind her, grinning and slobbering, hair plastered to his head with water from the Yellow Sea.

The little girls were tired now, the baby dragging at her grandmother's hand. It was far for such a little one to walk but she was too old to carry the child on her back, and her sister was too young. The old woman turned a soft face down toward the tiny child stumbling at her side. She loved these little girls, their brother too, but she was very old and would die before they were grown enough to take care of themselves.

Since Kun Soo died she had been sick. She was not sure what was wrong but one night she dreamed that she was being crushed beneath a rock and though she knew it was a dream she could not wake. She could hear the children's voices calling her but she could not move or open her eyes. Hissing was in her ears and then she dreamed that she was underneath black water, struggling for the surface, panicking.

She burst into wakefulness with both hands clutching at the air and her lungs cracking from the stress of trying to draw breath. For what seemed hours she lay flat on her back while the children cried and pulled at her, and after a while she sat up, and after a while longer, stood. Since then her skin had taken on a strange gray color, her chest felt heavy all the time, and increasingly she could not fill her lungs with breath. Twice she had felt a great weight bearing down on her and buckled under it, losing consciousness. Both times were brief but now she saw her death, like a distant figure on a deserted road, coming inexorably toward her.

They rounded another curve, labored up a slope, and stopped, the old woman with her eyes watering, one hand pressed flat against her chest. They had reached her friend's house now. It was a house much like her own, a low stone structure, but with clay tiling for the roof instead of asphalt. The two little girls squatted down against the rough stone fence and the old woman squatted beside them, reaching into her pocket for her cigarette. Two draws and she pinched it out again. She knew what she must do but she needed someone she could trust to tell her what it was.

She spoke softly to the children and they went together to her friend's front door.

Inside the house, the old woman found her friend was not alone. A cousin was there with her, pushing a needle up and down in the toe of a white sock, but when she understood that the old woman wanted to speak of something serious she gathered up her mending and took the children to her house across the street. For that whole day the old woman and her friend knelt together on the warm surface of the ondol floor, going through all the arguments the old woman had already been through time and time again, looking at each one this way and that, leaving no aspect unconsidered.

As the day wore on, a strange fearfulness climbed inside the old woman's body, as though speaking of such things brought them to life while only holding them inside her head did not. Five times during that long day she lost her breath and had to lean her back against the wall and push her legs out straight, holding down a rising feeling in her chest, as though she would drown in this conspiracy they made.

The first time it happened, her friend was calm and brought her ginseng tea steaming in a small white cup. The old woman took it gratefully, and holding it in both hands, brought the cup slowly to her mouth. At first the taste was bitter on her tongue but as she sipped its fragrance filled her head with flowers.

At the second attack, her friend said, "Why don't you go back home and think some more on this and come again next week?"

But the old woman was adamant, saying, "No, it is today this thing must be resolved."

"This decision is too hard for us to make," her friend said at the third attack. "We should go and see the geomancer."

The old woman made her face stiff. "No geomancer can decide this thing. It is a decision to be made by grandmothers alone."

Her old friend became quiet then, talking to herself inside her head, and after a while the reasoning went on between them once again.

At the fourth attack, her friend said nothing, just brought more tea and rubbed the old woman's legs and waited till it passed, and by the time the sun came down behind the house, making the fibers of the window paper glow like burning spiderwebs, the fifth attack had come and gone and the old woman lay with her neck against a bolster, all strength drained out of her.

Presently the light clicked on and her friend said softly, "See, here is my daughter Jung Hee home from work."

The old woman rose, tucked the loose strands of hair back into her bun, smoothed her crumpled blouse, and retied the knot that held it at the front. She accepted Jung Hee's bow and knelt once more, this time with Jung Hee too, and between them they completed their conspiracy.

When it was all done, she felt a little of her strength return. She went outside and crossed the street to where her old friend's cousin lived. The little girls had stayed with her all day, and the old woman blessed her for it, but her friend's cousin praised the children because they had played quietly all day and made no trouble for her. Now they saw their grandmother in the door and came running with their arms out, crying, "*Halmoni! Halmoni!*" but the old woman made them stand with her and say their thanks and make their bows before she took them back across the street. There her old friend looked at them with a sad face, giving them sesame-seed candy to take home, and the children, seeing her distress, pulled down their mouths as if to cry. "Come now," said their grandmother. "No need for that." And she took the baby's hand.

When they reached home, Dae Young was standing by the fence looking for them up and down the road. He ran to meet them, calling out complaints, but when he saw the way his grandmother bowed her shoulders down and the way her feet shuffled close against the ground, he took his little sisters' hands and led them home. Inside, he proudly showed them what he had found for them to eat today—a long ropy hank of seaweed in a plastic pack, three mung bean cakes, a long bright yellow pickled radish—but when his grandmother rolled out the bedding and lay down without so much as heating water, he seemed to understand that something large was happening to his family. He divided up the food, putting with it some of the sesame-seed candy his sisters had brought home, and took a bowl to his grandmother where she lay flat down with her eyes closed. But she refused it, so he set it carefully aside, and kneeling with his sisters on the now cold *ondol* floor, he ate, watching his grandmother with troubled eyes.

Next morning he rose early once again but did not leave the house to go foraging for food or coal, staying instead beside her, speaking sharply to his sisters when they made a noise or complained about the cold. The old woman slept all day and all night too, but the next morning she rose with strength and soon the little girls found themselves walking through the streets with *Halmoni* again, this time with their brother and also Aunt Jung Hee. It seemed colder still than yesterday because the wind was up, but as they went, no matter which way they turned along the slanting streets, the early-morning sun went on ahead of them, balanced in a circle of white fire, making the icicles hanging from the eaves look like the sparkling earrings of a queen. The old woman took this as a sign that what she planned to do was right.

Now it had been done, and the old woman plodded slowly back along the frozen streets of Inch'on with her head turned down. This morning, when she had led her three young grandchildren along these streets, a harsh wind had leaped out at her from every corner, rushing into her throat as though to snatch the sorrow out of it, wrenching tears out of her eyes.

Now the sky was still, ghost-gray and luminous, its belly sagging almost to the upturned corners of the gray tiled roofs.

The old woman's arms were heavy, her legs swollen from the ankle to the knee as though encased in stone, and although it was still early in the afternoon, she wanted to stretch her body out and close her eyes and let her hands rest at her sides. But she could smell snow coming and knew she must hurry to get home before it started to fall. She wished she had not worn her dead son's padded boots. They were warm, but she had had to wind her feet with rags to keep them on and they were very cumbersome. They seemed now to grow heavier with every step, as though to drag her back and make her undo this thing she had done today.

Beside her, Jung Hee walked silently, as though contemplating her part in what the two of them had done. She was a plain woman, with a stammer and a twisted upper lip. Because of it no man had come to ask for her, and neither matchmaker nor fortune-teller had had success in making an arrangement. Now, at almost thirty-five, she had watched two younger sisters marry and bear children and surely knew that she would never have a son, or any children of her own. And yet today she had conspired to give away the children of another. She seemed to walk inside her head, wrestling with her thoughts.

The old woman wanted to ask her what she thought—was it right, after all, this thing they had done today? But what did Jung Hee know except her own frustration? All her life she had been nothing but a housemaid in another's house. When the two old women first told her of their plan, she had resisted.

"How can I come with you and say I am the mother of another woman's children?" she had cried, and in the end her mother had commanded her.

The old woman pitied her, and pitied Mi Sook too. It would be a hard thing for her to find that her children had been spirited away like this, but what else was a grandmother to do with three young children and her body growing old? With no food to feed them, no money to buy coal or pay for electricity, no new coats to keep their arms from sticking down out of their sleeves like naked chicken legs this bitterest of winters, what else was she to do?

Her first thought had been of Kun Soo's daughter, Eun Hye, who had been so determined to have the children for herself. But Eun Hye had left no address and the old woman knew only that she lived in Pusan. Before she could discover her, she might be already dead. Anyway, if she had sent the children to Eun Hye, Mi Sook would certainly discover them and then what trouble there would be. No, this way was best. These children had seen trouble enough in their short lives and had no need of more. They would miss their family for a while, but they would not freeze to death, or starve, or turn to thieving in the streets, their faces growing sharp, eyes sideways in their heads, and in the end they would be better off. This way, too, Mi Sook would find it easy to get another husband. He would give her his own sons and she would forget Dae Young, and the little girls as well. This way a grandmother could go to join her ancestors in peace.

• • •

At the Social Welfare office, the people had been kind. The woman at the desk pushed out her round smooth face and smiled with teeth that seemed too many for her mouth. On her bright red jacket was a notice saying that her name was Mrs. Choi.

"How many, Grandmother?" said Mrs. Choi. "What ages?" Then she punched a button on her telephone, and without picking it up, said in an excited voice, "Miss Lee, I think you ought to come in here."

The woman called Miss Lee came in with papers in her hand. She was young and still unmarried, one of the new kind of women, with a smart haircut and her slacks creased in a sharp line down each leg. She made a bow, first to the old woman, then to Jung Hee. "Only three?" she said to Mrs. Choi.

"But the oldest is a boy, and very handsome."

"Yes, that is good. These might be satisfactory." Miss Lee crouched down before the children and asked their names.

The little girls were shy but their brother stood with one hand firmly on each sister's shoulder and spoke their names for them. "Tae Hee," he said, "is three years old. Li Na is five. And I am almost seven now. I am Dae Young. I am responsible."

Miss Lee laughed. "You are a good boy, Dae Young. Would you and your little sisters like toys to play with while you wait?"

Mrs. Choi came out from behind the desk with a box of toys. Dae Young refused to look, but Tae Hee took a yellow rubber duck. Li Na stood shyly with her toes turned in, hands in a twist behind her back, so Mrs. Choi set the box down on a long bench against the wall and, sitting down beside it, tapped her finger on the side. "Hm," she said, and then, "Aha!" She took out a large book with a paper cover and turned the pages slowly, showing Li Na bold, black-outlined pictures of dancing girls and children bowling hoops and flying kites. Then she took out a small box of crayons and began to give one of the dancing girls a bright pink dress. Li Na craned to see. "Here, you try," said Mrs. Choi, and she pushed the box aside and helped Li Na up onto the bench and showed her how to color in between the lines. Tae Hee climbed up next to them and watched, squeaking her rubber duck. Dae Young sat down too, with his head up and his hands set on his knees, looking straight ahead.

Miss Lee tapped her pen against the papers in her hand, looking at the children sitting on the bench. "Too thin," she said, "but healthy otherwise?"

The old woman said there was a sore spot on the older girl's head.

Miss Lee pursed her mouth and moved Li Na's hair aside with the tip of her pen. "A fungus of some kind, I think."

Mrs. Choi stopped coloring and looked too. "Fungus or poor eating."

The old woman started to be ashamed but Miss Lee took her hand and said, "Come over here and sit down at this table, Grandmother. It is not your fault about the sore spot on her head. You have done the best you can but it was right to bring them in. These children will have a good life, I promise you. You must not grieve for them." Then she asked her many questions, and Jung Hee too. The old woman was afraid that

Jung Hee would not give the right answers and Miss Lee would realize she was not the children's mother after all. But no, she had known these children almost all their lives and answered easily.

Miss Lee listened to the answers and filled out the papers with her head nodding and her face smiling as though something good was happening here. "Perhaps your children would like to go to America?" she said to Jung Hee.

Jung Hee made a strange noise like pebbles clattering in her throat, but the old woman made a hushing face, turning her head cautiously across her shoulder.

Miss Lee dropped her voice then, whispering about America.

The old woman thought about all this, trudging along, and she thought about America. She thought of how Jung Hee had given that strange groan, and it seemed to her that it held a kind of longing. Perhaps Jung Hee had a secret dream of going there. Perhaps she thought she could find a husband in America. Well, maybe so. The old woman had heard that Americans were different from Korean men, that in America wives did what they wanted and did not ask permission from their husbands. She had heard that an American who took a wife with children would take the children too. Such customs! It was hard to think of such a thing.

She looked sidelong at Jung Hee. In the cold air her twisted lip glowed like a shriveled purple plum. Perhaps in America she could find a man who did not care about it, or about her plain face either. He would give her sons and in return she would help him in his business. But now the old woman remembered another thing she had heard about America, how in the cities black men came in masks and shot Korean people in their stores and businesses. And yet, in spite of this, a man even of the lowest caste could gain wealth and have position in his town. A strange place, this America.

But what of all this anyway? What chance was there for someone like Jung Hee to go to such a place? It was an old woman's foolishness to think of such a thing.

Miss Lee had said, though, that her grandchildren might go. She said the women in America were very modern. They worked and grew rich and forgot to marry and have children. When they were too old to bear they searched for children to adopt, but there were not enough. Because of this, many children from the Inch'on orphanage were taken there.

The old woman thought about how her grandchildren might live in America. They would have a new father who would drive his own car every day and not fall off a roof and die, and a mother with her own car too, who did not run away and sleep at night in the back room of a coffee shop, neglecting to bring home money to put rice into her children's bowls. They would have a new grandmother too. She would be like the old women from America that she had seen in Inch'on, tourists come with their old husbands and old women friends to eat at the expensive seafood restaurants along the waterfront. She would wear bright clothes and curl her hair and look at her new grandchildren out of pale round eyes and frighten them. But she would love them, surely, and soon they would grow used to her. She would cook for them and they would eat everything and their bellies would grow round. Each day she would send them off to school with books, and each night help them climb up onto high beds shared with no one else. She would speak to them in English and after a while they would forget their mother tongue. They would forget their family. They would not come back to Inch'on.

The old woman shivered. There would be no one now, at the celebration of the harvest moon, to come and tend her grave. But she could not consider this. She had considered it already, and set it aside, while she was making her decision.

Beside her, Jung Hee was crying quietly into her hand. The old woman let her cry. It was good for her to do. As for herself, there could be no crying yet. She must give all her attention to making her feet go down the road. When she got home and lay down on her quilt, she would consider everything. Maybe then it would be time to cry.

Soon they reached the place where they must go in different ways. The old woman turned, holding out her hands, and Jung Hee took them, tilting down her head. Then she turned away and the old woman stood watching her until she disappeared around a corner of the road.

All morning the old woman had been firm and calm, and fear had not risen up to drown her as it had five times the day she talked with Jung Hee's mother. But now, standing here alone in the business section of the town, with strangers going in and out of doors, and motorbikes and bicycles and taxis making turmoil, she saw a businessman in a rich dark leather coat come down the street. He was tall and wide across the shoulders, with the strawlike hair of an American. As he passed, he looked down at her with his pale eyes as though she was not there, pushed through a door and vanished. The drowning started again, and the old woman leaned against the plate-glass window of the building at her back and breathed inside the top part of her chest. But darkness came behind her eyes and she felt herself slide down.

She knew she was sitting on the public street with her feet stuck out in front like any beggar woman but there was nothing she could do. She seemed to be inside the Social Welfare office once again, signing the forms to put her grandchildren into the orphanage. And now Jung Hee signed them too, stammering out her story—quietly, so the children would not hear—saying yes, she was their mother, and yes, her husband had fallen off a roof and died, and yes, Grandmother was old and very sick and must be tended to, and no, there was no money if she did not go to work, and no, there was no one else to take care of the children.

The old woman listened to all this with praise, and some surprise, because Jung Hee was making up embellishments to the story they had practiced between them, making the situation even more desperate. She was doing her best to help her mother's oldest friend.

The children sat on the wooden bench against the wall, not understanding what was happening to them. Their grandmother had told them nothing. It would have been too hard.

When all the papers had been signed, she simply turned away and left them there as though to go along the passage for a moment and come back. The last she saw of them, Tae Hee, her legs too short to reach the floor, was squeezing the yellow plastic duck against her ear, listening to it squeak. Li Na was taking out one crayon at a time and swirling color on the pages of her book, holding it up to Mrs. Choi with a shy delighted face. Dae Young, though, sat stiff and straight, refusing toys, watching his grandmother go out the door with dark, unfathomable eyes. Now it seemed to her that he had known what she was doing all along, and his face accused her. The darkness came up over her again.

When she came back to herself, she could not tell if she had been there propped against the wall for long or not. The street was strangely dim and mute and she thought she had lost both sight and hearing. Then she saw that it was snowing. Large flat flakes slid sideways through the sky, muffling sound and making it seem as though she was looking at the street through coarse white lace.

She looked down at her body. Snow had grown up around her legs and crept into the tops of her son's boots. From this she knew that she had been there a long time. She must be very cold, she told herself, but she felt neither cold nor warm, and very light, as though she were a ghost. No one had stopped to help her and no policeman asked her to move on, so perhaps it might be true. She sat there listening for her breath and could not hear it, and then came to her feet, moving easily. A battered blue taxi jerked to a stop beside the curb and the driver looked at her inquiringly but she had no money for him and motioned him away. He shrugged his shoulders and drove off, his wheels spinning in the snow.

She could not tell if it took many hours or only a few minutes to make her way back home, but the drowning feeling in her chest was gone, and her arms and legs were not heavy anymore. At first her son's boots held her back but she slipped out of them and came across the soft snow like a young girl dancing.

THE WORLD GLOWED WHITE and Mi Sook came through Inch'on's night streets easily. Beneath her feet the snow made squeaking sounds, and up above the sky seemed very high and black, ringing with the eerie clarity that follows snow. The moon looked down out of a narrowed eye.

In Mi Sook's purse she carried fifty thousand *won* to give the children's grandmother. She was happy about this and when the problem of where to get more when it was spent rose in her mind, she pushed it aside, thinking about how her mother-in-law would go to market first thing in the morning, how the two of them would cook all day, chopping and slicing, steaming fish, frying octopus, preparing soybean soup and fluffy rice and many side dishes of greens and cuttlefish and anchovies and pickled turnip—oh, they would have everything!—and how by the end of the day the children's stomachs would bulge out and she would take the picture book and sit with them and tell them the story of the turtle and the rabbit.

When she thought about the picture book, Hyun Joon rose in her mind. She shook her head and hurried up her steps. She must put that foolishness aside. There was no gain in sorrowing for what she could not have.

After Kun Soo's funeral she had gone back to the coffee shop with her mind in a tumultuous condition, convinced she had indeed, as Kun Soo had accused her, caused his death. Had she not, walking the streets at night or lying on her quilt, plotted ways for him to die? Had she not dreamed that he was in his coffin?

When first she saw him lying wrapped in his white shroud, his hands set on his breast and incense at his head and feet, she had shuddered deep inside. When Mrs. Park's sons lifted him into his coffin and she stood beside it looking down, she thought that she would faint because the sight was just the same as she had dreamed.

At that moment all the tumult of the funeral had died away. Her head seemed to expand and she was inside it looking out at Kun Soo's spirit, like a cloud standing in the corner of the room. At his side was a woman she knew was his first wife, at his side a twisted boy, and at his back were all his ancestors. They said nothing, not even to each other, just stood silently and looked at her, and she could feel them walking up and down inside her mind. They knew what she had thought, all the violent methods she had devised for Kun Soo's death. She had not imagined he would fall off a roof, but once she had arranged a spectacular crash for his fish truck, making it skip and hop and overturn and, skidding on its roof, smash into the pylon of a bridge in the way she had seen it happen on a television show. She hoped no one would ever tell her exactly what had happened with the truck for fear that it would be the same.

But she had never thrown him off a roof. That was not her fault. No, it was not her fault. And yet she knew it was. Kun Soo knew it too, his first wife as well. So did that awful son, and all his crowd of ancestors. They knew what she had done. She turned dizzy and began to sweat.

That night she did not sleep. She had always feared the shade of Kun Soo's first wife but now that she had seen her with the other shades she did not even dare to lie down on the bedding, instead pacing up and down the narrow veranda. "What am I to do?" she cried all through the night. "Oh, what am I to do?"

As the night wore on, a thought occurred to her. If by wishing she had brought about Kun Soo's death, then, also by wishing, had she not brought about the other half of her desire? She was free to marry Hyun Joon now.

When that thought first came to her she stopped, glancing back across her shoulder, and set it carefully aside. Not until all the business of the funeral was done, all Eun Hye's meddling with the children settled once and for all, and she was safely on the bus for Seoul did she dare to bring it out again. She had left the baby with her grandmother because she knew that this thought and its execution were going to take up all her concentration. Also, she would need to look her prettiest and a baby hanging from her back would make her look too old.

The bus was crowded and there was no seat for her. All the way to Seoul she clung to an upright pole with other people's bodies jammed against her. Usually she hated such a ride—the smell of sweat, of hair grease and cheap perfume, of passed wind, the feeling of entrapment—but today she barely noticed, too preoccupied with looking at this thought from every angle, turning it about and taking everything she could into account.

Yes, it was a good thought. And the further the bus carried her from Inch'on, the less she feared Kun Soo and his ancestors.

Back at the coffee shop, she said nothing of Kun Soo's death except to *Madame*, who lifted her shoulders in a sympathetic way and said, "Well, child, you must settle on a business for yourself. It is better than depending on a man." Mi Sook was not ready to listen to this talk and so she avoided *Madame*, making her own plans in her head.

But Hyun Joon did not appear as usual. She watched for him from first thing in the morning until she closed the shop at night but day came after day and still he did not appear. Well, she told herself, he is ashamed that he provoked my husband. When he has got over it he will come back. But Hyun Joon did not come.

Mi Sook applied her mind to this problem. Hyun Joon was an honorable man and his shame was very high because he had provoked Kun Soo, but if he knew of Kun Soo's death, his desire for her would overcome his shame. She must get word to him that she was free.

Well then, she would go weeping to the helper and tell her what had happened. Then she would go out for a walk—to give the girl an opportunity to run to all the tables telling every student. It would not be long before Hyun Joon heard and when he understood she was free of Kun Soo he would surely come.

But what if the helper did not tell? Or if she did, what if the news did not reach Hyun Joon? And if she did tell, and if Hyun Joon got the news, what if he did not come after all? What if he blamed himself for Kun Soo's death—because it was, in a sense, his fault for flirting with her—and did not come out of fear she would be angry with him? Or fear of her revenge? No, gossip would not bring him to her. Surely, though, he would soon come of his own accord. Yes, any day now he would come.

But still he did not come. Her day off for that month came and went and she did not dare go back to Inch'on in case that was the day he came. Her next day off she went walking in the frozen park, not strolling but rushing up and down in a frenzy looking for him. The park was almost empty but once she thought she saw him and broke into a run, but when she got closer it was not him at all, just some strange man. She knew she should go back to Inch'on but could not think about it. By now she had fully persuaded herself that Hyun Joon was the sort of modern man who would ignore old customs. Having married her, he would take her children as his own. Thus it was imperative she bring him to her, for her children's sakes.

When she could bear to wait no longer she said casually to

a table full of students, "Where is Hyun Joon? He has not been here for a while. Has he fallen ill?"

One of the students had been reading aloud from a piece of paper while the others tossed their hands about and interrupted with their own opinions. Now the student stopped reading, although he still held the paper up in front of him. They all turned and looked at her together.

"Oh, Hyun Joon," said the one with the paper. "He is too busy these days to come. He must do extra study to get ready."

"What is he getting ready for?"

"To go away to Purdue, of course. Soon he will take up his scholarship."

"Of course. How silly of me to forget. When will he leave?"

"I don't know. Soon. A day or two maybe."

"Then you must tell him to come and say good-bye to me," Mi Sook said. "I will miss him in the coffee shop." She kept her voice light and her manner joking, but inside she was in a panic. She had wasted all this time waiting for Hyun Joon while every day brought his departure closer.

The student smiled a teasing smile. "I will tell him you miss him, little sister." And he gave the paper a shake to straighten it and went on reading.

Mi Sook went out into the lane and stood with her fists clenched against the wall. "Let him come," she prayed. "Oh, let him come."

• • •

He came that night. Mi Sook was taken by surprise. She had not expected it to be so soon. When she opened the back door and the light behind her fell on him, she set her hand before her teeth and blushed. "Why hello, Hyun Joon."

Hyun Joon was carrying a white box tied up with a piece of yellow ribbon. He seemed awkward, passing it from one hand to the other as though he did not know what to do with it. "Well, Mi Sook, I am afraid it is not hello but good-bye I have come to say."

"What can you mean?"

"Tomorrow I will leave to take up my scholarship at Purdue University."

She motioned him to come inside. He took a half step back, glancing up and down the lane.

Mi Sook felt a small sound jump out of her throat, like the squeak of a baby bird. She spoke quickly, covering it up. "But you will come sometimes and drink coffee still. Surely it is not so far?"

Hyun Joon laughed. "Purdue is in America, in a place called Indiana."

"America? How can this be?"

"Why little Mi Sook, did you think Purdue was in Korea?"

Mi Sook felt her face flame red and she wanted to run away and hide. Instead she made herself look brave and laughed also. "How silly of me. What a silly thing I am. When will you come back? Will it be more than a month?"

"Mi Sook, do you know what a scholarship is?"

She looked at him.

"It is like a prize. It means you can go to a university and study there for no charge."

"For how long? A month?"

"More than a month, more than a year. I will be away for three years, maybe four if things go well. It depends on my hard work and my good luck."

"Four years? But then you will come back?"

"Oh yes. I am to take a position at Hyundai Engineering."

"That is a good job, yes?"

"A good job, yes."

"Enough for you to marry, yes?"

"Quite enough. I hope to marry soon after I return."

"You have your eye on someone, then?"

He smiled. "Yes, for a long time now."

"And do you think she will have you?"

"I know she will."

Mi Sook's heart, which had slunk down below her knees, began to climb again. It was turning out quite easy after all. Hyun Joon spoke openly, following without hesitation the path she led him down. Just a little further and he would be folding her in his arms and kissing her, asking her to wait for him until he came back home.

But she did not want to wait for that long time. No, she would lead him carefully until he asked instead for her to meet him in America, where they would be married and she would keep his house for him while he studied at the university. Her children would come too, and go to school, and every Sunday Hyun Joon would set aside his scholarship and take his family for an outing, to a park maybe, if they had parks in the cities of America, or maybe to this place Niagara Falls that *Madame* wanted to see. She would send a postcard back to her.

"Ah, Hyun Joon," she breathed, "you will be a good husband to this lucky girl."

He looked serious. "I hope so. It is all arranged."

"Arranged?"

"My wedding, it is all arranged. It has been arranged since I was very young, almost since I was born. My father and my fiancée's father went to school together. They are our neighbors now. I have grown up with my fiancée like a little sister and it is her father who has promised me the job at Hyundai Engineering. He is very high up in that company."

When Hyun Joon said "little sister," Mi Sook felt a shaft enter her heart. She had always thought of that expression as his special name for her. "Well then," she said brightly, "you are well provided for."

There was silence. Then, "My husband died."

"What did you say?"

"My husband, Kun Soo, died."

She had not meant to say it but now it was said she couldn't stop. Starting with the argument in the coffee shop, she told about the wreck of the fish truck, the fall from the roof, the stubborn dying in the storage shed, the accusations that it was her fault.

As she spoke, a subtle change came over Hyun Joon, a sort of tension, as though one by one each muscle in his body tightened, and Mi Sook understood that he had known about the fantasy she entertained for him. Humiliation clutched the corners of her mouth, drawing it up into a foolish smile. Her voice went faster, faster, higher, higher, and when she had told everything she leaned against the door frame, shaking, hardly able to support herself.

"I had not heard . . ." Hyun Joon began. Once more he glanced up and down the lane and for a moment Mi Sook thought he was going to run away.

But no, he made himself straight. "I had not heard," he said, "because I have been studying day and night to make my English good enough. But tonight I was out shopping for gifts to leave with my family and my fiancée when I happened to run into a few of the other students. They said you were asking after me so I came to say good-bye and now to offer you my sympathy as well."

Mi Sook pushed herself off the door frame and stood staring at him, a nub of anger growing in her heart.

"Because I am fond of you," Hyun Joon went on, "and your baby daughter also, I feel as though you are my little sister and I am sorry for your husband dying. I feel that in a way it is my fault. If I had not been in high spirits here that day then perhaps he would not have been so angry that he wrecked the truck."

"But it was not your fault he fell down from the roof."

"No, but still I feel sad for you about it." He seemed suddenly to notice the yellow-ribboned parcel, which, in his agitation, he had been passing once more hand to hand. "Here, I want you to have this." He thrust it at her. "Good luck, little sister Mi Sook. Good luck to you."

Then he was gone and Mi Sook was left with nothing but the parcel and the empty shop.

When the first rays of early morning sun fell through the window of the coffee shop they fell on Mi Sook sitting upright at the table Hyun Joon had always used, the parcel set before her. All night she had sat there without moving and it seemed to her that many people were inside her head, this one weeping in a loud, insistent voice, this one regretting and regretting, this one reproaching her for foolishness, this one saying angrily, "And why is Hyun Joon going to America when all this time he has sat right here making arguments against that place?" Another, sneering, said, "Look at you now. After all your plotting and your planning you have lost a husband whose only fault was to be too much in love with you and have gained nothing but a gift intended for another woman." Because it was obvious that Hyun Joon had not bought this gift for Mi Sook but for his fiancée.

Underneath these voices was another sound, a small child crying for its mother, and her own voice asking, "How will you feed them now? How will you feed them now?"

When the sun was fully up Mi Sook rose and, walking through the shop, pushed aside the swinging doors behind the counter and went into the bathroom. She washed her face and dried it with a towel. Then she went back to the table and in a single movement tore the yellow ribbon off the gift and lifted up the lid. Tissue paper was inside. Looking at it, she felt her fingers grow numb and awkward and so heavy that she had to rest them on the table and wait for feeling to return before, with delicate, slow movements, the way a soldier might defuse a bomb, she turned the tissue paper down.

It was the lucky gourd she and Hyun Joon had admired in the window of the jeweler's shop. *Wealth*, it said, and *Many Sons*. She lifted it and turned it in her hand, watching the red stones sparkle in the early-morning light.

A little before noon Mi Sook was standing in the slushy snow outside the jewelry store. In the window, another gourd turned on the little velvet-covered platform. It was similar to hers although not the same. *Long Life*, it said, and *Health*. It was surely worth a large amount of money. She pushed open the door.

The shopkeeper looked at her suspiciously when she asked if he would buy the gourd from her. "Where did you get this gourd?"

"The student, Hyun Joon, gave it to me as a gift."

"Ah yes, I remember him. He bought it only yesterday. A gift, you say? You waste no time in making money on this gift."

For a moment Mi Sook was afraid he would call the police and she would lose her gourd. But no, when he had examined her closely the shopkeeper curled his lip and laughed low in his throat.

Mi Sook felt the blood rush up her neck because she knew

what he was thinking, but she was determined to get money for the gourd. "How much will you give for it?"

The shopkeeper considered, looking first at her, then at the gourd. "Fifteen thousand *won.*"

Mi Sook had no idea what Hyun Joon had paid for the gourd but she knew the ways of shopkeepers. "No, it is not enough. Only yesterday it was bought right here in this very shop. It is worth at least . . ." She hesitated, fearing to name a price, but at last she countered with a price ten times what he had offered her.

The shopkeeper looked hard at her, a half smile on his face, then threw his hands in the air and turned away. "When you want to do business you may come back," he said and rattled through the screen of beads hanging on the door of his back room.

Mi Sook waited stubbornly. Even though the coffee shop might fill with customers and the helper be overrun with their demands, she was determined to stand right here until the shopkeeper gave her a good price.

He came back. "What, you are still here?" He set about arranging gold chains on a tray.

Mi Sook stood with the gourd in her hand. She knew if she made the next offer she would be the one to lose. She set it on the counter, making sure to hold it with her hand.

The shopkeeper slid his eyes across. "Well, because you are becoming a nuisance in my shop . . ." and he named a slightly higher price.

Mi Sook said nothing. She simply stood in his way when

he moved about the shop, holding the gourd in her hand.

The shopkeeper became agitated and began to bargain with her silence, edging his offer up five and ten *won* at a time, turning away from her with each small rise. But Mi Sook moved with him, bringing her body and the gleaming gourd up close in front of him, so that each time he turned away he must turn away again, like an animal trapped in a cage that is too small. And every time he turned, he edged the price up a little in a rising voice.

"Fifty thousand *won*," he said now, and turned so that his belly came up against the counter and Mi Sook could not get in front of him. Instead, she moved so close behind him she could feel the heat rise off his solid back.

Just then the plastic door beads rattled and a woman came from the back room. She had a heavy body and her jaw set in a grim expression. "What is this?" she said, and the shopkeeper slid sideways along the counter, furtively, as though she had caught him in some sort of misbehavior.

He looked quickly at the woman, then swung on Mi Sook with an angry movement. "Fifty thousand *won*. My last offer. You will make a poor man go bankrupt with your demands. Do I not have to pay my rent and feed my children, and look, here is my poor wife who must go on bare feet in the public street if I do not make a good business. Fifty thousand. I will give no more."

He sighed loudly in her face and for the first time Mi Sook flinched away, not from him but from the inflammatory smell of liquor on his breath. It was a smell she did not recognize, smooth and biting all at once, and for a moment she saw him out to dinner with his friends, tossing back first one glass, then another and another of something golden and expensive. "Seventy-five," she said and from the corner of her eye saw the man's wife set her feet apart and fold her arms across her chest.

Fifty thousand *won* was not so very much but it was a nice enough amount of money for a poor girl like Mi Sook, more than she could make down at the coffee shop for two months' work. She knew that if she sold the gourd on the street she would do poorly and maybe have it stolen into the bargain. And also this man was very fearful of his wife. With her here, she knew he would not go one *won* higher.

"I will do it," she said.

As she went out the door and turned across the window of the shop with her fifty thousand *won* tucked in the pocket of her padded coat, she stopped to look once more at the new gourd turning there. It was without doubt a handsome gourd. She sighed. If she had been lucky and made Hyun Joon marry her, she could have kept the other one.

A woman came and stood beside her, looking into the window. She carried a large shopping bag and was nicely dressed in high-heeled leather boots and a red wool coat with a wide black collar of some short-haired fur. Mi Sook knew it was not mink because her friendship with *Madame* had given her a discerning eye. "It is a nice gourd," she said, although she would not have spoken if the collar had been mink.

The woman glanced sideways. "Yes. I am looking for a gift for my new granddaughter. I think it might do."

"What do you think it might cost?"

The woman made a clicking with her tongue. "Maybe one hundred thousand *won*. Maybe two. But then, depending on what those red stones turn out to be, it could be more."

Mi Sook was not too disappointed. She knew she could not expect to get the full price of the gourd and after all, fifty thousand *won* was fifty thousand more than she had yesterday. Later that night, wrapped in her warmest clothes and with the fifty thousand *won* now tucked inside her blouse, she ran, crunching through the snow, to catch the last bus to Inch'on.

When she reached the house she was surprised to find it dark. The children's grandmother would never take them out, or go out herself, in freezing weather such as this. Apprehension touched her and she stepped quickly up the low step of the veranda and set her hand against the door. There she hesitated, remembering the ancestors, but at last she pushed it open.

"Halmoni?" she whispered, eyes wide in her head, but there was no reply. The house was still and dark and cold as death, the moonlight clinging to the window as though afraid to penetrate the room. Still in her shoes, she raised one arm in the air and edged out across the floor, and found the string of the electric light, and pulled. The light came on, swinging slowly on its cord. No one was there.

But of course no one was there. Who could survive this frozen house at night? She went to the coal box in the corner, and looking down at the few crushed pieces on the bottom, felt a deep heaviness settle on her heart. She had been cruel and selfish to stay away in Seoul so long, lost in the folly of a dizzy girl. She had thought only of herself, her mad obsession with Hyun Joon, and had given no consideration to the hunger of her children, leaving them with an old woman and no way to warm themselves.

She turned to the row of hooks along the wall beside the door and saw that her children's coats were gone, their shoes not in a row against the wall. Kun Soo's padded boots were missing also. So. Their grandmother had worn the boots and taken the children somewhere where they would not freeze to death.

Turning back into the room, she looked for some clue to what had happened there. Above the sink, the shelves that once held drying gourds were gone, and almost all the gourds gone too, the remaining ones stacked in the old woman's basket on one end of the counter. On the other end, a small white bowl was set. She went across and looked down into it. Arranged neatly on a clump of shriveled seaweed were a black bean cake, a yellow slice of pickled radish, a piece of sesame-seed candy, all frozen. She frowned down at the bowl, puzzling over this strange meal. Was it some kind of offering? Had the children's grandmother done this to appease the spirits before she took them off into the night?

But to make an offering would have taken time and they must have left in haste because the bedding had been left out in a crumpled heap. If there had been time, her mother-in-law would certainly have rolled it and set it up against the wall. It was her custom so to do. And look, the old woman had rushed off without her coat. It lay threadbare on the floor beside the bedding. What happened here? Mi Sook asked herself. Had the children's grandmother gone demented off into the night, wearing nothing warm except her dead son's boots? A cold hand took her by the heart, the sudden knowledge that the bedding had not been left unrolled from carelessness or haste.

Glancing once around the room, she slipped out of her shoes, stepped up onto the *ondol* floor, and setting one cautious foot before the other, advanced on the tumbled heap and with a trembling hand turned the top blanket down.

The old woman's eyes were open and for a moment Mi Sook thought she was still alive, but then she realized there were pools of ice across her eyes, as though she had been crying and the tears had gathered in her eye sockets and frozen there. Light glittered in the ice like life.

Once more she looked around the room, examining the shadows in the corners fearfully, but there was nothing. No ancestors, no old woman's vengeful spirit waiting to leap out and punish her for her neglectfulness. She knelt, and gently lifting the edge of the blanket, took the old woman's hand in hers. It was frozen solid, like a bunch of winter twigs, but Mi Sook imagined she felt a kindliness in it.

She had never loved her husband's mother. Even though she knew it was none of the old woman's fault but Kun Soo's, she had held a grudge against her about his first wife because she was the one who told her. She had sneered inside her head at the way the old woman bowed low to her son, despised her for clinging to the old traditions, for the way she spent hours crouched on the floor scratching at her gourds. Sometimes in the night, when Kun Soo was not home and she had woken up in terror of his first wife's ghost, she would roll roughly up against her mother-in-law, angry because this old woman was making her as superstitious as she was herself.

Now, thinking of how well her mother-in-law had fulfilled her duty to her grandchildren, loving them and making them soup and rice and pickling cabbage for the winter months, making sure the fire beneath the *ondol* floor was banked each night before they went to bed, and how she had gone cold and hungry with them on account of her, and now had died, frozen solid in this dark and empty house, she felt regret, even a sort of love. Her mother-in-law was, after all, very old. How could she change her ways?

All night she knelt there, rocking back and forth and mourning for this kind old woman, and for her children vanished in the night. For the first time in her life she felt alone.

Toward morning, when the cold had gone inside her bones and hollowed out the inside of her head, she had a vision. The old woman stood before her, shoulders stooped, a basket on her arm. Her face was soft. "Do not be afraid," she said. "Your children all are safe." She held the basket out and Mi Sook saw that it was full of gourds.

At that moment a mournful booming echoed through the house and Mi Sook leaped in panic to her feet. Stumbling hastily into her shoes, she started to flee, but as she sprang from the veranda to the ground, she stopped, and creeping cautiously inside again, snatched up the basket of dried gourds, then fled again, running for her life down the slippery street as though the spirits of Kun Soo and all his ancestors were swarming at her back, skidding on the ice, saving herself with a hand flung out against a fence.

The bronze voice of the temple bell declared another day.

DAE YOUNG STOOD WITH HIS LEGS SET in the playground of the orphanage, shaking like a heatwave in the cold late afternoon. He was all alone now. The big girls who had sprung out to hit his sisters on the head with sticks had gone inside. The other children followed when the bell for dinner rang. Dae Young, though, had stayed outside. He refused to eat dinner with those hateful girls. And he had not been afraid of them today. He had seen them spring out from behind the bush when his sisters reached the bottom of the slide and tumbled on the ground. They jumped on them and waved their sticks and hit them on the head.

He was on the swing, standing on the wooden seat, pumping and pumping with his knees bent and then straight and then bent again. But when he saw his sisters on the ground with their hands over their ears, something red came rushing up into his head, and with the momentum of the swing he leaped down onto the back of one of the big girls. Soft bodies thrashed and twisted under him and then his little sisters were running for the house and he was on his feet with the two big girls standing back to back, swinging their sticks this way and that to hold him off. The other children were around them in a circle, shouting and jeering, bawling encouragement to Dae Young or insults at the girls, jumping up and down to see over each other's heads.

Dae Young charged through the two girls' swung defenses with his fists held hard and tight and pounded at their arms and bellies and against their breasts, kicking at their knees. The big girls flung down their sticks, and plunging through the caterwauling crowd, ran off toward the house while he stood shouting after them. Almost at once the bell rang to call the children in for dinner and suddenly Dae Young was standing in the playground all alone and shaking head to toe with rage.

His shaking lessened now, then stopped, but still he stood glaring at the side wall of the house as though daring the big girls to come back for him. The big girls were very bad. They had no right to hit his little sisters. No one had the right to hit his sisters except him, no one in the world.

Inside his chest there rose a longing for the safe arms of his grandmother. He did not understand where *Halmoni* had gone. Surely she would come soon and take them home. *Halmoni* was very kind. Sometimes she scolded him but she never hit him, and she was always gentle with his sisters. He remembered how she used to tell him it was bad for him to hit his sisters, even if they disobeyed him. He had often seen his father hit his mother, though. He pondered on it. Why was it that a man could hit his wife but a brother could not hit his sisters? Then something like a dream came inside his head and he squatted on his haunches to examine it.

It was late at night, very black inside the house, and the family lay together on the *ondol* floor, he closest to the wall, then his grandmother, his two small sisters, and closest to the door, his mother. His father was not there, but that was not unusual. He often came home very late, sometimes not until the sun was making feathered patterns in the sky. Dae Young had woken cold because the blankets had been pulled aside and the night's supply of coal below the *ondol* floor had burned away. He thought of getting up and putting on his padded jacket but he was still weighed down by sleep and lay there, chilly and irresolute, until he slid back into semiconsciousness.

Afterwards he would think about what happened next as a bad dream. He would not speak of it to anyone and when his father told him he had fallen in the street and gashed his face against the sharp edge of a rock, he would tell himself that after all it really was a dream. But deep inside his head he knew that it was real.

At first the scuffling and his mother's screams were not to be remarked upon. She often screamed when his father came home early in the morning. It was a usual thing and it would pass. He rolled onto his side and closed his eyes and waited for his mother to come running and sweep his baby sister up into her arms and dart out of the door. Then his father would stand in the doorway with his fist up in the air and curse his wife and curse his luck and then come back and lie down with his toes pointing straight up in a little hill beneath the blanket, and after a while his mouth would fall open and he would make loud noises like a rattling train, his breath going up into the air and falling down around his family until one by one they coughed and set their hands against their mouths and left him there to sleep alone.

But this time was somehow different, and Dae Young rolled as if in sleep, and squinting through his eyelids, saw his grandmother squatting up against the wall with his little sister Li Na in her arms, rocking back and forth and moaning in her throat. His mother, with her blouse and hair in disarray, was rushing for the door. Now he heard her foot thump on the wooden board of the veranda, now heard her run across the yard. And this time his father did not follow to curse her from the door but crouched with his face against his hands, red blood bursting from between his fingers.

Dae Young rolled away and made his body very small and after that he did not know what happened, only that his mother had gone off alone and left the baby screaming on the floor, and that his father wore a bandage on his face and said he had fallen in the street.

It occurred to Dae Young now that his mother had done that to his father with the knife his grandmother kept on a high shelf in the kitchen. That knife was very sharp. Once he took it from the bench where she was making dinner and ran it lightly down his finger the way she did to test it. Even that small touch made the surface of his skin open and a tiny line of blood came out. His grandmother turned and snatched the knife away and scolded him. "It is too sharp for a little boy to play with," she said. "You could slit a pig's throat with that knife." And she began to tell him stories about when she was a child and lived on a farm out in the countryside.

Dae Young forgot about playing with the knife and sat down cross-legged on the floor, listening with all his head. He loved these stories. He loved his grandmother more than anyone, although he knew he was supposed to love his father best. But his father frightened him, with his loud voice and his breath that smelled like fire. *Halmoni's* voice was soft and low. Her breath smelled like the wind. She made him seaweed soup and steamed rice cakes and once she brought back from the market a plastic sack of squid no bigger than his baby sister's hand, and still alive. She took her knife and sliced each one exactly down the middle while the legs on each side waved at her. Then she put all the waving legs into a pot with hot paste and strips of crackling dark green seaweed and other things too and made squid soup for him. He loved his grandmother, and respected her. She had seen a pig's throat slit.

The day his father was brought home dying by his friends, the scar that ran from eye to chin went white, like a streak of lightning down the left side of his face. His mother had done that, he knew that now. Perhaps, though, on that morning of the blood, she had tried to slit his throat. She must be very bad.

He tried a sentence in his head, and then he said it tentatively out loud. "*Ama* is bad," he said, the words making a little cloud in the air before his face.

He pulled back, watching the cloud grow thin and wide and

231

vanish. Then he said it again, louder and louder, screaming at her, until he was taken over by it and he could hear his father screaming at her with him in his head. Father and son, they stood together in the playground of the orphanage shouting, "Bad *Ama!* Bad! Bad *Ama!*" until the fat teacher came running out and crouched down in front of him and took him by the arms, hissing in his face for him to stop.

Now he saw that all the children had come running out behind her, chopsticks and spoons still in their hands, and stood, some in socked feet, staring at him, mouthing his words after him. He fell silent and bowed his head before the teacher, but when she tried to pull him close and comfort him he twisted out of her arms and ran down to the far end of the yard. There he flung himself against the high wire fence and clung to it in silence until the dark came down.

Then the fat teacher came again and took him by the hand and led him inside to the kitchen, where she filled his bowl with special pieces she had saved for him. "Eat, little one. You have to eat to stay alive."

Late next afternoon, Dae Young was once more standing in the yard, this time beside the gate. His little sisters stood each side of him and he held their hands in his. He glanced side to side, then peered out at the street, then side to side again.

The man called Father had been to talk to him today. The fat teacher called him to come inside and when he came he found his sisters sitting with big eyes in the room where all the children slept together on the floor. The fat teacher smiled and held her hand against his cheek. "Sit down, little one." He sat, the warm floor a comfort at his bottom but in his head a small, uncomfortable eye.

The Father was wearing that black shirt and that white collar with nowhere to open it at the front. He talked to Dae Young and his sisters in his odd Korean accent, saying things like, "Your grandmother is very old. Your mother can't afford. You are only six years old, but it is important that you understand what has happened to your family."

"Seven. I am seven."

"Seven in Korean years," whispered the fat teacher, who was kneeling on the floor behind him. "But the Father counts birthdays in American. To him you are only six years old."

Thinking of it standing here before the gate, Dae Young felt his anger start to burn again. First these people took away his clothes. They made him stand naked in a tub of water so hot he could barely put his feet in it, and then a maid poured water on his head and scrubbed and scrubbed his skin until he thought it would all come off and then she made him put on someone else's pants and socks and shirt.

He didn't like the shirt. It was stiff and had an ugly red pattern with squares and stripes, but when he complained she said it was a cowboy shirt from Texas, where everyone wore shirts like that and hats so big you could climb inside them and rode horses everywhere and drank beer and whiskey and shot each other with long guns in the street.

While she told him this, snapping shut the shiny metal fasteners on the shirt, Dae Young looked down scornfully at her bent head. He knew she was just trying to make him stand still and not be a nuisance to her. When she had finished snapping the buttons and tucking the shirt inside his pants he stood there with his arms hanging down and looked straight ahead and refused to move at all.

So then they cut his hair. A barber came with clippers and put a box on a chair and lifted him up onto it by the armpits like a baby and cut his hair so short that when he put his hand up to feel, it was standing straight up on his head like the bristles of a broom. He hated it.

He hated what they did to his sisters too. They scrubbed them too and put them into other people's clothes. Li Na's hair they twisted into two short braids that stuck out behind her ears and tied a bright pink ribbon to each one. They gave her someone else's sneakers to wear outside to play and she was happy with them because they had a little picture of a duck above the heel. But Dae Young thought she looked stupid with her two braids sticking out behind her ears like that. When he saw what happened to his baby sister Tae Hee, though, he was insulted, and all the barber did was laugh and say, "Sorry, I thought she was a boy."

Then they made them stand against a wall while they took photographs of them in their strange clothes and ugly haircuts. First they said, "Put your back against the wall," and then, "Turn sideways," and when Dae Young said, "Why are you taking pictures of us?" one of the big girls who was watching said, "So the police can find you if you run away," and grinned, and the barber, who was sitting at the table now, shoveling noodles into his mouth with chopsticks and a spoon, said, "Go on, get out of here," and she went away.

After that the big girls told his sisters what to do and wouldn't let him be in charge of them. When the fat teacher wasn't looking they pinched their arms and backs and made them cry and when she came to see they put their arms around them, or took Tae Hee on their backs to give her rides, or lifted Li Na on the swing with the red seat and pushed her up into the air. When the fat teacher went away again, they tripped and dropped Tae Hee on the ground, or pushed the swing so hard Li Na opened her mouth wide and couldn't scream and when they let her off she threw up down the front of someone else's clothes. They wouldn't let him be responsible. And now this Father thought that he was only six years old.

He didn't trust him, this enormous foreign man with his enormous pale nose sticking out and his eyes made into twisty shapes by the thick lenses of his heavy, black-framed glasses. Dae Young had bowed to him when he came into the room and also when he left, because he was an older man, but when the Father talked he just looked straight ahead, trying not to hear his words.

"We hope to find another family for you," the Father said. "If you are very lucky you might go to America."

That was when Dae Young turned to look at him.

"Would you like that, little one?" the fat teacher asked him with a smiling face.

He didn't look at her, all his attention on the Father.

Now all his attention was on the orphanage's wire front gate, and on the street beyond. He didn't want to go to America. Especially he didn't want to go to Texas. He didn't want to wear a cowboy hat or ride a horse. He didn't want to wake up every day and wear this ugly shirt. He didn't want another family. He wanted his grandmother.

It would be easy. He would simply open the gate when no one was looking and lead his sisters off along the street. At first they would walk slowly, like children on an outing to the park, so as not to draw attention. But when they turned the corner he would hoist Tae Hee on his back and tell Li Na to hold on to his belt and they would run and run until they got back home to *Halmoni* and everything would be all right.

The day his father came home on the board, he turned his head and looked at him. "My son," he said, "you must be responsible." On the day that he was buried in the ground, *Halmoni* put her arm around him and said, "Kun Soo's son, my grandson, you are now the head man of your family. You must take care of your sisters. You must be responsible."

And he had been responsible. He had worked hard every day to be responsible. At the general store he had done odd jobs and Mr. Hong had rewarded him with coins and odds and ends of food. He had pushed and pulled at boxes at the fish warehouse and Mr. Shin had sometimes let him have a fish head, sometimes a whole fish. He had learned to send his baby sister store-to-store to beg. She was cute and almost always had some small success, coming out with a handful of scorched rice candy, a miniature fruit yogurt drink, sometimes a little pot of soft fruit gel.

He had learned also to creep under the plastic covers on the market stalls, and where the stalls stood edge to edge, to slip his hand up in between, or to walk nonchalantly by, snatching up a peach here, a handful of chestnuts there, a yellow apple. He had brought home a pickled radish, a pocketful of rice, a pack of instant noodles, coca-cola in a can. He had begged from the butcher a package of meat trimmings and stolen from the fish market a pollock for his grandmother to cook. He had begged cigarettes for her from the construction workers at the wine shop where his father used to drink, and a bowl of soup from Mrs. Kim who was the owner. Once he even slipped away with three t-shirts and a bundle of new socks from a big store on a busy street of town.

While the weather was not cold he had done well enough, but then the bitter wind came down, the street vendors folded up their stalls, and the snow fell day after day, week after week, piling up across the coal merchant's backyard so that to find a single piece of coal he had to dig and dig until his hands and arms and the knees and legs of his pants were soaked and froze against his skin, while he carried home barely enough coal to make a fire to dry them out again.

He burned up all the odds and ends of wood his father had collected in the storage shed, and when it was all gone he hauled the wooden ladder out into the yard and jumped on it until the rungs came loose and then fed them to the fire. Even the long sides he dragged inside and rammed under the floor, and when the nearer end was burned, he waited till the fire died down and scraped the ash aside and crawled in underneath to get the unburned end and hauled it back to feed another fire. He tore down the shelves where his grandmother set her gourds to dry and burned them up, and burned the drier gourds, and then went out to forage on construction sites. But the snow was getting higher all the time, and anyway he was too late. Others had come before him and all the loose wood had been carted off.

In those days he began to be afraid. His stomach ached and rocked inside him and a burning came up in the back of his throat. But when he tried to vomit nothing came, just a thin, foul-smelling fluid. His sisters cried a lot and then they didn't cry. Their heads seemed to grow too big for their bodies and their eyes were very big and black. Sometimes they slept all day and all night too.

Once his grandmother lay down beside them with her hands against her sides and didn't answer even when he shouted loudly close against her head. His sisters woke, though, and when they saw him shouting in a panic at their grandmother, they shouted too, and wailed and cried so much he wished he had not woken them. But then *Halmoni* woke up and he was glad. His panic did not leave though. It was always with him after that, a small animal crouched inside his chest.

He understood now that his family was starving and it made him brave. He walked boldly into stores and with barely a glance to left or right seized food off the shelves and hid it in his jacket or his pockets, sometimes in his hat or in a sock. And for the most part his boldness went unnoticed. Only twice did a store owner call the police to chase him and both times he easily escaped because they came in their big car with siren wailing and red lights flashing, making a commotion on the street while, bulging in odd places from his stolen merchandise, he slipped quietly back home.

Sometimes on the way back home from foraging for food, hunger would overwhelm him and he would crouch down in an alley or underneath a bridge, and tearing the top off a pack of noodles or the wrapping off a pack of mung bean cakes, begin to wolf them down. But then he would hear *Halmoni*'s voice saying, "My grandson, you must be responsible," and shame would creep behind his ears and on his neck because he had eaten the food he was bringing to his sisters. Then he would fold down the top or roll back the plastic wrap, and cramming what was left inside his jacket, he would run home fast, pushing his legs as hard as they would go, then even harder, because if he ran fast enough his hunger would go away and he could give everything he had to his sisters and his grandmother and ask for none of it himself. Yes, he had been responsible. His grandmother would welcome him back home.

MI SOOK THOUGHT ABOUT HER CHILDREN all the time with a kind of wistfulness, like a child left out of a game. Sometimes she thought about them living in Eun Hye's nice big Western-style house—Where else would they be?—with a bedroom each, a four-ring stove for cooking, a dishwasher, a tumble dryer for their clothes, an *ondol* floor in every room, and, best of all, an indoor bathroom with a high flush toilet that was never broken.

In the corner of the kitchen, Mi Sook saw a narrow stairway leading down to Eun Hye's husband's clock shop. She saw Dae Young going down the stairs to help his new father in the shop, picking up parcels for him and making deliveries and learning how a shop was run and how a clock that would not run was made to run. She saw Eun Hye's husband take his hand, and chatting to the child of this and that, walk with him through the streets.

Soon they came to the harbor—which in Mi Sook's imagination was the same as the one in Inch'on because that was the only one she knew—and went into a big warehouse like the fish warehouse where Kun Soo used to work. Here they walked back and forth, inspecting the packing and stacking and loading of dried seaweed in the same way Mr. Shin used to supervise the packing and stacking and loading of fish. Eun Hye's husband explained everything to Dae Young and the child listened carefully because he understood that one day all this would be his.

Then Mi Sook saw her little girls in pretty dresses frilled at the neck and knee playing on a swing in the yard of Eun Hye's house, or pretending to be mothers with a baby doll they fed from a tiny bottle, or maybe they had Barbie dolls with yellow hair and many sets of clothes and tiny plastic shoes. When they grew hungry, Eun Hye, whom they now called *Ama*, brought them yogurt sodas on a rosewood serving table, and snacks of dumplings, sesame-seed cookies, sticky rice wrapped in crisp sheets of her husband's seaweed like miniature bedding rolls.

Sometimes Mi Sook fancied she lived in the house with them, in a room of her own, where the children came creeping at night to sleep against their other mother. She puzzled over this problem of two mothers and decided that the children would call her "Little *Ama*" and Eun Hye "Big *Ama*" because she was the oldest. Eun Hye would be like a mother to Mi Sook too, or maybe an older sister.

But when she bled each month Mi Sook remembered she was not a child or a little sister but a full-grown woman. Then her longing for her children was like an illness. Her head ached and her belly twisted and wrenched painfully inside her as though trying to give birth. She became feverish, her joints made little snapping noises when she moved, and her ankles swelled. Sometimes, when she could not get up off her quilt even to wash and dress, she had the helper send out for her sister and lay down in her room all day, alternately sleeping and waking to hunch over her belly and moan in a way she never had before.

On these days she dared not think about her children living with Eun Hye because she feared they were not there, but altogether lost. Then she blamed herself and blamed herself for losing them. If she had not been swallowed up in her fantastic scheme to get Hyun Joon as a father for them, they would be with her still. She dreamed about them every night, sometimes waking in horror because she saw them but did not recognize their faces and when she spoke to them they turned away as from a stranger. Other times she dreamed that she was very old and dying on her bed. She called out for her children, calling and calling day and night, but no one knew for whom she called and no one fetched them to her.

Sometimes she would wake from these dreams resolved to go back to the house in Inch'on, where she would search through everything to find that piece of paper on which Eun Hye had written her address. She would rise and dress and roll her bedding up against the wall, and with a few coins for her bus fare tucked inside her blouse, set off down the lane. But at the bus stop she would stand stupidly, letting one bus pass and then another until it was too late to get to Inch'on before dark. Then she would turn and go back to the coffee shop, telling herself that after all the slip of paper was long gone. And who knew what would be waiting for her in that empty house?

Other times she planned how she would go to visit Jung Hee's mother. These were the grandchildren of her oldest friend. Surely she would know what had become of them? But then she thought Jung Hee's mother would not know at all because her house was far to walk, too far for an old sick woman in the cold.

So then, she would knock on the doors of all the neighbors close around the house and make inquiries of them. Perhaps her mother-in-law had left a message for her, or someone had heard news about her children. Perhaps they were waiting for her at a neighbor's house. Mrs. Park's, maybe. It would be logical. Mrs. Park was comfortably off and lived just across the alleyway. If the children's grandmother had fallen sick and knew that she was dying, she could perhaps have gathered strength enough to take them across to her, or she might have sent them on their own. Or maybe when she died the children went there of their own accord.

But then she thought of Mrs. Park's strong sons. What if she came knocking on the door and Mrs. Park was angry with her, saying in a loud voice that she was a thoughtless, selfish mother and deserved no children? What if she called her two strong sons to throw her in the street and all the neighbors came to point at her and curse her for the way she had let a good old woman die alone? Then a worse thought came into Mi Sook's head: What if the children's grandmother had not died of illness but from lack of food? And what if her children had starved to death as well? If they were dead she could not go back to Inch'on because she was to blame. Mrs. Park would call her sons to hold her arms behind her back while she dialed her telephone and called for the police.

By the time Mi Sook reached this stage in her fearful suppositions, her fears and guilts had risen up to weave themselves into a web so fantastical and sticky that the more she twisted and turned in planning how to get her children back, the more immobile she became. All the things that had happened to her since she met Kun Soo came back and she lived through them again, blaming herself and saying, "Don't do this, do that," trying to cut out the bad parts and keep only the good, but she could never figure out a way to do it. For hours she would lie there, churning and churning in her mind until she feared she would go insane, and always everything was just the same. Then she would mourn for her children, and for Kun Soo, who had loved her even though he had his troubles, and for the old woman her mother-in-law who was kind to her, and for herself because she was nothing after all but a poor girl in a coffee shop. At last exhaustion would spread its heavy body over hers and weigh her down unconscious all the long afternoon and evening and on all through the night.

By morning, though, the horrors would be gone and she would rise early to work on a new gourd. She did this carefully, first walking slowly up and down the shelves she had constructed in her room, searching for a gourd with a shape fitting the pattern she had in mind. The shelves were rough but functional and on them sat drying gourds of every shape and size. At last she took one down, and sliding out a coffee-filter carton from below the bottom shelf, she squatted on the floor. Reaching into it, she took up a small blunt knife and began slowly and carefully to scrape off the rotten outer layer of the gourd to reveal the pure gleaming surface underneath, letting the dry skin rustle down into the box.

In the corner of the room, set on a board, were a pot of lacquer with a brush attached inside the lid, a tiny pointed knife, some pots of paint, a set of tiny pointed brushes. When the gourd was scraped to her satisfaction she dropped the knife into the coffee-filter box and slid the box back into place below the bottom shelf. Then she wiped the gourd all over carefully with the corner of her apron and carried it across to the corner, where she set it on the board. She sat back on her heels, and linking her fingers left hand into right, turned her hands outwards, flexing them. She cupped them loosely, palms up, in her lap and turned her eyes down on them, letting the image of the finished gourd appear like a projection of her mind. Then she took up the gourd in her left hand, the tiny pointed knife in the other, and began to carve the characters for *Health, Long Life, Wisdom,* and other worthy attributes. Sometimes she made a pattern out of her imagination or copied from something she had seen.

When she first took the gourds out of her mother-in-law's basket she had found, hidden at the bottom, the picture book Hyun Joon had given her, and sometimes she tried to carve pictures like the ones in that. But they had many complicated lines and she was not yet good at it.

While she scraped and carved she told herself that one day she would become skillful with these gourds. She would not ruin them by cutting into them before they were properly dried out. Her hand would not shake when she carved the characters or painted them on. The lacquer would not run down in ugly yellow stripes. Soon she would never need to throw one in the trash and one day she would make a gourd as lovely as the one Hyun Joon had given her. Then she would sell it and make another one. And then another. And when she had made enough money to pay someone to make an investigation, she would discover Eun Hye's address in Pusan. She would put on a new dress and comb her hair, and taking her best gourd, wrap it as a gift. Then she would go to visit.

She imagined this visit so often that it became like a favorite movie in her mind. Eun Hye would meet her at the door. "Mi Sook," she would say with a smiling face, "how nice it is to see you after this long time."

Then Mi Sook would take the gift between her hands and offer it to her, and Eun Hye would say, "Come, Mi Sook, come inside." She would bring green tea on a little serving table and apologize. "The children are not here. They are all at school, where they do very well. You must wait until they return." She would open the gift Mi Sook had brought, exclaiming over its beauty, and set it on a shelf for the children to see when they came home, and for the rest of the morning the two women would chat and laugh together like two old friends.

In the middle of this, Eun Hye's husband would come up from the clock shop for his midmorning snack. He would bow to Mi Sook with tears in his eyes, thanking her for the three beautiful and handsome and very smart children she had given him. He would tell her he was very happy to be the father of her children and beg her not to take them from him. Eun Hye would beg too, with her hands under her chin. Mi Sook would be kind. Even though she would soon have enough money to take care of her own children, she would allow Eun Hye and her husband to keep them.

Just before noon, she and Eun Hye would walk together to collect the children from their school. The children would jump with happiness to see her and they would all go back to Eun Hye's house, where they would eat and drink and have a pleasant afternoon talking about what they had done since last they saw each other. The children would love her and be grateful to her for giving them the opportunity to have a kind mother and a father with enough money to send them to school with brand-new book bags filled with books and packs of colored pencils. They would tell her all the things they had learned, and she would be proud of them.

Eun Hye's husband would join them later in the afternoon. "They will go to university, of course."

"The girls will go as well?"

"Boys. Girls. It makes no difference."

When it was time to go Mi Sook would slip quietly into the kitchen, where she would set an envelope discreetly on the counter. It would not be much, not enough to pay expenses for the children, but it would give her back her face. And soon it would be more. Eun Hye would smile at her when she came back from the kitchen but neither of them would mention it. Then Mi Sook would go back to Seoul.

All this Mi Sook thought about with a pleased expression on her face while she worked hard on her gourds, and when the first knock of the morning came on the back door, she put her work aside and went to take delivery of a load of cakes or sticky buns. These days immediately after her attacks of misery were her best. She managed the coffee shop like an old friend and when things were slow she left the helper in charge and went to stand before the jeweler's window, examining the latest gourd he had there on display. Then she went back to her room and tried to copy it.

As each gourd was done she set it on a shelf next to the last one she had made. They were all in order from the first one she had completed to the last and she examined them from time to time, noting the progression in her skill.

DAE YOUNG HAD A FRIEND NOW. His name was Jae. They became friends at the Christmas party. On that day the whole
orphanage washed themselves all over and dressed in the best
clothes they could find and stood in two rows in the entryway.
The door opened and a big black man dressed up like a soldier
stuck his head inside.

"Okay, folks!" he said, and Dae Young knew he was American.

The children laughed and imitated him. "Okay, folks!" they
shouted and followed him outside to where three troop trucks
had been driven up into the yard by American soldiers in uni-
forms and Korean soldiers too. The soldiers packed the children in the trucks and drove them to a military base where
there were donkey rides and games and all the food they could
eat, hamburgers and hot dogs and popcorn and coca-cola that
came rushing from a hose that stuck out of a shiny red machine.
Dae Young liked the popcorn and the coca-cola but he had
never eaten hamburgers or hot dogs and refused to try them.

That Christmas was the first time he met Santa Claus. Dae
Young didn't care for him. His baby sister cried when they sat

her on his knee and Li Na pulled his beard because the other children told her it was fake, but Dae Young refused to have anything to do with him. He slunk along the back wall of the auditorium, looking for a way out, and found a door that wasn't locked. He went through and when he closed it quietly behind him, there was Jae, backed up against the wall, watching the door with anxious eyes. When he saw Dae Young he said, "Okay, folks!" in an American voice.

Dae Young laughed. "Okay, folks!" he said.

Together they crept along the passageway, opening a door here, a door there, turning a corner, pushing hard together on a heavy door that led out to a slippery, oily-smelling yard. And then they were in a place like a shed where military vehicles were lined up row on row, trucks and jeeps and troop trucks like the ones that had brought them to the party. They pulled at their door handles and none of them was locked so they climbed into a jeep and took turns pretending they were driving. Then they climbed up under the back flap of a troop truck and sat facing each other on the seats that ran along each side, rocking back and forth and poking their fingers underneath the canvas and making shooting sounds.

But then a soldier caught them. "Oh, ho!" he said, lifting up the flap. "What have we here?"

He was very big, with all his hair shaved off so that his head looked like a white balloon. He stood grinning down at them.

"Want to look around?"

That evening was the first thing Dae Young had enjoyed

since he was locked up in the orphanage. The soldier was nice. He didn't care that they were being bad. He didn't try to make them go back and talk to Santa Claus or ride a donkey round a ring. He had a bunch of keys. "Here, I'll show you," he said and opened doors and showed them rooms with guns and boxes full of things he said were bombs and hand grenades, and let them start a truck.

He could speak Korean, although some of his words sounded strange and when they talked to him he said, "What's that?" a lot and they had to say it all again but slower.

He said his name was Sergeant Cox but they could call him Sarge. "When I was transferred here I didn't want to come," he said. "But now I like it. I like Korean girls and little kids. I even like the food."

When it was time to go he said, "Wait, I've got something here for you," and digging in the pocket of his pants, he produced some coins, which he shuffled in his palm and picked out two, laying one in each boy's hand. "That's five hundred *won* apiece," he said. "To maybe bring you luck. I hope you get adopted."

Dae Young didn't want good luck to be adopted but he had never seen a coin like this before. It had a picture of a flying bird. He closed his hand on it and bowed his thanks, eyes turned down to Sarge's huge shiny boots, then up the hefty legs and thighs inside the camouflage fatigues, the robust crotch, the massive chest, broad spread of shoulders, solid neck, and set on top, Sarge's blunt shadowed jaw and whitely grinning teeth, his kindly eyes.

A picture of a building came inside Dae Young's head, a tall one going up into the sky, with sunny, spreading rooms where he could take his sisters and his grandmother and Jae to live, where all the closets would be filled with food and the *ondol* floors would never lose their heat and no big girls with sticks would be allowed. He thought that if Sarge could be his father it might not be so bad to be adopted after all. After that he kept Sarge's coin inside his sock. When he walked he could feel its lucky bird pressing on the bottom of his foot, bringing him good luck.

And it had brought him luck, because now he and Jae were friends. They did everything together, even though Jae was almost twelve years old. They played outside together, came one behind the other late for meals, refused to eat the little colored stones called vitamins. Instead they slipped them in their pockets and later climbed together on the fence and threw them at the passing cars, or at the magpies who gathered on the fence beside the compost pit, waiting for the cook to throw away new ends of vegetables. They begged from the delivery men who brought the food and coal, took turns saying curse words to the man who brought the mail. Sometimes they wrestled with each other on the bedding when they were supposed to be asleep. Then the other children giggled and the fat teacher came and made them stand against the wall, but not together.

But even though the two boys joined each other in their small rebellions, they never joined together in the biggest one. They talked about it, yes. They planned. They gave each other tips and good advice. But when they ran away, they went alone.

Dae Young had tried now to escape a dozen times. The first four times he took his sisters, but Li Na could not run fast enough and cried, and Tae Hee clutched him so tightly with her arms around his neck that he could not breathe and before long they were caught. On the fifth and sixth attempts his sisters pulled away when he tried to take their hands so those times he went alone, and six times after that without even trying to take them, telling himself that once he made it safely back home to his grandmother she would send for them to come home in the orphanage's little bus. But always someone saw him leave, the maid or the fat teacher or the handyman or one of the big girls, and then there would be footsteps running after him, or the orphanage bus would pull up just ahead. Twice a police car had come beside him and a policeman jumped out with his arms spread and he was caught again. Jae also had tried many times to run away, and like Dae Young he had been caught.

Today the two boys had lit a fire on the frozen pond with scraps of twigs and paper. They sat beside it trying to keep warm and pretending to be Eskimos. They knew about Eskimos now. On TV there had been a movie that showed them chewing leather for their boots inside their igloos and fishing through the ice. It showed a little boy squat down in the snow to pee without wetting himself. Jae said they had magic underpants. Dae Young wished he had magic underpants as well. He had peed in the bedding every night since the Father first came to talk to him, and he was ashamed. The teachers did not know because many of the children peed at night and when they woke in the morning the bedding was soaked, the floor one big stinky puddle. The maids hauled the bedding out into the yard and hosed it down and hung it by the fire to dry, but it still smelled bad and sometimes was still damp when they rolled it out across the floor at night. By the morning it was soaked again. The teachers shook their heads and told them they would send the guilty children out for salt when they discovered them. Dae Young did not know why they wanted salt. Perhaps they would sprinkle it on the floor and the sharp smell of the pee would not climb into their noses when they woke up in the morning. He wanted all the children in the orphanage to have magic underpants. He wanted Jae to be his brother.

But now Miss Lee was at the orphanage. Dae Young recognized her. She was the lady from the Social Welfare office, the one who had talked a long time with *Halmoni*, writing on a piece of paper, and then sent her away, holding him back from running after her. Today she had a camera on a long black cord slung around her neck. She had come when they were eating lunch and all the children stood to make their bows and then sat down again. The fat teacher put her spoon and chopsticks down and went to stand with Miss Lee beside the door.

Dae Young watched them nervously. He had great respect for Miss Lee, and feared her too. She was very powerful. She could take children from their grandmothers and put them in the orphanage and no one stopped her. When he saw her turn and look at him and then turn back and talk some more to the fat teacher, he put his mouth close to Jae's ear and as soon as lunch was done they pulled their coats and mittens on and came far down into the yard beside the fence to play the rubber-band game. The magpies were sitting in a row along the fence, watching them and dropping steaming yellow pats onto the snow and cawing to each other.

But here was the fat teacher come to find him. She was standing at the corner of the house calling out his name. Miss Lee stood shivering beside her with the camera in her hand.

Dae Young crouched very low, ignoring them. He turned back the finger flap of his right mitten and jabbed his stick into a pile of dirty snow, deep down amongst the buried rubber bands. He flicked it and a rubber band flew out. Both boys turned to see where it had fallen but at that moment a magpie swooped down with a rattling cry and carried it away.

"Good luck for you today," said Jae.

But Dae Young didn't feel there would be luck for him today, not with Miss Lee stepping carefully down the yard toward him in her black coat and high-heeled shoes. His two sisters were behind her with the fat teacher, Tae Hee with her hair combed flat against her head, Li Na with new red ribbons on her braids.

Miss Lee said, "Come and climb up on the slide for me," and he obeyed because Miss Lee was very powerful.

Miss Lee pulled off one glove and tucked it in her pocket. She held the camera up with her finger on the button and said, "Smile everyone," but Dae Young didn't smile. His sisters did, and they slid down and stood here and there for Miss Lee to take more photographs. But Dae Young turned away.

That evening, lying in amongst the other children on the bedding, Jae said, "You are too lucky, having your photograph made."

Then the other children started to talk about it and Dae Young discovered that this photograph was an important thing. The photographs that were made when they first came to the orphanage were not important, just for the fat teacher to show to the police when they ran away. These ones, though, were different. They would be sent away to a family that might adopt him.

Dae Young lay awake. In the dim light he could see the photographs of children pinned against a piece of corkboard on the wall. He knew now that these were children who had been adopted. He could not see them clearly but he knew they were smiling. He also knew that some of them looked frightened.

He thought about his grandmother. He could not understand why she had left him here so long. He wished he had made a better smile for Miss Lee's photograph. He hoped Li Na had not smiled enough to show her rotten teeth. He pressed his right foot down onto the instep of his left to feel Sarge's coin inside his sock.

THE WEEKS WENT BY. A bitter winter gave way to a reluctant spring. The harsh Siberian wind lashing down across Korea like a vicious tongue had lost its edge. At first a crack of blue appeared, widened, and like a forearm swept across a misted windowpane, swept its way horizon to horizon. Ice melted off back streets and alleys, and the spent charcoal growing in them like a mold was hauled away. New blossoms rioted in the parks, the students began their springtime riots in the streets.

Now Seoul entered that brief lovely time between harsh freeze and the long stifling days of summer when the air was so heavy that spilled water would sit all day on hot cement without evaporating. The wind blew soft and warm, not enough to tear off hats or lift the women's skirts but just enough to keep the traffic fumes cleared out. Buds swelled and blossomed on the cherry tree outside the window of the coffee shop and two tiny birds flew in and out with bits of fluff and straw and feathers in their beaks.

Mi Sook went outside each day, standing with her head

turned up to see what progress they had made, and on the day a little bird came darting down at her, flapping its wings and pecking at her head, she knew that there were eggs.

All winter she had stayed inside, working with shivering concentration on her gourds, not putting a foot out the door to take one of the walks she used to take, wrapped up and stamping through the frozen streets with her nose tingling, coldness ringing in her head. Now her mood lightened and she began to walk again.

One day she found herself outside the park where she had followed Hyun Joon on that afternoon they spent together, and turned into it, and walked.

Here was the pond, the carp rising red and golden to the surface to be fed. Here were the little boys with tops, the children flying kites. Shading her eyes, she looked up at the sky. A fish, a butterfly, a dragon kite. Here was the kiosk where Hyun Joon had bought the newspaper and yogurt drinks. Here was the bench where they had sat. Behind it red azaleas bloomed and a plum tree stretched out flower-laden arms. The bench's seat was slightly curved, the back tilted at a comfortable angle. It was all just as it had been that day. It seemed so long ago. Mi Sook sat down and turned her face up to the sun, and shut her eyes, and dreamed.

She saw, against the wall of a poor house, a gourd vine pushing out its first spring blooms. Soon it was high enough to reach the roof. A young girl came from inside the house. A woman came out after her. Together they examined the gourds growing on the vine, touching first this one, then that, examining each one's shape, the length and beauty of its curving neck. This one, they decided, was the loveliest.

The woman came to look at it each morning when the white flowers on the vine were folding up their petals, and again at evening when they opened up their faces to the moon. Over the season, the gourd ripened, its outer casing hardened, and one day the woman came with a knife. Holding one hand at its base so it would not fall, she sliced through the stem above its neck.

Now Mi Sook saw another woman riding in the back seat of an elegant black car. She wore a pale pink business suit made of heavy slub silk of the highest quality and gave instructions to the driver. Soon the car came to a halt and the driver sprang to open her door. She got out and came through the narrow walkways of a street market. Behind her came the driver, carrying a basket on his arm. She went stall to stall inspecting all the gourds, accepting this, rejecting that.

She came to the woman who had grown the special gourd. "Good morning," she said, and bowed.

"Good morning," the woman said, bowing in return. "I have the gourd I promised you." And she brought it out from underneath the stall.

The woman in the business suit examined it, turning it in her hands, examining the color and the elegance of shape. "This is well done," she said at last. "I will pay what we agreed."

Now the woman in the suit was coming back into her shop in Seoul. She took the key out of her pocket and unlocked the door. The driver followed her, carrying the basket. They walked through the shop, past shelves lined with carved and decorated gourds, and climbed a staircase at the back. Here the driver set the basket on the end of a long table where girls sat along each side making lucky gourds in every shape and color and for all occasions. The girls looked up at him and made remarks and laughed, flirting with him, and he preened a little before he went back down the stairs.

Now, working carefully, the woman in the suit took each gourd she had bought that day out of the basket and set them on the shelves of the workshop with the other gourds set there to dry. The special gourd she set on a shelf at the far end of the room. She would work on that herself.

The street door rattled and the woman in the suit went downstairs in time to see a wealthy-looking woman enter. She had short curled hair and wore a bright yellow silk dress with a bow on the left hip and gathers falling out of it. She did not notice the owner of the shop at first because her attention was on the gourds ranged up and down the walls and in an elegant central display of multitiered glass shelves. The edges of these shelves were beveled like the facets on a chandelier and the display was lit from underneath, the light reflected and reflected so that the gourds glinted and shimmered in a rainbow pool of radiance. The woman in the yellow dress stood a long time before this display, pressing her hands together and making little noises of appreciation.

The owner of the shop made a small cough in her throat and, turning, took down a gourd from a locked glass cabinet behind her, setting it on the counter. The lady in yellow came smiling to the counter and took the gourd and turned it round and round, touching it only with the tips of her fingers, holding them flat so that her bright painted nails would not damage the lacquered surface of the gourd. She read the Korean characters out loud: *Good Luck, Long Life, Many Sons.*

"A beautiful gift for your daughter on her wedding day," said the storekeeper.

"Yes," said the customer, "it is well done. I will pay what we agreed." And she took from her purse an amount of money one thousand times what the storekeeper had paid for the special gourd upstairs.

The storekeeper wrapped the gourd in soft white tissue and packed it in a box. She bowed the customer politely from the store, standing in the sunny doorway to watch her walk away.

People bustled back and forth along the street. Some of them were local merchants. They all knew the woman in the doorway. "Good afternoon," they said, making small respectful bows—because this woman was becoming very wealthy.

The woman greeted them all. Above her head, its elegant gold lettering sparkling in the sun, the bright red shop sign read *The Lucky Gourd Shop*.

Mi Sook smiled. The sadness that for so long had sat inside her heart had walked away into the park. Now she stopped her dreaming and fell to making plans. Soon she would need an amount of money to buy sharp knives, a large supply of gourds, some semiprecious stones, feathers, lacquer, paint, brushes, all the extra things needed to make high-class gourds like in the jeweler's window. Then there would be rent and salary for the workers. But where to lay her hand on such a sum?

A shadow came across the sun. "Hello," a voice said.

He was a tall man but she could not see him well because the sun was behind him, making him into a flat dark outline.

"Hello," said Mi Sook cautiously.

He moved and she could now see that he wore military fatigues. Above were the big nose and shaved blond head of an American GI.

"Do you mind if I sit here with you?" he said, pronouncing the Korean words carefully. His pale eyes looked directly into hers.

Mi Sook thought of the painted girls walking up and down outside the U.S. military base and turned her head aside, looking at the little chunks of gravel by his enormous boot. She gathered her feet beneath her, intending to get up and walk away, but something made her hesitate. She set her hands on each side of her legs and pushed on the hard wood of the bench, but it seemed to soften under her. She looked up at the soldier. "Sit down," she said.

His name was Frank, he told her, apologizing for his poor Korean. He had been here for more than three years now and although he had studied the Korean language in America and had practiced every day since he came here, he was still not good at it. It went too fast. He was not used to speaking fast, or listening fast either.

He had been lonely since he came, he told her. He missed his mom and pop and three young brothers, none of whom were soldiers. Here the winter was too cold and the summer so humid he could hardly breathe, even at night. He came from Bakersfield, he said, a desert town where the air was always dry.

"Is that near Purdue?" asked Mi Sook, and he laughed and shook his head, but he didn't tell her where it was. She looked at his big head and his eager pale blue eyes and working mouth, and it was frightening and rude the way he stared into her eyes.

Frank talked and talked, telling her many things about himself, and she listened, struggling to understand the foreign intonations of his words. He told her he had not had a pretty girl to talk to since he left home. He had had a girlfriend then, in Bakersfield, and they went out together all the time. She had a red car, a convertible, and they would drive out into the desert with the top down and the hot wind rushing in their hair, or go up into the mountains, spinning round the bends and shouting, or maybe they would drive a long way to the beach and swim. Once they went window shopping on Rodeo Drive in Hollywood.

Mi Sook's eyes grew large at this. "Hollywood I know," she said. "Many movie stars live there and they are rich."

Frank laughed. "Oh yes, very *very* rich." He told her he had not been with a girl since he left Bakersfield. He asked if he could walk her home.

She told him no.

"Okay," he said. "Okay. But can I meet you here again?"

"Perhaps."

"Tomorrow then?"

"Perhaps next week."

"Okay," he said. "I get the message. Next week, then."

Later that day, Mi Sook went to sit at the little table in the window of *Madame*'s wedding shop. She wanted to tell *Madame* about Frank, but she knew what she would say. "Bah," she would say. "What for do you need this man?" So she said nothing, flicking through the bridal fashion magazines.

After a while she stopped looking at the brides and began to notice things in the backgrounds of the pictures, also to pay attention to the advertisements shouting at her out of almost every page. Here was a shiny long black car, here an older woman in a white fur coat, here a gold watch glistening with diamonds. One page had a picture of a foot and ankle. The foot wore a high-heeled bright red shoe and around the ankle was a fine gold chain. Here was a lady in lace underwear, just a bra and panties, with her pale bare stomach all exposed. She held her arms above her head and her breasts were very big, with shadows in between. Mi Sook examined her face. Her eyes were almost closed and she pouted out her lips and did not look at all ashamed.

She turned the page and spent a long time looking at a picture of a table in a dining room. It was of fine dark shining wood with sparkling dishes, white with golden rims, and sparkling crystal glasses. In the middle of the table was an enormous bowl of pink and white chrysanthemums. No food

was on the plates and no people sitting at the table, just a thin
lady in an evening dress standing with one hip stuck out at a
peculiar angle and one hand held out toward the table as
though to say, "See what I have here. See how rich I am." Mi
Sook turned the page. Here was half a face with long blond
hair and perfect skin, its bright pink half mouth mocking her.
She slammed the magazine shut.

"So what is your trouble today, child?" said *Madame*'s voice
behind her.

Mi Sook pushed her chair back and squirmed around to
look up at *Madame*. "I have met a man," she said.

"Aha."

"He is American."

Madame said nothing.

"I met him in the park."

Madame pulled out the chair across from Mi Sook and sat
down. "Yes, this could well be trouble for you, child.".

THE GIANT MULBERRY TREES that grew down one side of the orphanage's yard were so old that their bottom limbs hung low enough for the children to climb up into them. The trees had broken out in berries and they ate all they could reach, then the braver children climbed high up into the branches.

Dae Young and Jae were the bravest and they climbed the highest, shaking the branches so that the berries fell onto the ground with soft, wet, plopping sounds. The other children stood below, trying to catch them before they hit the ground, scooping them up in handfuls, feasting, mouths stained bright black with mulberry blood. But their clothes were also stained, and the laundry women complained about it. The mulberry trees were banned.

Dae Young and Jae made a game out of the ban. When no adults were around they climbed onto a lower branch, wrapped their arms around a higher one, and bounced and bounced until the whole tree shook and shuddered, clattering its upper branches against the orphanage's green tiled roof, blotching it with mulberries.

The fat teacher came running out, waving her arms. "You are frightening the little ones who are taking their nap," she cried. "You are giving the cook a headache. How can she make dinner for you with these branches beating on the roof so that the racket makes her head burst?"

Sometimes she punished them by making them stand against the wall. "You must learn to be still and quiet," she said. "Do not move until I come out again." But when she went inside they squatted down and played jacks with pebbles, springing upright when they heard the door flap back against the wall.

Soon the two boys became naughty heroes to the other children. When the fat teacher came running out to make them stand against the wall, they jumped down from the tree and ran to hide, and no one gave away their hiding place. The big girls would have liked to but now that Jae was Dae Young's friend they did not dare. When Dae Young and Jae were not around, though, they still hit his little sisters on the head with sticks. Since their photographs were taken they had hit them even more. Sometimes Li Na cried quietly in the night but in the day she did everything the big girls told her, even when they hit her. All this made Dae Young angry in his head and so he misbehaved.

Today Dae Young and Jae were taking turns to scramble up into the lower branches of the mulberry tree closest to the kitchen. Bouncing mightily to make a strong rhythm, they beat its branches hard against the roof. First Jae bounced while Dae Young stood guard, listening for the door to flap against the wall. Then it was Dae Young's turn to bounce and Jae's to stand guard.

Dae Young was bouncing now. When Jae came rushing he leaped down from the tree and the two of them ran to hide around the corner of the building, where there was a large stand of bamboo. Here they wedged themselves, the hard knobbed stems pressing up against their ears and cheeks while they listened to the fat teacher threatening the other children. When they heard the door flap shut again they squeezed out, rubbing their cheeks where the bamboo had left knobbly patterns, and ran to bounce again.

Now Jae was bouncing, Dae Young standing guard. He heard the door flap back and at the same time an enormous crack. As he ran to hide in the bamboo he passed Jae tangled up amongst the fallen branches of the mulberry tree, but the fat teacher was coming and he did not dare stop.

The Father was called in to talk with Jae. Dae Young was frightened Jae would tell that he also had been part of it, but no one came for him and he was proud Jae had not told, but also sad because he had brought trouble on his friend.

The Father gave Jae a saw and told him he must help the handyman. For more than a week he labored every day to saw the fallen branches and stack them into piles. Dae Young asked if he could help and the handyman said, "Ah," in a knowing way and gave him a small saw. But he was not good with it and soon gave up, laboring instead to stack the wood in piles. At first he was fearful that Jae would not be his friend anymore but it turned out worse than that because as soon as the wood was cut and stacked Jae was sent to live in another part of the orphanage with the older boys. He was taken away, crying and struggling with the driver and the big boy who had come to get him, in the orphanage's van.

Dae Young went into the house to find the fat teacher. She was in the kitchen with a towel around her head, poking a spoon into the pots of food the cook was boiling up for dinner. She smiled at him.

"I want to know why Jae was sent away."

The fat teacher pulled him away from the hot front of the oven and crouched down with one hand on each arm. "Because you are a good boy," she said with a coaxing face, "and Jae is a bad influence on you. We cannot send you to a family in America if you are bad, can we? It would be a great shame for our country. You must be a good boy from now on so you can be adopted."

One of the big girls was waiting in the entryway beside the door. "It is too late for you now," she said. "You are a naughty boy and will never be adopted."

"I don't care." He tried to go past her to the yard but she blocked his way, pushing at his shoulders with her hands and making her eyes small and mean. "Jae will never be adopted either because he is naughty too," she said. "And anyway he is twelve years and too old. No one wants him now."

Dae Young felt anger marching in his head. He looked boldly up into the big girl's mocking face. "You are naughty too," he said. "You are naughtier even than Jae. And you are older than Jae too. No one wants you either. You are a very bad girl and will have to live here all your life."

She swung her arm to hit him but he dodged underneath, and trembling with anger and bravery, ran out into the yard. But he had seen tears start in the big girl's eyes. It made him feel uncomfortable and itchy in his cowboy shirt.

That night he ran away again and this time no one saw him go. He hadn't planned it. He just couldn't go to sleep. He lay listening to the breathing and moaning of the other children and thought about the time Jae rolled over in the dark and whispered in his ear, "Every night before I go to sleep, I rub Sarge's coin and wish to be adopted." He thought about the big girl saying Jae would never be adopted and his head grew tight, as though it was about to burst.

He shoved the blanket to one side, and slipping his feet into his sneakers at the door, crept out to sit on one end of the see-saw. The white scar where the limb had been ripped off the mulberry tree glowed pale. He shuffled one foot in the sawdust, then the other. He stood, kicking at it with both feet, watching it fly around his ankles in a misty cloud, then turned and looked at the blank wall of the orphanage, at the high black windows where the kitchen was, at the upward curving corners of the roof. He tilted his head back on his neck and looked up at the sky and it was full of stars, more even than a pomegranate's seeds. He looked for the moon but could not find it. A light wind lifted his hair. It was warm and smelled of fish and garlic and his grandmother. He crouched down and laced up his sneakers, turned, and crept across the yard.

The gate was fastened with a padlock as it always was at night but his sneakers made only a small squeak on the wire, the gate's hinge barely rattled, the thump of his descent was no louder than a squirrel jumping branch to branch. For a moment he stood as he had landed just outside the gate, legs spread, knees bent, arms held out for balance. Nothing moved except the pale cloud of his breath going out and out. He took a cautious step, another, and another.

Now he was running through the yellow circles of the street lamps, running and running, around corners and along alleys, stumbling against trash cans, down streets where light seeped out around the shutters of shops and houses, making odd patterns on the ground, running and running with his heart pumping and his legs pumping and his eyes bursting from his head, and all the time the night grew dark and darker. Men's voices called roughly out of sight and someone coughed and spat, doors clacked, feet clattered on an overpass above his head, a shrill voice laughed. Once he heard someone crying, the same wailing sound his grandmother had made all that dreadful night after his father died. And now the wind came swirling up the street, blowing plastic bags and sheets of news-paper into his face. A kicked can rattled from an alleyway in front of him and then a face looked round the corner and a hand came out. He ran and ran.

He was running on a highway now, close along the white line at the edge. Engines jerked and roared beside him, lights flooded and faded, flooded again, horns argued at his back, scattering his wits, and then, behind, a single rising cry, red flashing lights, a shout, "Hey! Hey!" He swiveled, dashed out across the road. An eighteen-wheeler truck hauled on its brakes, blasting its distress into the night, while he stood frozen in its path. The glaring lights bore down on him. He shut his eyes.

But now strong arms were lifting him. A car door opened, slammed. The sound of traffic dimmed. A disembodied voice called out his name. A policeman sat beside him with his arm across his back. He wanted to pee.

The policeman in the front seat of the car stopped talking to the radio and twisted around. "Hey, kid," he said, "have you run off again?"

Dae Young made his chest big and his voice loud. "I am going to see my grandmother. She is expecting me."

The policeman pushed his hat back. "Listen, kid," he said, "if your grandmother wanted you at home, why would she put you in the orphanage?"

Dae Young watched him, waiting for the answer, but the policeman just pulled his hat straight on his head and turned back to the front and started up the car.

DESPITE ALL *MADAME*'S WARNINGS, Mi Sook went on meeting Frank down at the park every Sunday afternoon and sometimes on a weekday also. She mentioned nothing to *Madame*, and never brought him to the coffee shop. Having heard the students rant against America, she knew he would not be well received. If the students should decide she had become a GI's whore it would be bad for business and also she would lose her friends.

Whatever *Madame* or the students might have concluded if they saw the two of them together, the truth was that Frank never put his hands on her, he never offered money. He spoke softly to her and was always as polite as he knew how to be. Unlike Korean men, he opened doors and let her go through first, he bent his head and asked what she would like to do today, he never asked for any sort of deference from her, and when she was cheerful in his company, he smiled and smiled with big, white, perfectly straight teeth.

At first they walked around the park and talked, and then they walked about the streets, Mi Sook making sure to guide him into streets far from the coffee shop. When she saw a mother with a baby on her back or scrambling at her side, she turned her eyes away and said bright, funny things to Frank. One day he bought her lunch, nothing fancy, just steamed buns and deep-fried octopus on sticks from a pushcart near the railway station, where they sat under the tarpaulin cover and shared a bottle of *soju*.

Mi Sook was not sure why she kept on meeting him. She didn't like him the way she used to like Hyun Joon. He was nice enough, although she didn't like the way he was so big. Sometimes, when she saw him from behind, she caught her breath at the size of him, the massive back, the legs like two tree trunks. His hands also were too big, and, as though he sensed her intimidation, it was a long time before he ventured to hold her elbow when they crossed a street.

He never talked the way Hyun Joon used to talk, about stories and history and politics and how to make a better life for the Korean people. He never asked if she could read, he never seemed to read himself, although he seemed to watch things on his television that were not on hers. She asked him how he did this and he laughed his big deep laugh. "We get U.S. TV on the base," he said, but he didn't tell her how. Then he asked if she would like to come and see the base and she said no.

"Maybe one day you would like to come there to a dance?"

She made a small impatient movement of her hand.

"Okay," he said. "Okay."

"I wish," he said, "you'd been around at Christmas. You

could have come and helped us with the orphans' party. You'd be good with kids, I think."

Mi Sook felt her insides tighten. "No, I am not good with kids."

"Come on, don't be like that. You'd have liked it. It's a party just for little kids. Korean kids are cute as buttons, aren't they just? There's this orphanage in Inch'on full of them and we have a party for them every Christmas. It's a lot of fun, with games and tons of food and donkey rides and Santa Claus and gifts for all of them and Christmas carols playing. It's just like when we were kids back home." He laughed in a sighing way. "Cute kids. Can't help feeling sorry for them, though. Come on, don't be like that. You'd love 'em, I know you would."

But Mi Sook turned nervously away and went back early to the coffee shop complaining of the cold, although the cold she felt was all inside.

That night she woke up from a dream about her children but could not remember it, not even if it made her smile or cry. She would not meet Frank again, she told herself. And yet she did. More and more the helper called her sister in to help her in the coffee shop while Mi Sook, with her hair brushed shiny and her face made up, went off all afternoon or evening on some errand she never spoke about.

One day *Madame* came down the lane behind the shop and smacked her hand against the door. The helper opened it and jerked her head toward the back room, where Mi Sook was standing before her mirror with her hairbrush in her hand. *Madame* stuck her square face through the door and looked at her. "You do not come to visit me," she said. "I thought you must have fallen ill."

Mi Sook tossed her hair back with a nervous gesture. "These days I am so busy with my gourds I cannot come."

The helper, who was listening behind *Madame*, giggled with her hand across her teeth. *Madame* turned. "Something is funny, yes?" But Mi Sook glared and the helper went away.

Madame turned back. "It is the American?"

Mi Sook set down the brush. "*Madame* . . ."

"Child, what is it you want from him?"

Mi Sook could give no satisfactory answer to this question and at last *Madame* went off, shaking her head and muttering.

Walking to the park that day, Mi Sook found the question rattling in her head. "Child, what is it you want from him?" *Madame*'s voice asked, "What is it you want?" and each time she asked, the answer seemed to Mi Sook to grow more and more important. All her life she had relied on *Madame* for advice and it had never let her down. But now she had gone against it and she knew there had to be a satisfactory reason to bring back to *Madame*. But she did not know what it should be.

On Korean Independence Day, Frank took her to a proper restaurant for dinner where the waiter treated her as though she were rich. He held her chair back for her while she sat down and then slid it close up to the table. He shook her napkin out and bowed and kept his eyes turned down when he handed her the narrow folder with the dishes listed in a curling hand. He filled her wine glass even when she drank only a sip, until she set her hand across the top and frowned at him.

Then he went to stand behind a pillar, watching to see what she might need, and when Frank paid the money for the meal, he scooped the tip up off the table with a beaming face and bowed and smiled her out to the front door.

Frank took her to a movie then. It was very dark and their seats were so close that she could feel the heat rise out of him. After a while he slid his arm along the seat behind her while she sat stiff as a statue of the Buddha, so aware of him and his strange soapy smell that she saw nothing of the screen. Toward the movie's end she let him hold her hand.

That night she let him kiss her, just a little kiss, no more than a brush of lips before she pulled away and turned to start the long walk back home to the coffee shop. But she had not gone far when she sensed him following. She turned the wrong way down a street, walking very fast and wondering what to do, and then stood still, then turned, and he was gone. When she started up again she felt him there again. It frightened her and she ran, darting first down one alley, then another, until she was sure he was no longer there.

For three weeks after that she did not meet him in the park, but spent all her spare time working on her gourds. At the end of these three weeks she held a completed gourd up in her hand and smiled and said aloud, "Now I have a business for myself," and took it next door to show *Madame*.

"Ai-yi!" *Madame* said when she saw it. "Here, set it here so I can look at it." She went to the little table by the window and cleared away the fashion magazines. "Set it right here in the middle where the light is good."

Mi Sook followed her and set it down. *Madame* walked slowly from one side of the table to the other, bending to turn the gourd from time to time, peering closely at it through her black-rimmed half glasses. At last she straightened, smiling. "This is well done, child. What will you do with it?"

"I will sell it and save the money for my business."

"Who will you sell it to?"

"The jeweler in the next street."

Madame looked dubious. "And how much will he pay, this jeweler?"

"Maybe as much as fifty thousand *won*."

Madame clicked her tongue. "Child, child," she said. "This is no way to make your fortune. Such a gourd is worth . . ." She tossed her hands about.

Mi Sook looked at *Madame's* blunt tossing fingers. "I know," she said, "I know. The jeweler will sell it for six or maybe even ten times that amount but I think that fifty thousand is all he will offer a poor girl, so what am I to do?"

Madame brought in her hands and set them one on each of Mi Sook's shoulders. "Come, come, child. Do not distress yourself. That is the way of business and the jeweler is not to be blamed for it. You must pay attention to *Madame*. It is not the one who makes the item but the one who sells it to the customer who gets the profit." She turned Mi Sook slightly, gesturing with her head toward the ceiling. "Look at those girls upstairs sewing their hearts out on my machines. Do they get rich? No. And yet they make the dresses. It is I, *Madame*, who makes the profits because I am the owner of the store."

Mi Sook pulled away, making her back straight and her shoulders square. "One day I will be an owner too. Then I will make the profits, but for now I must not complain. Whatever I can get will make my savings higher. Complaining to myself will not."

Madame made a noise like a snort, and clenching her fist she held it in the air the way the students did when they were rioting. "Foolish child," she said in a loud voice, and Mi Sook realized that for the first time since she had known her, *Madame* was angry with her. "Foolish child," she said again, "have you learned nothing from sitting in my shop year after year? Have you not understood one tiny thing? Have I not told you to use the people that you know to help you in your business? Have I not told you never undersell yourself? Always you must keep your prices high and your goods selective. You sell cheap down at the jeweler and you will never get your prices up again." She picked the gourd up from the table, holding it out to Mi Sook in both hands. "Look at this gourd, child. *Look* at it. What do you see?"

"A decorative gourd with writing on the base that says, *Wealth* and *Many Sons*."

"Eh! No! Look again. You see a special gift. Something to give your daughter when she marries. Something unique, not another like it. Now, look around you. What else do you see?"

"I see a store called Madame's Bridal—Oh, *Madame!*"

"Oh, *Madame*, indeed! How soon can you make more of these?"

• • •

It was another three weeks before Mi Sook went again to meet Frank in the park. By then she had commissions for six more gourds with *Wealth* and *Many Sons* for weddings, three with *Good Luck* and *Health* for one hundred–day celebrations, and one with *Long Life* and *Happiness* for a sixtieth-year celebration. When she saw him sitting patiently with his hands between his knees, she knew he had waited for her just like that every Sunday for the past six weeks and she felt sorry for him and apologized.

But he apologized in turn—for following her and frightening her. "Oh Babe," he said, "I'm sorry. I didn't mean to frighten you. I just couldn't bear for you to vanish off into the streets the way you do and no way to get in touch except to sit every Sunday in the park hoping you'll come." And he gave her a gift, a fine gold chain to hang around her neck.

Madame inspected it. "Where did you get this?"

Mi Sook shifted her feet.

"From the American?"

Mi Sook looked at *Madame*'s troubled face. Again she seemed to hear her ask, "Child, what is it you want from him? What is it you want?" Now an answer bubbled up into her head. "*Madame*, you said yourself I should use the people I know to help me in my business."

Madame looked from Mi Sook to the gold chain around her

neck, her expression meditative. Mi Sook braced for her opinion. But *Madame* just held her hand out for the chain and going to the bottom of the stairs, called down her girl who made the little pillows for the wedding rings. She gave her instructions to make a tiny pillow of jade-green velvet and when it was done she set it inside one of Mi Sook's completed gourds and set the gold chain on the pillow. "*Voila!*" she said. "A jewelry box with jewelry. It will bring a grand price."

Then she looked at Mi Sook as though waiting for the answer to a question and Mi Sook turned her head aside and blushed. "Do not think I have become a GI's whore."

Madame tilted her head side to side. "Okay, I will not think it."

"Where is the gold chain?" Frank said next time they met.

"It was stolen from my neck," she said. "It snapped almost at a touch it was so fine."

Next week Frank brought her another, thicker, chain that had a safety clasp. For this *Madame* got more than for the first. Taking only a small commission, she passed on the rest to Mi Sook, who added it to her savings in yet another candy box. Before long she had fallen into the way of walking Frank along certain streets, where she would happen up against a window full of pretty things and point at this and that, exclaiming. And he called her "Babe" and bought her something every time.

Some of these pretty things she wore when she was with him and some she passed on to *Madame* to sell, and all the time the money in her candy boxes grew. One day she collected them all up, packed them in a paper sack, and carried them through the streets to the big gray office building that housed the credit union. She pushed through the rotating door and went inside.

The clerk watched with a smirking smile while she emptied the contents of the candy boxes on his desk. "I must count this?" he said.

"I have counted it already. It is written on this paper."

He pushed his glasses up the bridge of his nose with one finger and examined the scrap of paper she pushed across the desk.

He pushed it back to her. "It is not enough."

"But I have been saving for a long time now."

"Then you must save longer. It is not enough."

Mi Sook collected her money without looking at his face and went back to the coffee shop. There she took the small gray pad she used to write the totals for the till each evening and made herself a schedule. If she was to have a business for herself, she must work harder every day and later every night. She must think about her children in Pusan.

AT THE ORPHANAGE, the Father had a globe. On it he showed Dae Young and his sisters Korea and America. "Your new father is an important man," he said. "He works for the American government in a big bank. He has a swimming pool in his garden and a big car. You are very lucky."

Dae Young looked at him. "Will he let me drive this car?"

The Father laughed. "Of course. When you are old enough. Until then, you can ride in it any time you want."

"Can I sit in the front?"

"You can sit anywhere you want."

The fat teacher interrupted. "See, little one, what I told you has come true. You are a good boy now. You eat. You do not run away. And so you have a brand-new family. They will be proud of you. And look, here I have photographs. Here are two big brothers and also a big sister."

She turned to the little girls, who clung together on the floor watching their brother's face. "Look, here is your new big sister. See her pretty yellow hair? See how long it is, and how it curls, just like a Barbie doll."

Tae Hee turned her eyes down to the photograph without moving her head but Li Na shrank away.

"What?" said the fat teacher. "You do not like your sister? Come now, you will make her sad." She thrust the photograph toward Li Na, who slid her hands behind her back.

"Come now, look, a lovely sister for you."

Li Na looked up at her from underneath her bangs. "Will this big sister hit us with a stick?"

The fat teacher turned the photograph around and looked closely at it with her forehead wrinkled up. She laughed a jerky little laugh. "What a funny question. No, of course she will not hit you with a stick. She will love you. And your brothers also will love you. And here is your new mother. See how kind she looks?"

Li Na looked at Dae Young but he was holding a photograph in each hand, concentrating first on this one, then on that. She put both arms around her little sister and together they looked at the new mother with frightened, smiling faces.

Dae Young didn't care about the mother, or the sister. He looked at the two brothers. They both had yellow hair, one curly and one straight, and both of them were big, although not as big as Sarge. They grinned at him like Sarge, though, with big white shining teeth.

The new father smiled as well, but with a serious face. He wore gold-rimmed glasses and his hair was not yellow but a sort of light brown color with his forehead going back into it on each side like a pair of wings. He didn't look at all like

Sarge. Dae Young liked the brothers but it was the father's photograph he slipped into the pocket of his shirt.

That night he lay in bed and thought about his new father. He didn't understand about the government or the bank and he had never seen a swimming pool, but he was proud about the car. He dreamed he was riding in it. He was in the front seat and a man like a taxi driver was behind the steering wheel. Where was his new father? He turned to find him in the back seat but no one was there.

"Stop, stop," he told the driver. "We must go back and find my *apba*."

The driver turned his head and smiled with rotten teeth. "*Apba* is dead," he said.

Dae Young woke with his chest heaving and tears flying from his eyes. Although he was ashamed he could not stop. He lay there in the dark with the fumes from the pee-soaked bedding rising up to sting his eyes and cried so hard that the fat teacher came running with her hair on end and treated him kindly. She helped him wash and dress again in clean clothes and knelt in front of him and pulled his head against her big soft breast and stroked his neck. "Hwish, hwish, little one," she said. "Everything has turned out well for you. Hwish. Hwish." And he leaned against her breast and cried hard until his head was so filled up with tears he could hardly breathe. It was the first time he had cried since his Korean father died.

Now he could not go to sleep. The fat teacher had made him a bed in the corner of the kitchen so he would not have to lie down in the pee again, but his arms and legs would not stay still. At last he crept outside and sat down on the see-saw with his knees drawn up, staring at the mulberry trees along the fence. As he watched, tiny lights rose from the grass and flickered underneath the trees. Soon they flashed and twinkled to the very top.

FRANK WAS WORRIED. "Oh Babe," he said, "you come to see me less and less. Are you becoming tired of me?"

"I must work hard. It takes up all my time."

"You are not tired of me?"

Mi Sook looked up at him. Behind his head an airplane dragged its forking silver tail across the sky. "I am not tired of you."

"Why don't you ever wear that chain I bought for you?"

She turned her eyes down. "I am saving it."

"For what?"

"For when I go with you to something very special." And she turned her eyes back up to him again.

Frank's big face flushed with pleasure. "Well then, Babe, we'll make it a *real* special occasion." And he made an arrangement to take her out to dinner at a big hotel the following week. "Wear one of those pretty dresses Korean girls wear," he said, excitement gleaming off his teeth. "I bet you'd look good enough to eat in one of those."

This worried Mi Sook because she had never owned a *hanbok*, but then she went next door to see *Madame*.

Madame screwed up her face. "What is this for?"

"For an occasion. Nothing."

"I do not think much of it."

"Come, *Madame*, have I not made many gourds? Am I not almost ready for my business? Surely you are pleased with me?"

Madame grumbled and muttered but she went upstairs and came down with a big box full of tissue paper. Underneath the tissue paper was a brand-new *hanbok*, its bright blue and yellow sleeves folded stiffly across the stiff pink skirt. "Here," she grunted, thrusting the box at Mi Sook. "You may use this. It is a wedding *hanbok* but no matter. This American of yours will never know the difference. Do not soil it. It is waiting for a customer."

The next week Mi Sook did her hair carefully and put on a new color of lipstick, a deep purply red, and went to meet Frank wearing the borrowed *hanbok*. *Madame* had also lent her an elegant jade pin for her hair, carved at one end like a dragon's head and at the other like its tail. When Frank saw her his eyes grew big. "Why, Babe," he said. "Why, Babe."

He was not wearing his fatigues that day. Instead he wore a proper uniform, dark green with creases down the legs, and colored strips of ribbon and little silver medals on his breast, and shoes so shiny they were like two black mirrors on his feet.

Mi Sook smiled. "So handsome," and his teeth spread wide and wider in his face.

He ate almost no dinner, although he ordered lavishly and

the waiter came often with a bottle and a white napkin on his arm. He told Mi Sook she was beautiful, the loveliest thing he had ever seen, and why didn't she wear those dresses all the time? She expected him to ask about the chain—she was ready with a story that it didn't suit the color of her *hanbok*—but he seemed to have forgotten. For the first time he asked about her family. Where was their house? Did they have servants and a garden with a high stone fence? Where did her father work? Was he with Hyundai? Dae Woo? Samsung? Was he an independent businessman? Maybe he ran a trading company?

Mi Sook laughed.

"What then?"

She looked mysterious and dipped her head.

"Will you introduce me to him soon? I'd like to meet your dad."

She dipped her head again.

And then Frank set aside his napkin. Reaching across the table, he took her hand. "My tour is almost up," he said. "In one month's time I'm going home. I want you to come too."

The waiter coughed beside them.

"Just the check," Frank said, and while the waiter went to get it ready he put his hand into his breast pocket and drew out a small embroidered satin purse, red with a gleaming golden snap.

"I want you to have this," he said, sliding it across the table. "It's an engagement ring."

• • •

Mi Sook carried the *hanbok* back to *Madame*. She stood watching her spread it on the counter of the shop and fold it carefully back into the box. When the tissue paper was all tucked in and the lid pressed down, she set the little satin purse down on the counter.

"What is this?" said *Madame*. She snapped it open, and dropping the ring onto her palm, she picked it up between two fingers and held it up, its gold glinting and its diamond flashing in the light. "What is this?" She peered at Mi Sook over her glasses. "Now you will *marry* this American?"

Mi Sook tipped her head from side to side.

"Now you will go home to *America* with him? But what about your children?"

"They will come too, of course."

"He has told you this?"

"He is American."

"That is as may be, but has he told you he will take your children?"

Mi Sook fidgeted.

"Ah. And what about your business?"

"I can have my business in America."

Madame eyed her narrowly. "And do you know that Americans will want to buy your lucky gourds? What if they do not? Where will your business be then?"

Mi Sook pouted. "So then I will not go. I will have my business here." She looked at the diamond sparkling in *Madame*'s hand. "This ring, how much is it worth?"

Madame dropped the ring back into the purse. "Ah, no, do

not do this, Mi Sook. Do not sell this ring. A gold chain is one thing, an opal pin, a bracelet. Such things are gifts and you may do with them as you please. But a ring like this is not a gift. It is a promise made between you. Here child, if you will not marry him you must give it back." She pressed the little purse into Mi Sook's hand and closed her fingers over it. "And anyway, this man is just a soldier, not so rich." She turned away, turned back. "I do not think you ought to marry him."

On Sunday, Mi Sook tucked the little purse inside her blouse and walked down to the park. It would be easy. She would turn her eyes down in apology and hand Frank back his ring. When he said, "Oh, Babe," she would say, "But I must have my business here. I must be independent." Then he would say, "But you can have a business in America," and she would say, "But I have three children I must care for." And he would say . . . What would he say? Would he be angry with her for not telling him about the children? Would he snatch his ring and walk away? Or would he say, please let him say, "But you must bring them too." No, this was foolish dreaming. This was the fantasy that led her chasing down the road behind Hyun Joon, the fantasy that made her lose her children. She must not be foolish a second time. No, she would go to Frank and tell him plainly, "I will not marry you," and give him back his ring. But this ring was surely worth . . . how much? More than the lucky gourd Hyun Joon had given her? Yes, surely more than that. Into her head came Kun Soo's whining voice: "How am I to build my nest egg if I must give every penny that I earn out of my hand?" She brushed the thought aside. She was not like Kun Soo. She would not trick some poor girl into marrying without telling her about a wife and five grown daughters, also a crazy son. No, she would not do a thing like that. But wait, she had not told Frank about three children or a husband who was dead. Was she no better than Kun Soo, then, with his bragging and his dyed black hair?

Now she was at the entrance to the park, now stepping slowly down the path. She stopped. Just ahead of her went Frank's broad back and shiny big black boots. He went around a curve. She followed him. But when she reached the curve she turned across the grass, coming up behind him where he sat on the wooden park bench where he always waited for her. Bushes were between them but she could see his big arms spread out along the bench's back. She slipped her hand into her blouse and drew out the little purse.

Just then Frank turned his head to watch a small boy throwing a fish kite up into the sky. She saw him smile. He looked so kindly sitting there she felt her heart go soft. She slipped the ring back into her blouse, and edging her way between two bushes, came out into the space behind him. He was looking up and down the path, stretching his neck out to see as far as he could.

Inside the softness of her heart Mi Sook felt a fluttering as though a tiny bird were struggling to escape. She took one step back, then two. She thought of how *Madame* had said, "He is just a soldier, not so rich." She had married Kun Soo, whom she thought was rich, and had been disappointed. What if she married Frank and was once more disappointed? She could not run home to the coffee shop from Bakersfield.

Now she was back behind the bushes, her breath coming harshly in her throat as though she had run a long distance very fast. A small boy appeared beside her, staring up. "What are you doing in the bushes? Are you playing hidey-seek?" She hissed at him, flapping her hands to make him go away, and his face swelled up bright red and accusing. She flapped again, and made an angry face. Mucus spun out of his nose and he twisted round and ran, calling, "Help me, help," to someone out of sight. She peered between the branches to see if Frank had heard the child's commotion, but no, he sat there on the bench looking up and down the path, then at his watch, then up and down the path.

A hundred times Mi Sook parted the bushes, meaning to go to him. A hundred times she let them drop. Eventually Frank put his big right hand over his watch, twisted it on his wrist, and looked down at it again. He stood up, walking back and forth along the path with his face pulled down and glum. Now he came toward her looking miserable, now he walked away. The third time he walked away from her, she turned and ran.

Twice more Mi Sook went to meet him in the park and both those times she ran away. The last time she went she knew she must decide today because it had been a month and now he would go home to America. Once more she drew the little purse out of her blouse, once more she put it back, but no matter how she willed herself to do it, she could not part the bushes and approach him. That day she stood a long, long time. That day Frank did not stand up and pace the path. Instead, he sat with his elbows on his knees and his hands hanging down between his legs. He hung his head down too, staring at the ground. At last, when the sky began to dim, he gave a great push on his knees and rose. For a moment he turned toward the bushes where Mi Sook hid as though he knew that she was there, as though he had known it all along. She felt a hot flush rising on her neck. Her hand went out.

But he had turned away, and by the time she had her wits about her once again and ran behind to catch him up, she was just in time to see him walk out of the park. By the time she reached the street he was nowhere to be seen.

ONE WEEK LATER, ON THE MONDAY, Mi Sook once more nudged through the credit union's glass rotating door. In her arms she carried the paper sack of candy boxes. The bank clerk saw her come and frowned but when she pushed the slip of paper across the desk to him, he smiled a tiny tight-mouthed smile and gestured to the paper sack. One by one Mi Sook took out the candy boxes, lifted off their lids, and tipped the contents out onto his desk.

As each box appeared, the bank clerk smiled another tiny smile, each one less tight-lipped than the one before, and when all the boxes had been emptied out, he kept the last smile on his face and with efficient agile fingers separated the notes and coins and ordered them in piles, counting softly to himself and tapping numbers into a large black adding machine on the corner of his desk, lifting his eyes from time to time to glance at Mi Sook's set, determined face, then dropping them again.

Mi Sook did not look at him at all. She watched the narrow roll of paper edge up out of the machine and slither down the desk front, growing long and longer. When it began to curl around her feet, she knew it was enough.

ACKNOWLEDGMENTS

My thanks go to the following people for their cultural advice: Young Chung; So Young Choo; Da Weo Chung; Hye Won Lee; Yunsil So; Young and Jung Sohn; NaNa and RiRi Yang; Keon-Woo Lee of the Asian Development Bank, Manila; Cherl Baik Seung, deputy mayor of Inch'on, and his assistant, Gweon Kim Jong; Ted J. Choi of KIC Incorporated, Seoul, and his assistant, C. O. Ahn; and Colonel Mark H. Gerner, Eighth U.S. Army, South Korea. Thanks to my fellow writers for their critical reviews: Mary Golding Hogya, Bonni Goldberg, Geraldine Connolly, Bibi Reed, Natasha Saje, Nancy Black, and Catherine McLean. Thanks also to my tenacious agent, Miriam Altshuler; Fred Ramey, who acquired and edited the manuscript for hardback publication; the dedicated and wonderfully supportive staff of MacMurray & Beck-MacAdam/Cage; and Kimberly Kanner, of Washington Square Press, who acquired and edited this paperback edition. And lastly, thanks to my three Korean children for their memories; to my three Caucasian children for their good fellowship; and to my husband for his many trips to Asia, leaving me with no date and long lovely hours alone to read and write.

Two chapters of this novel were previously published as the *Literal Latté* prizewinning story, "A Decision of Grandmothers." An adapted version of four other chapters was published as the *Georgia State University Review* prizewinning story, "Coin with Lucky Bird." Further adapted excerpts were published as the *Crucible* prizewinning story, "Goblin Child."

THE
LUCKY GOURD
SHOP

A NOVEL

Joanna Catherine Scott

A Readers Club Guide

ABOUT THIS GUIDE

The following questions and author interview are intended
to help you find interesting and rewarding approaches to
your reading of Joanna Catherine Scott's *The Lucky Gourd Shop*.
We hope this guide enriches your enjoyment
and appreciation of the book.

For a complete listing of our Readers Club
Guides, or to read the guides online, visit

http://www.SimonSays.com/reading/guides

Background to **The Lucky Gourd Shop**
Joanna Catherine Scott

Fifteen years ago, while living in the Philippines, my husband and I adopted three Korean children (one boy and two girls). We knew that their father was dead, that their grandmother was old and sick, and if not dead already, would die soon. We did not know, though, what had become of their birth mother. The adoption papers said the mother and the grandmother together put the children in the orphanage. When the children first learned English, they told us this was not the case, that the woman with their grandmother was not their mother, but Grannie's friend. Their mother ran away, they said. She was a bad mother.

This hit a tender nerve in me. In Australia, I married at the very young age of 19 and had three children. Then the feminist revolution turned the world upside down and many marriages fell apart, including mine. I lost those children—my husband got custody of them. I was severely criticized, and some labeled me a bad mother. As you may imagine, the effects of this went deep into my emotions, and even though I was reunited with my children later on, I still retained a great deal of guilt.

Because of this, when I heard the accusation flung against this unknown Korean woman by her children, I wanted to defend her. At the time, though, I could do no more than reassure them, telling them things like, "No, Ama was not bad. Things happened she could not control. She tried her best."

When the children reached adolescence, they became curious about their mother and we tried to find her, but did not succeed. After the letter from Korea came, as described in the novel's prologue, they did not want to continue searching. Instead, they came up with the idea that I should take all the information we had and make out of it a novel about their birth mother. At first, I reacted against this, but as I thought more about it, it occurred to me that it could be my opportunity to defend this woman. To do that I needed to explain her.

And so I set myself to reading everything I could find about Korea: its culture, history, short stories (the primary form of modern Korean fiction), memoirs, essays, poetry. In all these, I was searching for an understanding of my children's mother. I thought of her as Mi Sook and before long she obsessed me. What was she like? What did she think? How had she been raised? Why had she married a man so much older than herself, a man with children of her age? Why had she, on one occasion, become so angry with him that she slashed his face with a knife? Why had she run away after his funeral? How had she reacted when she came home and found her children had vanished?

We did know certain facts about the family, most dramatically, that the father, who drove a fish truck and worked in construction, had fallen off a roof, and refusing help, died a stubborn, raging death in a storage shed in his backyard. In my research, I learned that, traditionally, Koreans believe it is unlucky for a man to be taken dead into his own house, so I wanted to know why, by insisting on a death outside his house, this man had apparently put an intentional curse on his family.

One day, a sentence dropped into my head: "In Korea, in a poor back street of Inch'on, a man has fallen off a roof." As soon as I had that I knew I had a novel. Why? Because it had the feeling of a story starting. I knew who this man was—Mi Sook's husband—but I did not know him, or why he had fallen off the roof, or whether his relationship to Mi Sook had anything to do with it. I did not know the causes and effects, and the peculiar province of the novel is the exploration of causes and effects. I was ready to begin what would become *The Lucky Gourd Shop*.

The writing went quickly, taking just three months. By the time it was done, that beginning sentence had dropped away. I had needed it only as a mechanism to propel me into the story. I was nervous about letting my children read the manuscript since it was by no means a "teenage" novel, but they surprised me by embracing the story as their own. When I saw that, I asked myself, Have I done the right thing giving them a fiction as their story, with characters that I invented, action that I invented? Am I giving them something false on which to build their lives? But these are intelligent human beings: although they took it as their own and believed it was their story, they also understood it was a fiction. The human mind is remarkable in that it can hold two conflicting beliefs at the same time.

The Lucky Gourd Shop tells the birth mother's story in a way that shows the working of her mind and the effect of her life circumstances on her behavior. I think that for her children it has made her into what she was: a young girl tossed about by poverty and happenstance, rather than a shadowy, unsympathetic figure who abandoned them. If I have done this much for them by writing it, I think I have done well.

The other thing that has been valuable for them is that I managed to present their native culture to them from the inside, by which I mean in a way that shows how it would have been for their own family. It is one thing to read books on social customs, or to visit the country, but *The Lucky Gourd Shop* shows, in an imaginative way, what it would have been like for them to be Koreans in the situation into which they were born.

I have been asked by Koreans how, as an American, I managed to get so thoroughly inside the Korean psyche. I do not know how to answer that question except by saying that when I write, I make sure my research is exhaustive. In the case of *The Lucky Gourd Shop*, I had the advantage of having visited the places I needed to describe, and of knowing the basic facts of what happened to the family. I also had an certain understanding of the personalities involved, descriptions of the house and a sense of the violence it contained, an account of the father's death and funeral, the children's experiences in the orphanage, and many other details given to me like gifts out of my son's memory. These I was able to take and lay out like the undergirding of a building and on them construct the novel. Also, I think my own experience allowed me to enter imaginatively into the psyche of a mother who has lost her children.

I am often asked whether it was difficult adopting three children all at once. The answer is, yes, extremely difficult. Adopted children have unique problems of their own. At first, there are all the problems of language and cultural adaptation, then, once puberty strikes, all sorts of separation traumas well up out of their subconscious and manifest themselves in nightmares, rages, suicidal urges, and a range of other difficult behaviors which, tumbled on top of the normal tumult of adolescence, can at times stir up into a frightening brew.

One issue I personally found difficult to deal with was the "head man" concept they brought with them regarding the boy. When his father died, he became the family head. With this came responsibility for the safety and guidance of his sisters. And so it was to him they turned for decision making. When they were expected to behave in ways they did not understand, they would have meetings and confer together, and he would give the orders. If he did not agree with something I directed them to do, he would simply countermand me.

So there was, for some time, a problem with my authority as mother. Also, his sisters fully expected to defer to him and wait on him like little wives. It took years to bring them out of this. However, I'm as pig-headed as any Korean male, and I prevailed. I'm happy to say that, these days, the boy is sought after by women because he treats them with unusual deference and consideration, and neither of the girls takes nonsense from any sort of male.

As adults, the three are still extremely close. However much we and their adoptive siblings love them, and they us, their own familial bond is something that cannot be replaced. They can see each other in each other's faces, hear each other in each other's voices, identify with each other's fits of rage or taste in clothes or jokes, and speculate about their birth parents based on characteristics that they share. This sort of commonality is precious. The traumas we admittedly went through in raising them were worth it just for that. If we had not taken them, the chances are that the baby would have been adopted separately, while the older two would have had much less chance of finding a new home. Had that happened, the boy would have been devastated. He would have thought that he had failed in his responsibility toward his little sister.

When the children are older, perhaps they will pursue their birth mother until they find her. That's something for them to decide and not for me: she's their mother, not mine. It's not my place, although I certainly would help. It's an enormous thing to happen to somebody— to be reunited with a birth mother. There is no predicting whether the reunion will be one of joy or tragedy, and so I feel strongly that it's up to them to make the decision, when they are ready. I also realize they may never be ready. They may decide that they prefer to visit their birth mother in their imaginations.

In closing, let me emphasize that although *The Lucky Gourd Shop* deals with death, despair and poverty, none of these is its underlying theme. Rather, it deals with that unique quality of the human animal, the ability to turn away, to make from the disaster of the past the best that can be made.

Reading Group Questions and Topics for Discussion

1. Discuss *The Lucky Gourd Shop*'s innovative narrative structure. Start by considering the brief, first-person prologue in which Scott makes it clear that, while Dae Young's "twigs and sticks of memory" are used as its foundation, the story itself is constructed from imagination. How is the reader's relationship with the third person narrator affected by this prologue?

2. *The Lucky Gourd Shop* is the outgrowth of an intensely personal and therapeutic project—an invaluable gift from a mother to her adopted children. How, and at what points, did this knowledge affect or contribute to your sense of intimacy and connection to the scenes you were reading?

3. In what ways might the epigraph about separation and memory by Kim Sowol speak to the motivations underlying Scott's novel? And to the action and themes of the story itself?

4. Discuss how Scott's spare use of dialogue throughout *The Lucky Gourd Shop* contributes to the novel's tone and mood. What kind of novel is this? How would you describe Scott's writing style to a friend?

5. "No matter how much anger a man has inside him, it cannot protect him against a bullet in the head." Here, as Kun Soo's mother reflects on her husband's death at the hands of the North Koreans, Scott quietly underscores the desperation and rage which has become Kun Soo's tragic inheritance. Discuss this in relation to the next generation: In what ways does Dae Young— whose frustration and bewilderment we come to know intimately at the orphanage near the end of the novel—also become the bearer of this legacy?

6. What specific roles do faith and superstition play in shaping the life paths taken by Kun Soo and Mi Sook? To start with, consider the vivid scene between Kun Soo and the White Shaman.

7. Describe your emotions and reactions to each of the characters' personal journeys as you read this book. Compare your reactions to Scott's narrative in the early chapters to those in later chapters.

8. The quest for stability, contentment, and even rebirth is a guiding concern in *The Lucky Gourd Shop*. Throughout the course of the novel, both Mi Sook and Kun Soo's mother reflect repeatedly on the elusiveness of such a quest. With the fading specter of Japanese colonialism, the more recent nightmare of the Korean War, and the continuing aggressive posture of North Korea, neither woman has ever known anything but a world of roiling uncertainty and flux. In discussing Scott's vivid and sensuous evocation of Korea in the 1970s and '80s, consider the specific techniques she uses to saturate her story with a sense of this deep-seated cultural uncertainty and flux.

9. What were your understandings about Korean history and culture before reading Scott's novel? What surprised you most as you read? In what specific ways have Scott's images and depictions come to inform, challenge, or even contradict your previous notions?

10. Scott starkly captures the historically male-based nature of Korean culture, and also gives us glimpses, most notably in the character of Madame, of the rise of feminist resistance. Consider Scott's novel through the lens of gender: What specific examples can you cite from the novel to either refute or support the argument that the women in this novel collectively come out on the losing end in their struggle to define themselves independently from men?

11. One of the most affecting moments in the novel is Scott's presentation of the final hours of Kun Soo's mother. Here, in understated, memory-laced paragraphs, she invests her novel with its thematic center. Reread the snowstorm scene, ending with the lyrical (and loaded): "At first her son's boots held her back but she slipped out of them and came across the soft snow like a young girl dancing." What are the ideas, images, and guiding themes emerging in these pages—and how do they inform the novel as a whole?

12. What sort of person is Madame? Consider the glimpse we're given of her personal history. In what ways is she the most striking and subversive character in this novel?

13. Along with Madame, construct brief biographical sketches of the principle and supporting characters in this story. What are the motivations underlying their actions and choices?

14. Is there a hero/heroine in this story? Kun Soo's mother? Mi Sook? Dae Young? Make a case for each.

15. What are the various roles dreams play—thematically, metaphorically, and literally—in the course of Scott's narrative? Consider in particular the significance of dreams in Mi Sook's life. Do her vivid imagination and capacity for fantasy ultimately liberate or betray her? Explain.

16. In the emotional realm inhabited by Scott's characters— Mi Sook, Kun Soo, and Dae Young, in particular—what are the similarities and distinctions between "dreaming" and "escaping"?

17. Consider the ways in which not only dreams but also ghostly visions function in the world of this novel as potent forces affecting the events of human life.

18. Unpack Scott's use of Mi Sook's elusive lucky gourd shop as an intricate, multilayered metaphor. Why do you suppose the author chose it as her title? What meanings and associations does the title evoke?